Leen Volwer

PENGUIN BOOKS

985

BLANDINGS CASTLE

P. G. Wodehouse was born in 1881, and educated at Dulwich College. He was in the Hong Kong and Shanghai Bank for two years and then got a job on the 'By The Way' column of the old *Globe*. His first stories were school stories written for *The Captain*, in one of which Psmith made his first appearance. He paid a visit to America in 1904, and another in 1909, when he sold two short stories for $300 apiece, and decided to remain there. Eventually he sold a serial to the *Saturday Evening Post*, and for the next twenty-five years almost all his books appeared first in this magazine. In 1906 he wrote some lyrics to music by Jerome Kern, and some years later he formed a partnership with Guy Bolton, which resulted in a number of shows and straight plays. Mr Wodehouse worked at plays with George Grossmith and Ian Hay and has made some adaptations. He has written seventy books.

P. G. WODEHOUSE

Blandings Castle

and Elsewhere

PENGUIN BOOKS

Penguin Books Ltd, Harmondsworth, Middlesex, England
Penguin Books Australia Ltd, Ringwood, Victoria, Australia

—

First published by Herbert Jenkins 1935
Published in Penguin Books 1954
Reprinted 1966

—

Copyright © P. G. Wodehouse, 1935

—

Made and printed in Great Britain
by Hazell Watson & Viney Ltd,
Aylesbury Bucks
Set in Monotype Garamond

All the characters in this book
are purely imaginary and have
no relation whatsoever to
any living person

Contents

Preface

EXCEPT for the tendency to write articles about the Modern Girl and allow his side-whiskers to grow, there is nothing an author to-day has to guard himself against more carefully than the Saga habit. The least slackening of vigilance and the thing has gripped him. He writes a story. Another story dealing with the same characters occurs to him, and he writes that. He feels that just one more won't hurt him, and he writes a third. And before he knows where he is, he is down with a Saga, and no cure in sight.

This is what happened to me with Bertie Wooster and Jeeves, and it has happened again with Lord Emsworth, his son Frederick, his butler Beach, his pig the Empress and the other residents of Blandings Castle. Beginning with SOMETHING FRESH, I went on to LEAVE IT TO PSMITH, then to SUMMER LIGHTNING, after that to HEAVY WEATHER, and now to the volume which you have just borrowed. And, to show the habit-forming nature of the drug, while it was eight years after SOMETHING FRESH before the urge for LEAVE IT TO PSMITH gripped me, only eighteen months elapsed between SUMMER LIGHTNING and HEAVY WEATHER. In a word, once a man who could take it or leave it alone, I had become an addict.

The stories in the first part of this book represent what I may term the short snorts in between the solid orgies. From time to time I would feel the Blandings Castle craving creeping over me, but I had the manhood to content myself with a small dose.

In point of time, these stories come after LEAVE IT TO PSMITH and before SUMMER LIGHTNING. PIG-HOO-O-O-O-EY, for example, shows Empress of Blandings winning her first silver medal in the Fat Pigs class at the Shropshire Agricultural Show. In SUMMER LIGHTNING and HEAVY WEATHER she is seen struggling to repeat in the following year.

THE CUSTODY OF THE PUMPKIN shows Lord Emsworth passing through the brief pumpkin phase which preceded the more lasting pig seizure.

And so on.

Bobbie Wickham, of MR POTTER TAKES A REST CURE, appeared in three of the stories in a book called MR MULLINER SPEAKING.

The final section of the volume deals with the secret history of Hollywood, revealing in print some of those stories which are whispered over the frosted malted milk when the boys get together in the commissary.

P. G. WODEHOUSE

BLANDINGS CASTLE

CHAPTER I

The Custody of the Pumpkin

THE morning sunshine descended like an amber shower-bath on Blandings Castle, lighting up with a heartening glow its ivied walls, its rolling parks, its gardens, out-houses, and messuages, and such of its inhabitants as chanced at the moment to be taking the air. It fell on green lawns and wide terraces, on noble trees and bright flower-beds. It fell on the baggy trousers-seat of Angus McAllister, head-gardener to the ninth Earl of Emsworth, as he bent with dour Scottish determination to pluck a slug from its reverie beneath the leaf of a lettuce. It fell on the whit-flannels of the Hon. Freddie Threepwood, Lord Emsworth's second son, hurrying across the water-meadows. It also fell on Lord Emsworth himself and on Beach, his faithful butler. They were standing on the turret above the west wing, the former with his eye to a powerful telescope, the latter holding the hat which he had been sent to fetch.

'Beach,' said Lord Emsworth.

'M'lord?'

'I've been swindled. This dashed thing doesn't work.'

'Your lordship cannot see clearly?'

'I can't see at all, dash it. It's all black.'

The butler was an observant man.

'Perhaps if I were to remove the cap at the extremity of the instrument, m'lord, more satisfactory results might be obtained.'

'Eh? Cap? Is there a cap? So there is. Take it off, Beach.'

'Very good, m'lord.'

'Ah!' There was satisfaction in Lord Emsworth's voice. He twiddled and adjusted, and the satisfaction deepened.

'Yes, that's better. That's capital. Beach, I can see a cow.'

'Indeed, m'lord?'

'Down in the water-meadows. Remarkable. Might be two yards away. All right, Beach. Shan't want you any longer.'

'Your hat, m'lord?'

'Put it on my head.'

'Very good, m'lord.'

The butler, this kindly act performed, withdrew. Lord Emsworth continued gazing at the cow.

The ninth Earl of Emsworth was a fluffy-minded and amiable old gentleman with a fondness for new toys. Although the main interest of his life was his garden, he was always ready to try a side line, and the latest of these side lines was this telescope of his. Ordered from London in a burst of enthusiasm consequent upon the reading of an article on astronomy in a monthly magazine, it had been placed in position on the previous evening. What was now in progress was its trial trip.

Presently, the cow's audience-appeal began to wane. It was a fine cow, as cows go, but, like so many cows, it lacked sustained dramatic interest. Surfeited after a while by the spectacle of it chewing the cud and staring glassily at nothing, Lord Emsworth decided to swivel the apparatus round in the hope of picking up something a trifle more sensational. And he was just about to do so, when into the range of his vision there came the Hon. Freddie. White and shining, he tripped along over the turf like a Theocritan shepherd hastening to keep an appointment with a nymph, and a sudden frown marred the serenity of Lord Emsworth's brow. He generally frowned when he saw Freddie, for with the passage of the years that youth had become more and more of a problem to an anxious father.

Unlike the male codfish, which, suddenly finding itself the parent of three million five hundred thousand little codfish, cheerfully resolves to love them all, the British aristocracy is apt to look with a somewhat jaundiced eye on its younger sons. And Freddie Threepwood was one of those

younger sons who rather invite the jaundiced eye. It seemed
to the head of the family that there was no way of coping
with the boy. If he was allowed to live in London, he piled
up debts and got into mischief; and when you jerked him
back into the purer surroundings of Blandings Castle, he
just mooned about the place, moping broodingly. Hamlet's
society at Elsinore must have had much the same effect on
his stepfather as did that of Freddie Threepwood at Blandings on Lord Emsworth. And it is probable that what induced the latter to keep a telescopic eye on him at this
moment was the fact that his demeanour was so mysterious-
ly jaunty, his bearing so intriguingly free from its customary crushed misery. Some inner voice whispered to Lord
Emsworth that this smiling, prancing youth was up to no
good and would bear watching.

The inner voice was absolutely correct. Within thirty
seconds its case had been proved up to the hilt. Scarcely
had his lordship had time to wish, as he invariably wished
on seeing his offspring, that Freddie had been something
entirely different in manners, morals, and appearance, and
had been the son of somebody else living a considerable distance away, when out of a small spinney near the end of the
meadow there bounded a girl. And Freddie, after a cautious
glance over his shoulder, immediately proceeded to fold
this female in a warm embrace.

Lord Emsworth had seen enough. He tottered away
from the telescope, a shattered man. One of his favourite
dreams was of some nice, eligible girl, belonging to a good
family, and possessing a bit of money of her own, coming
along some day and taking Freddie off his hands; but that
inner voice, more confident now than ever, told him that
this was not she. Freddie would not sneak off in this furtive
fashion to meet eligible girls, nor could he imagine any
eligible girl, in her right senses, rushing into Freddie's arms
in that enthusiastic way. No, there was only one explanation. In the cloistral seclusion of Blandings, far from the
Metropolis with all its conveniences for that sort of thing,
Freddie had managed to get himself entangled. Seething

with anguish and fury, Lord Emsworth hurried down the stairs and out on to the terrace. Here he prowled like an elderly leopard waiting for feeding-time, until in due season there was a flicker of white among the trees that flanked the drive and a cheerful whistling announced the culprit's approach.

It was with a sour and hostile eye that Lord Emsworth watched his son draw near. He adjusted his pince-nez, and with their assistance was able to perceive that a fatuous smile of self-satisfaction illumined the young man's face, giving him the appearance of a beaming sheep. In the young man's buttonhole there shone a nosegay of simple meadow flowers, which, as he walked, he patted from time to time with a loving hand.

'Frederick!' bellowed his lordship.

The villain of the piece halted abruptly. Sunk in a roseate trance, he had not observed his father. But such was the sunniness of his mood that even this encounter could not damp him. He gambolled happily up.

'Hullo, guv'nor!' he carolled. He searched in his mind for a pleasant topic of conversation – always a matter of some little difficulty on these occasions. 'Lovely day, what?'

His lordship was not be diverted into a discussion of the weather. He drew a step nearer, looking like the man who smothered the young princes in the Tower.

'Frederick,' he demanded, 'who was that girl?'

The Hon. Freddie started convulsively. He appeared to be swallowing with difficulty something large and jagged.

'Girl?' he quavered. 'Girl? Girl, guv'nor?'

'That girl I saw you kissing ten minutes ago down in the water-meadows.'

'Oh!' said the Hon. Freddie. He paused. 'Oh, ah!' He paused again. 'Oh, ah, yes! I've been meaning to tell you about that, guv'nor.'

'You have, have you?'

'All perfectly correct, you know. Oh, yes, indeed! All most absolutely correct-o! Nothing fishy, I mean to say, or anything like that. She's my *fiancée*.'

A sharp howl escaped Lord Emsworth, as if one of the bees humming in the lavender-beds had taken time off to sting him in the neck.

'Who is she?' he boomed. 'Who is this woman?'

'Her name's Donaldson.'

'Who is she?'

'Aggie Donaldson. Aggie's short for Niagara. Her people spent their honeymoon at the Falls, she tells me. She's American and all that. Rummy names they give kids in America,' proceeded Freddie, with hollow chattiness. 'I mean to say! Niagara! I ask you!'

'Who is she?'

'She's most awfully bright, you know. Full of beans. You'll love her.'

'Who is she?'

'And can play the saxophone.'

'Who,' demanded Lord Emsworth for the sixth time, 'is she? And where did you meet her?'

Freddie coughed. The information, he perceived, could no longer be withheld, and he was keenly alive to the fact that it scarcely fell into the class of tidings of great joy.

'Well, as a matter of fact, guv'nor, she's a sort of cousin of Angus McAllister's. She's come over to England for a visit, don't you know, and is staying with the old boy. That's how I happened to run across her.'

Lord Emsworth's eyes bulged and he gargled faintly. He had had many unpleasant visions of his son's future, but they had never included one of him walking down the aisle with a sort of cousin of his head-gardener.

'Oh!' he said. 'Oh, indeed?'

'That's the strength of it, guv'nor.'

Lord Emsworth threw his arms up, as if calling on Heaven to witness a good man's persecution, and shot off along the terrace at a rapid trot. Having ranged the grounds for some minutes, he ran his quarry to earth at the entrance to the yew alley.

The head-gardener turned at the sound of his footsteps. He was a sturdy man of medium height, with eyebrows that would have fitted a bigger forehead. These, added to a red and wiry beard, gave him a formidable and uncompromising expression. Honesty Angus McAllister's face had in full measure, and also intelligence; but it was a bit short on sweetness and light.

'McAllister,' said his lordship, plunging without preamble into the matter of his discourse. 'That girl. You must send her away.'

A look of bewilderment clouded such of Mr McAllister's features as were not concealed behind his beard and eyebrows.

'Gurrul?'

'That girl who is staying with you. She must go!'

'Gae where?'

Lord Emsworth was not in the mood be to finicky about details.

'Anywhere,' he said. 'I won't have her here a day longer.'

'Why?' inquired Mr McAllister, who liked to thresh these things out.

'Never mind why. You must send her away immediately.'

Mr McAllister mentioned an insuperable objection.

'She's payin' me twa poon' a week,' he said simply.

Lord Emsworth did not grind his teeth, for he was not given to that form of displaying emotion; but he leaped some ten inches into the air and dropped his pince-nez. And, though normally a fair-minded and reasonable man, well aware that modern earls must think twice before pulling the feudal stuff on their *employés*, he took on the forthright truculence of a large landowner of the early Norman period ticking off a serf.

'Listen, McAllister! Listen to me! Either you send that girl away to-day or you can go yourself. I mean it!'

A curious expression came into Angus McAllister's face – always excepting the occupied territories. It was the look of a man who has not forgotten Bannockburn, a man conscious of belonging to the country of William Wallace and Robert the Bruce. He made Scotch noises at the back of his throat.

'Yr' lorrudsheep will accept ma notis,' he said, with formal dignity.

'I'll pay you a month's wages in lieu of notice and you will leave this afternoon,' retorted Lord Emsworth with spirit.

'Mphm!' said Mr McAllister.

Lord Emsworth left the battle-field with a feeling of pure exhilaration, still in the grip of the animal fury of conflict. No twinge of remorse did he feel at the thought that Angus McAllister had served him faithfully for ten years. Nor did it cross his mind that he might miss McAllister.

But that night, as he sat smoking his after-dinner cigarette, Reason, so violently expelled, came stealing timidly back to her throne, and a cold hand seemed suddenly placed upon his heart.

With Angus McAllister gone, how would the pumpkin fare?

The importance of this pumpkin in the Earl of Emsworth's life requires, perhaps, a word of explanation. Every ancient family in England has some little gap in its scroll of honour, and that of Lord Emsworth was no exception. For generations back his ancestors had been doing notable deeds; they had sent out from Blandings Castle statesmen and warriors, governors and leaders of the people: but they had not – in the opinion of the present holder of the title – achieved a full hand. However splendid the family record might appear at first sight, the fact remained that no Earl of Emsworth had ever won a first prize for pumpkins at the Shrewsbury Show. For roses, yes. For tulips, true. For spring onions, granted. But not for pumpkins; and Lord Emsworth felt it deeply.

For many a summer past he had been striving indefatigably to remove this blot on the family escutcheon, only to see his hopes go tumbling down. But this year at last victory had seemed in sight, for there had been vouchsafed to Blandings a competitor of such amazing parts that his lordship, who had watched it grow practically from a pip, could not envisage failure. Surely, he told himself as he gazed on its golden roundness, even Sir Gregory Parsloe-Parsloe, of Matchingham Hall, winner for three successive years, would never be able to produce anything to challenge this superb vegetable.

And it was this supreme pumpkin whose welfare he feared he had jeopardized by dismissing Angus McAllister. For Angus was its official trainer. He understood the pumpkin. Indeed, in his reserved Scottish way, he even seemed to love it. With Angus gone, what would the harvest be?

Such were the meditations of Lord Emsworth as he reviewed the position of affairs. And though, as the days went by, he tried to tell himself that Angus McAllister was not the only man in the world who understood pumpkins, and that he had every confidence, the most complete and unswerving confidence, in Robert Barker, recently Angus's second-in-command, now promoted to the post of head-gardener and custodian of the Blandings Hope, he knew that this was but shallow bravado. When you are a pumpkin-owner with a big winner in your stable, you judge men by hard standards, and every day it became plainer that Robert Barker was only a makeshift. Within a week Lord Emsworth was pining for Angus McAllister.

It might be purely imagination, but to his excited fancy the pumpkin seemed to be pining for Angus too. It appeared to be drooping and losing weight. Lord Emsworth could not rid himself of the horrible idea that it was shrinking. And on the tenth night after McAllister's departure he dreamed a strange dream. He had gone with King George to show his Gracious Majesty the pumpkin, promising him the treat of a lifetime; and, when they arrived, there in the corner of the frame was a shrivelled thing the size of a pea. He woke, sweating, with his Sovereign's disappointed screams ringing in his ears; and Pride gave its last quiver and collapsed. To reinstate Angus would be a surrender, but it must be done.

'Beach,' he said that morning at breakfast, 'do you happen to – er – to have McAllister's address?'

'Yes, your lordship,' replied the butler. 'He is in London, residing at number eleven Buxton Crescent.'

'Buxton Crescent? Never heard of it.'

'It is, I fancy, your lordship, a boarding-house or some such establishment off the Cromwell Road. McAllister was accustomed to make it his headquarters whenever he visited the Metropolis on account of its handiness for Kensington Gardens. He liked,' said Beach with respectful reproach, for Angus had been a friend of his for nine years, 'to be near the flowers, your lordship.'

Two telegrams, passing through it in the course of the next twelve hours, caused some gossip at the post office of the little town of Market Blandings.

The first ran:

> *McAllister,*
> > *11 Buxton Crescent*
> > > *Cromwell Road*
> > > > *London*
> *Return immediately – Emsworth*

The second:

> *Lord Emsworth*
> > *Blandings Castle*
> > > *Shropshire*
> *I will not – McAllister*

Lord Emsworth had one of those minds capable of accommodating but one thought at a time – if that; and the possibility that Angus McAllister might decline to return had not occurred to him. It was difficult to adjust himself to this new problem, but he managed it at last. Before nightfall he had made up his mind. Robert Barker, that broken reed, could remain in charge for another day or so, and meanwhile he would go up to London and engage a real head-gardener, the finest head-gardener that money could buy.

It was the opinion of Dr Johnson that there is in London all that life can afford. A man, he held, who is tired of Lon-

don is tired of life itself. Lord Emsworth, had he been
aware of this statement, would have contested it warmly.
He hated London. He loathed its crowds, its smells, its
noises; its omnibuses, its taxis, and its hard pavements.
And, in addition to all its other defects, the miserable town
did not seem able to produce a single decent head-gardener.
He went from agency to agency, interviewing candidates,
and not one of them came within a mile of meeting his re-
quirements. He disliked their faces, he distrusted their
references. It was a harsh thing to say of any man, but he
was dashed if the best of them was even as good as Robert
Barker.

It was, therefore, in a black and soured mood that his
lordship, having lunched frugally at the Senior Conservative Club on the third day of his visit, stood on the steps
in the sunshine, wondering how on earth he was to get
through the afternoon. He had spent the morning rejecting
head-gardeners, and the next batch was not due until the
morrow. And what – besides rejecting head-gardeners –
was there for a man of reasonable tastes to do with his time
in this hopeless town?

And then there came into his mind a remark which Beach
the butler had made at the breakfast-table about flowers in
Kensington Gardens. He could go to Kensington Gardens
and look at the flowers.

He was about to hail a taxicab from the rank down the
street when there suddenly emerged from the Hotel Mag-
nificent over the way a young man. This young man proceeded to cross the road, and, as he drew near, it seemed to
Lord Emsworth that there was about his appearance something oddly familiar. He stared for a long instant before he
could believe his eyes, then with a wordless cry bounded
down the steps just as the other started to mount them.

'Oh, hullo, guv'nor!' ejaculated the Hon. Freddie,
plainly startled.

'What – what are you doing here?' demanded Lord Emsworth.

He spoke with heat, and justly so. London, as the result

of several spirited escapades which still rankled in the mind
of a father who had had to foot the bills, was forbidden
ground to Freddie.

The young man was plainly not at his ease. He had the
air of one who is being pushed towards dangerous mach-
inery in which he is loath to become entangled. He shuffled
his feet for a moment, then raised his left shoe and rubbed
the back of his right calf with it.

'The fact is, guv'nor —'

'You know you are forbidden to come to London.'

'Absolutely, guv'nor, but the fact is —'

'And why anybody but an imbecile should want to come
to London when he could be at Blandings —'

'I know, guv'nor, but the fact is —' Here Freddie, having
replaced his wandering foot on the pavement, raised the
other, and rubbed the back of his left calf. 'I wanted to see
you,' he said. 'Yes. Particularly wanted to see you.'

This was not strictly accurate. The last thing in the
world which the Hon. Freddie wanted was to see his
parent. He had come to the Senior Conservative Club to
leave a carefully written note. Having delivered which, it
had been his intention to bolt like a rabbit. This unfore-
seen meeting had upset his plans.

'To see me?' said Lord Emsworth. 'Why?'

'Got – er – something to tell you. Bit of news.'

'I trust it is of sufficient importance to justify your
coming to London against my express wishes.'

'Oh, yes. Oh, yes, yes-yes. Oh, rather. It's dashed important. Yes – not to put too fine a point upon it – most
dashed important. I say, guv'nor, are you in fairly good
form to stand a bit of a shock?'

A ghastly thought rushed into Lord Emsworth's mind.
Freddie's mysterious arrival – his strange manner – his odd
hesitation and uneasiness – could it mean —? He clutched
the young man's arm feverishly.

'Frederick! Speak! Tell me! Have the cats got at it?'

It was a fixed idea of Lord Emsworth, which no argument would have induced him to abandon, that cats had

the power to work some dreadful mischief on his pumpkin and were continually lying in wait for the opportunity of doing so; and his behaviour on the occasion when one of the fast sporting set from the stables, wandering into the kitchen garden and finding him gazing at the Blandings Hope, had rubbed itself sociably against his leg, lingered long in that animal's memory.

Freddie stared.

'Cats? Why? Where? Which? What cats?'

'Frederick! Is anything wrong with the pumpkin?'

In a crass and materialistic world there must inevitably be a scattered few here and there in whom pumpkins touch no chord. The Hon. Freddie Threepwood was one of these. He was accustomed to speak in mockery of all pumpkins, and had even gone so far as to allude to the Hope of Blandings as 'Percy'. His father's anxiety, therefore, merely caused him to giggle.

'Not that I know of,' he said.

'Then what do you mean?' thundered Lord Emsworth, stung by the giggle. 'What do you mean, sir, by coming here and alarming me – scaring me out of my wits, by Gad! – with your nonsense about giving me shocks?'

The Hon. Freddie looked carefully at his fermenting parent. His fingers, sliding into his pocket, closed on the note which nestled there. He drew it forth.

'Look here, guv'nor,' he said nervously. 'I think the best thing would be for you to read this. Meant to leave it for you with the hall-porter. It's – well, you just cast your eye over it. Good-bye, guv'nor. Got to see a man.'

And, thrusting the note into his father's hand, the Hon. Freddie turned and was gone. Lord Emsworth, perplexed and annoyed, watched him skim up the road and leap into a cab. He seethed impotently. Practically any behaviour on the part of his son Frederick had the power to irritate him, but it was when he was vague and mysterious and incoherent that the young man irritated him most.

He looked at the letter in his hand, turned it over, felt it. Then – for it had suddenly occurred to him that if he wished to ascertain its contents he had better read it – he tore open the envelope.

The note was brief, but full of good reading matter.

Dear Guv'nor,

Awfully sorry and all that, but couldn't hold out any longer. I've popped up to London in the two-seater and Aggie and I were spliced this morning. There looked like being a bit of a hitch at one time, but Aggie's guv'nor, who has come over from America, managed to wangle it all right by getting a special licence or something of that order. A most capable Johnny. He's coming to see you. He wants to have a good long talk with you about the whole binge. Lush him up hospitably and all that, would you mind, because he's a really sound egg, and you'll like him.

Well, cheerio: *Your affectionate son,*

Freddie

P.S. – You won't mind if I freeze on to the two-seater for the nonce, what? It may come in useful for the honeymoon.

The Senior Conservative Club is a solid and massive building, but, as Lord Emsworth raised his eyes dumbly from the perusal of this letter, it seemed to him that it was performing a kind of whirling dance. The whole of the immediate neighbourhood, indeed, appeared to be shimmying in the middle of a thick mist. He was profoundly stirred. It is not too much to say that he was shaken to the core of his being. No father enjoys being flouted and defied by his own son; nor is it reasonable to expect a man to take a cheery view of life who is faced with the prospect of supporting for the remainder of his years a younger son, a younger son's wife, and possibly younger grandchildren.

For an appreciable space of time he stood in the middle of the pavement, rooted to the spot. Passers-by bumped into him or grumblingly made *détours* to avoid a collision. Dogs sniffed at his ankles. Seedy-looking individuals tried to arrest his attention in order to speak of their financial affairs. Lord Emsworth heeded none of them. He remained where he was, gaping like a fish, until suddenly his faculties seemed to return to him.

An imperative need for flowers and green trees swept upon Lord Emsworth. The noise of the traffic and the heat of the sun on the stone pavement were afflicting him like a nightmare. He signalled energetically to a passing cab.

'Kensington Gardens,' he said, and sank back on the cushioned seat.

Something dimly resembling peace crept into his lordship's soul as he paid off his cab and entered the cool shade of the gardens. Even from the road he had caught a glimpse of stimulating reds and yellows; and as he ambled up the asphalt path and plunged round the corner the flower-beds burst upon his sight in all their consoling glory.

'Ah!' breathed Lord Emsworth rapturously, and came to a halt before a glowing carpet of tulips. A man of official aspect, wearing a peaked cap and a uniform, stopped as he heard the exclamation and looked at him with approval and even affection.

'Nice weather we're 'avin',' he observed.

Lord Emsworth did not reply. He had not heard. There is that about a well-set-out bed of flowers which acts on men who love their gardens like a drug, and he was in a sort of trance. Already he had completely forgotten where he was, and seemed to himself to be back in his paradise of Blandings. He drew a step nearer to the flower-bed, pointing like a setter.

The official-looking man's approval deepened. This man with the peaked cap was the park-keeper, who held the rights of the high, the low, and the middle justice over that section of the gardens. He, too, loved these flower-beds, and he seemed to see in Lord Emsworth a kindred soul. The general public was too apt to pass by, engrossed in its own affairs, and this often wounded the park-keeper. In Lord Emsworth he thought that he recognized one of the right sort.

'Nice – ' he began.

He broke off with a sharp cry. If he had not seen it with his own eyes, he would not have believed it. But, alas, there was no possibility of a mistake. With a ghastly shock he realized that he had been deceived in this attractive stranger. Decently, if untidily, dressed; clean; respectable to the outward eye; the stranger was in reality a dangerous criminal, the blackest type of evil-doer on the park-keeper's index. He was a Kensington Gardens flower-picker.

For, even as he uttered the word 'Nice', the man had stepped lightly over the low railing, had shambled across the strip of turf, and before you could say 'weather' was busy on his dark work. In the brief instant in which the park-keeper's vocal chords refused to obey him, he was two tulips ahead of the game and reaching out to scoop in a third.

'Hi!!!' roared the park-keeper, suddenly finding speech. ' 'I there!!!'

Lord Emsworth turned with a start.

'Bless my soul!' he murmured reproachfully.

He was in full possession of his senses now, such as they were, and understood the enormity of his conduct. He shuffled back on to the asphalt, contrite.

'My dear fellow —' he began remorsefully.

The park-keeper began to speak rapidly and at length. From time to time Lord Emsworth moved his lips and made deprecating gestures, but he could not stem the flood. Louder and more rhetorical grew the park-keeper and denser and more interested the rapidly assembling crowd of spectators. And then through the stream of words another voice spoke.

'Wot's all this?'

The Force had materialized in the shape of a large, solid constable.

The park-keeper seemed to understand that he had been superseded. He still spoke, but no longer like a father rebuking an erring son. His attitude now was more that of an elder brother appealing for justice against a delinquent junior. In a moving passage he stated his case.

' 'E Says,' observed the constable judicially, speaking slowly and in capitals, as if addressing an untutored foreigner, ' 'E Says You Was Pickin' The Flowers.'

'I saw 'im. I was standin' as close as I am to you.'

' 'E Saw You,' interpreted the constable. ' 'E Was Standing At Your Side.'

Lord Emsworth was feeling weak and bewildered. Without a thought of annoying or doing harm to anybody, he seemed to have unchained the fearful passions of a French Revolution; and there came over him a sense of how unjust it was that this sort of thing should be happening to him, of all people – a man already staggering beneath the troubles of a Job.

'I'll 'ave to ask you for your name and address,' said the constable, more briskly. A stubby pencil popped for an instant into his stern mouth and hovered, well and truly moistened, over the virgin page of his notebook – that dreadful notebook before which taxi-drivers shrink and hardened bus-conductors quail.

'I – I – why, my dear fellow – I mean, officer – I am the Earl of Emsworth.'

Much has been written of the psychology of crowds, designed to show how extraordinary and inexplicable it is, but most of such writing is exaggeration. A crowd generally behaves in a perfectly natural and intelligible fashion. When, for instance, it sees a man in a badly-fitting tweed suit and a hat he ought to be ashamed of getting put through it for pinching flowers in the Park, and the man says he is an earl, it laughs. This crowd laughed.

'Ho?' The constable did not stoop to join in the merriment of the rabble, but his lip twitched sardonically. 'Have you a card, your lordship?'

Nobody intimate with Lord Emsworth would have asked such a foolish question. His card-case was the thing he always lost second when visiting London – immediately after losing his umbrella.

'I – er – I'm afraid – '

'R!' said the constable. And the crowd uttered another happy, hyena-like laugh, so intensely galling that his lordship raised his bowed head and found enough spirit to cast an indignant glance. And, as he did so, the hunted look faded from his eyes.

'McAllister!' he cried.

Two new arrivals had just joined the throng, and, being of rugged and nobbly physique, had already shoved themselves through to the ringside seats. One was a tall, handsome, smooth-faced gentleman of authoritative appearance, who, if he had not worn rimless glasses, would have looked like a Roman emperor. The other was a shorter, sturdier man with a bristly red beard.

'McAllister!' moaned his lordship piteously. 'McAllister, my dear fellow, do please tell this man who I am.'

After what had passed between himself and his late employer, a lesser man than Angus McAllister might have seen in Lord Emsworth's predicament merely a judgement. A man of little magnanimity would have felt that here was where he got a bit of his own back.

Not so this splendid Glaswegian.

'Aye,' he said. 'Yon's Lorrud Emsworruth.'

'Who are you?' inquired the constable searchingly.

'I used to be head-gardener at the cassel.'

'Exactly,' bleated Lord Emsworth. 'Precisely. My head-gardener.'

The constable was shaken. Lord Emsworth might not look like an earl, but there was no getting away from the fact that Angus McAllister was supremely head-gardener-esque. A staunch admirer of the aristocracy, the constable perceived that zeal had caused him to make a bit of a bloomer.

In this crisis, however, he comported himself with masterly tact. He scowled blackly upon the interested throng.

'Pass along there, please. Pass along,' he commanded austerely. 'Ought to know better than block up a public thoroughfare like this. Pass along!'

He moved off, shepherding the crowd before him. The Roman emperor with the rimless glasses advanced upon

Lord Emsworth, extending a large hand.

'Pleased to meet you at last,' he said. 'My name is Donaldson, Lord Emsworth.'

For a moment the name conveyed nothing to his lordship. Then its significance hit him, and he drew himself up with hauteur.

'You'll excuse us, Angus,' said Mr Donaldson. 'High time you and I had a little chat, Lord Emsworth.'

Lord Emsworth was about to speak, when he caught the other's eye. It was a strong, keen, level grey eye, with a curious forcefulness about it that made him feel strangely inferior. There is every reason to suppose that Mr Donaldson had subscribed for years to those personality courses advertised in the magazines which guarantee to impart to the pupil who takes ten correspondence lessons the ability to look the boss in the eye and make him wilt. Mr Donaldson looked Lord Emsworth in the eye, and Lord Emsworth wilted.

'How do you do?' he said weakly.

'Now listen, Lord Emsworth,' proceeded Mr Donaldson. 'No sense in having hard feelings between members of a family. I take it you've heard by this that your boy and my girl have gone ahead and fixed it up? Personally, I'm delighted. That boy is a fine young fellow.'

Lord Emsworth blinked.

'You are speaking of my son Frederick?' he said incredulously.

'Of your son Frederick. Now, at the moment, no doubt, you are feeling a trifle sore. I don't blame you. You have every right to be sorer than a gumboil. But you must remember – young blood, eh? It will, I am convinced, be a lasting grief to that splendid young man —'

'You are still speaking of my son Frederick?'

'Of Frederick, yes. It will, I say, be a lasting grief to him if he feels he has incurred your resentment. You must forgive him, Lord Emsworth. He must have your support.'

'I suppose he'll have to have it, dash it!' said his lordship unhappily. 'Can't let the boy starve.'

Mr Donaldson's hand swept round in a wide, grand gesture.

'Don't you worry about that. I'll look after that end of it. I am not a rich man – '

'Ah!' said Lord Emsworth rather bleakly. There had been something about the largeness of the other's manner which had led him to entertain hopes.

'I doubt,' continued Mr Donaldson frankly, for he was a man who believed in frankness in these matters, 'if, all told, I have as much as ten million dollars in the world.'

Lord Emsworth swayed like a sapling in the breeze.

'Ten million? Ten million? Did you say you had ten million dollars?'

'Between nine and ten, I suppose. Not more. You must remember,' said Mr Donaldson, with a touch of apology, 'that conditions have changed very much in America of late. We have been through a tough time, a mighty tough time. Many of my friends have been harder hit than I have. But things are coming back. Yes, sir, they're coming right back. I am a firm believer in President Roosevelt and the New Deal. Under the New Deal, the American dog is beginning to eat more biscuits. That, I should have mentioned, is my line. I am Donaldson's Dog-Biscuits.'

'Donaldson's Dog-Biscuits? Indeed? Really! Fancy that!'

'You have heard of Donaldson's Dog-Biscuits?' asked their proprietor eagerly.

'Never,' said Lord Emsworth cordially.

'Oh! Well, that's who I am. And, as I say, the business is beginning to pick up nicely after the slump. All over the country our salesmen are reporting that the American dog is once more becoming biscuit-conscious. And so I am in a position, with your approval, to offer Frederick a steady and possibly a lucrative job. I propose, always with your consent, of course, to send him over to Long Island City to start learning the business. I have no doubt that he will in time prove a most valuable asset to the firm.'

Lord Emsworth could conceive of no way in which Freddie could be of value to a dog-biscuit firm, except possibly as a taster; but he refrained from damping the other's enthusiasm by saying so. In any case, the thought of the young man actually earning his living, and doing so three thousand miles from Blandings Castle, would probably have held him dumb.

'He seems full of keenness. But, in my opinion, to be able to give of his best and push the Donaldson biscuit as it should be pushed, he must feel that he has your moral support, Lord Emsworth – his father's moral support.'

'Yes, yes, yes,' said Lord Emsworth heartily. A feeling of positive adoration for Mr Donaldson was thrilling him. The getting rid of Freddie, which he himself had been unable to achieve in twenty-six years, this godlike dog-biscuit manufacturer had accomplished in less than a week. What a man! felt Lord Emsworth. 'Oh, yes, yes, yes!' he said. 'Yes, indeed. Most decidedly.'

'They sail on Wednesday.'

'Capital!'

'Early in the morning.'

'Splendid!'

'I may give them a friendly message from you? A forgiving, fatherly message?'

'Certainly, certainly, certainly. Inform Frederick that he has my best wishes.'

'I will.'

'Mention that I shall watch his future progress with considerable interest.'

'Exactly.'

'Say that I hope he will work hard and make a name for himself.'

'Just so.'

'And,' concluded Lord Emsworth, speaking with a paternal earnestness well in keeping with this solemn moment, 'tell him – er – not to hurry home.'

He pressed Mr Donaldson's hand with feelings too deep for further speech. Then he galloped swiftly to where Angus McAllister stood brooding over the tulip bed.

'McAllister!'

The head-gardener's beard waggled grimly. He looked at his late employer with cold eyes. It is never difficult to distinguish between a Scotsman with a grievance and a ray of sunshine, and Lord Emsworth, gazing upon the dour man, was able to see at a glance into which category Angus McAllister fell. His tongue seemed to cleave to his palate, but he forced himself to speak.

'McAllister ... I wish ... I wonder ...'

'Weel?'

'I wonder ... I wish ... What I want to say,' faltered Lord Emsworth humbly, 'is, have you accepted another situation yet?'

'I am conseederin' twa.'

'Come back to me!' pleaded his lordship, his voice breaking. 'Robert Barker is worse than useless. Come back to me!'

Angus McAllister gazed woodenly at the tulips.

'A' weel —' he said at length.

'You will?' cried Lord Emsworth joyfully. 'Splendid! Capital! Excellent!'

'A' didna say I wud.'

'I thought you said "I will",' said his lordship, dashed.

'I didna say "A' weel"; I said "A' weel",' said Mr McAllister stiffly. 'Meanin' mebbe I might, mebbe not.'

Lord Emsworth laid a trembling hand upon his shoulder.

'McAllister, I will raise your salary.'

The beard twitched.

'Dash it, I'll double it!'

The eyebrows flickered.

'McAllister ... Angus ...' said Lord Emsworth in a low voice. 'Come back! The pumpkin needs you.'

In an age of rush and hurry like that of to-day, an age in which there are innumerable calls on the time of everyone, it is possible that here and there throughout the ranks of those who have read this chronicle there may be one or two who for various reasons found themselves unable to attend the last Agricultural Show at Shrewsbury. For these a few words must be added.

Sir Gregory Parsloe-Parsloe, of Matchingham Hall, was
there, of course, but it would not have escaped the notice
of a close observer that his mien lacked something of the
haughty arrogance which had characterized it in other
years. From time to time, as he paced the tent devoted to
the exhibition of vegetables, he might have been seen to
bite his lip, and his eye had something of that brooding
look which Napoleon's must have worn at Waterloo.

But there was the right stuff in Sir Gregory. He was a
gentleman and a sportsman. In the Parsloe tradition there
was nothing small or mean. Half-way down the tent he
stopped, and with a quick, manly gesture thrust out his
hand.

'Congratulate you, Emsworth,' he said huskily.

Lord Emsworth looked up with a start. He had been
deep in his thoughts.

'Eh? Oh, thanks. Thanks, my dear fellow, thanks,
thanks. Thank you very much.' He hesitated. 'Er – can't
both win, eh?'

Sir Gregory puzzled it out and saw that he was right.

'No,' he said. 'No. See what you mean. Can't both win.
No getting round that.'

He nodded and walked on, with who knows what vultures gnawing at his broad bosom. And Lord Emsworth –
with Angus McAllister, who had been a silent, beard-
waggling witness of the scene, at his side – turned once
more to stare reverently at that which lay on the strawy
bottom of one of the largest packing-cases ever seen in
Shrewsbury town.

A card had been attached to the exterior of the packing-
case. It bore the simple legend:

PUMPKINS. FIRST PRIZE

CHAPTER 2

Lord Emsworth Acts for the Best

THE housekeeper's room at Blandings Castle, G.H.Q. of the domestic staff that ministered to the needs of the Earl of Emsworth, was in normal circumstances a pleasant and cheerful apartment. It caught the afternoon sun; and the paper which covered its walls had been conceived in a jovial spirit by someone who held that the human eye, resting on ninety-seven simultaneous pink birds perched upon ninety-seven blue rose-bushes, could not but be agreeably stimulated and refreshed. Yet, with the entry of Beach, the butler, it was as though there had crept into its atmosphere a chill dreariness; and Mrs Twemlow, the housekeeper, laying down her knitting, gazed at him in alarm.

'Whatever is the matter, Mr Beach?'

The butler stared moodily out of the window. His face was drawn and he breathed heavily, as a man will who is suffering from a combination of strong emotion and adenoids. A ray of sunshine, which had been advancing jauntily along the carpet, caught sight of his face and slunk out, abashed.

'I have come to a decision, Mrs Twemlow.'

'What about?'

'Ever since his lordship started to grow it I have seen the writing on the wall plainer and plainer, and now I have made up my mind. The moment his lordship returns from London, I tender my resignation. Eighteen years have I served in his lordship's household, commencing as under-footman and rising to my present position, but now the end has come.'

'You don't mean you're going just because his lordship has grown a beard?'

'It is the only way, Mrs Twemlow. That beard is

weakening his lordship's position throughout the entire country-side. Are you aware that at the recent Sunday school treat I heard cries of "Beaver!"?'

'No!'

'Yes! And this spirit of mockery and disrespect will spread. And, what is more, that beard is alienating the best elements in the County. I saw Sir Gregory Parsloe-Parsloe look very sharp at it when he dined with us last Friday.'

'It is not a handsome beard,' admitted the housekeeper.

'It is not. And his lordship must be informed. As long as I remain in his lordship's service, it is impossible for me to speak. So I shall tender my resignation. Once that is done, my lips will no longer be sealed. Is that buttered toast under that dish, Mrs Twemlow?'

'Yes, Mr Beach. Take a slice. It will cheer you up.'

'Cheer me up!' said the butler, with a hollow laugh that sounded like a knell.

It was fortunate that Lord Emsworth, seated at the time of this conversation in the smoking-room of the Senior Conservative Club in London, had no suspicion of the supreme calamity that was about to fall upon him; for there was already much upon his mind.

In the last few days, indeed, everything seemed to have gone wrong. Angus McAllister, his head-gardener, had reported an alarming invasion of greenfly among the roses. A favourite and respected cow, strongly fancied for the Milk-Giving Jerseys event at the forthcoming Cattle Show, had contracted a mysterious ailment which was baffling the skill of the local vet. And on top of all this a telegram had arrived from his lordship's younger son, the Hon. Frederick Threepwood, announcing that he was back in England and desirous of seeing his father immediately.

This, felt Lord Emsworth, as he stared bleakly before him at the little groups of happy Senior Conservatives, was the most unkindest cut of all. What on earth was Freddie doing in England? Eight months before he had married the only daughter of Donaldson's Dog-Biscuits, of Long

Island City, in the United States of America; and in Long
Island City he ought now to have been, sedulously pro-
moting the dog-biscuit industry's best interests. Instead of
which, here he was in London – and, according to his telegram, in trouble.

Lord Emsworth passed a hand over his chin, to assist
thought, and was vaguely annoyed by some obstacle that
intruded itself in the path of his fingers. Concentrating his
faculties, such as they were, on this obstacle, he discovered
it to be his beard. It irritated him. Hitherto, in moments of
stress, he had always derived comfort from the feel of a
clean-shaven chin. He felt now as if he were rubbing his
hand over seaweed; and most unjustly – for it was certainly
not that young man's fault that he had decided to grow a
beard – he became aware of an added sense of grievance
against the Hon. Freddie.

It was at this moment that he perceived his child approaching him across the smoking-room floor.

'Hullo, guv'nor!' said Freddie.

'Well, Frederick?' said Lord Emsworth.

There followed a silence. Freddie was remembering that
he had not met his father since the day when he had slipped
into the latter's hand a note announcing his marriage to a
girl whom Lord Emsworth had never seen – except once,
through a telescope, when he, Freddie, was kissing her in
the grounds of Blandings Castle. Lord Emsworth, on his
side, was brooding on that phrase 'in trouble', which had
formed so significant a part of his son's telegram. For fifteen
years he had been reluctantly helping Freddie out of
trouble; and now, when it had seemed that he was off his
hands for ever, the thing had started all over again.

'Do sit down,' he said testily.

Freddie had been standing on one leg, and his con-
strained attitude annoyed Lord Emsworth.

'Right-ho,' said Freddie, taking a chair. 'I say, guv'nor,
since when the foliage?'

'What?'

'The beard. I hardly recognized you.'

Another spasm of irritation shot through his lordship.

'Never mind my beard!'

'I don't if you don't,' said Freddie agreeably. 'It was dashed good of you, guv'nor, to come bounding up to town so promptly.'

'I came because your telegram said that you were in trouble.'

'British,' said Freddie approvingly. 'Very British.'

'Though what trouble you can be in I cannot imagine. It is surely not money again?'

'Oh, no. Not money. If that had been all, I would have applied to the good old pop-in-law. Old Donaldson's an ace. He thinks the world of me.'

'Indeed? I met Mr Donaldson only once, but he struck me as a man of sound judgement.'

'That's what I say. He thinks I'm a wonder. If it were simply a question of needing a bit of the ready, I could touch him like a shot. But it isn't money that's the trouble. It's Aggie. My wife, you know.'

'Well?'

'She's left me.'

'Left you!'

'Absolutely flat. Buzzed off, and the note pinned to the pin-cushion. She's now at the Savoy and won't let me come near her; and I'm at a service-flat in King Street, eating my jolly old heart out, if you know what I mean.'

Lord Emsworth uttered a deep sigh. He gazed drearily at his son, marvelling that it should be in the power of any young man, even a specialist like Freddie, so consistently to make a mess of his affairs. By what amounted to a miracle this offspring of his had contrived to lure a millionaire's daughter into marrying him; and now, it seemed, he had let her get away. Years before, when a boy, and romantic as most boys are, his lordship had sometimes regretted that the Emsworths, though an ancient clan, did not possess a Family Curse. How little he had suspected that he was shortly about to become the father of it.

'The fault,' he said tonelessly, 'was, I suppose, yours?'

'In a way, yes. But —'

'What precisely occurred?'

'Well, it was like this, guv'nor. You know how keen I've always been on the movies. Going to every picture I could manage, and so forth. Well, one night, as I was lying awake, I suddenly got the idea for a scenario of my own. And dashed good it was, too. It was about a poor man who had an accident, and the coves at the hospital said that an operation was the only thing that could save his life. But they wouldn't operate without five hundred dollars down in advance, and he hadn't got five hundred dollars. So his wife got hold of a millionaire.'

'What,' inquired Lord Emsworth, 'is all this drivel?'

'Drivel, guv'nor?' said Freddie, wounded. 'I'm only telling you my scenario.'

'I have no wish to hear it. What I am anxious to learn from you – in as few words as possible – is the reason for the breach between your wife and yourself.'

'Well, I'm telling you. It all started with the scenario. When I'd written it, I naturally wanted to sell it to somebody; and just about then Pauline Petite came East and took a house at Great Neck, and a pal of mine introduced me to her.'

'Who is Pauline Petite?'

'Good heavens, guv'nor!' Freddie stared, amazed. 'You don't mean to sit there and tell me you've never heard of Pauline Petite! The movie star. Didn't you see "Passion's Slaves"?'

'I did not.'

'Nor "Silken Fetters"?'

'Never.'

'Nor "Purple Passion"? Nor "Bonds of Gold"? Nor "Seduction"? Great Scott, guv'nor, you haven't lived!'

'What about this woman?'

'Well, a pal introduced me to her, you see, and I started to pave the way to getting her interested in this scenario of mine. Because, if she liked it, of course it meant everything. Well, this involved seeing a good deal of her, you understand, and one night Jane Yorke happened to come on us having a bite together at an inn.'

'Good God!'

'Oh, it was all perfectly respectable, guv'nor. All strictly on the up-and-up. Purely a business relationship. But the trouble was I had kept the thing from Aggie because I wanted to surprise her. I wanted to be able to come to her with the scenario accepted and tell her I wasn't such a fool as I looked.'

'Any woman capable of believing that —'

'And most unfortunately I had said that I had to go to Chicago that night on business. So, what with one thing and another — Well, as I said just now, she's at the Savoy and I'm —'

'Who is Jane Yorke?'

A scowl marred Freddie's smooth features.

'A pill, guv'nor. One of the worst. A Jebusite and Amalekite. If it hadn't been for her, I believe I could have fixed the thing. But she got hold of Aggie and whisked her away and poisoned her mind. This woman, guv'nor, has got a brother in the background, and she wanted Aggie to marry the brother. And my belief is that she is trying to induce Aggie to pop over to Paris and get a divorce, so as to give the blighted brother another look in, dash him! So now, guv'nor, is the time for action. Now is the moment to rally round as never before. I rely on you.'

'Me? What on earth do you expect me to do?'

'Why, go to her and plead with her. They do it in the movies. I've seen thousands of pictures where the white-haired old father —'

'Stuff and nonsense!' said Lord Emsworth, stung to the quick – for, like so many well-preserved men of ripe years, he was under the impression that he was merely slightly brindled. 'You have made your bed, and you must stew in it.'

'Eh?'

'I mean, you must stew in your own juice. You have brought this trouble on yourself by your own idiotic behaviour, and you must bear the consequences.'

'You mean you won't go and plead!'

'No.'

'You mean yes?'

'I mean no.'

'Not plead?' said Freddie, desiring to get this thing clear.

'I refuse to allow myself to be drawn into the matter.'

'You won't even give her a ring on the telephone?'

'I will not.'

'Oh, come, guv'nor. Be a sport. Her suite's Number Sixty-seven. You can get her in a second and state my case, all for the cost of twopence. Have a pop at it.'

'No.'

Freddie rose with set face.

'Very well,' he said tensely. 'Then I may as well tell you, guv'nor, that my life is as good as over. The future holds nothing for me. I am a spent egg. If Aggie goes to Paris and gets that divorce, I shall retire to some quiet spot and there pass the few remaining years of my existence, a blighted wreck. Good-bye, guv'nor.'

'Good-bye.'

'Honk-honk!' said Freddie moodily.

As a general rule, Lord Emsworth was an early and a sound sleeper, one of the few qualities which he shared with Napoleon Bonaparte being the ability to slumber the moment his head touched the pillow. But that night, weighed down with his troubles, he sought unconsciouness in vain. And somewhere in the small hours of the morning he sat up in bed, quaking. A sudden grisly thought had occurred to him.

Freddie had stated that, in the event of his wife obtaining a divorce, he proposed to retire for the rest of his life to some quiet spot. Suppose by 'quiet spot' he meant Blandings Castle! The possibility shook Lord Emsworth like an ague. Freddie had visited Blandings for extended periods before, and it was his lordship's considered opinion that the boy was a worse menace to the happy life of rural England than botts, greenfly, or foot-and-mouth disease. The prospect of having him at Blandings indefinitely affected Lord Emsworth like a blow on the base of the skull.

An entirely new line of thought was now opened. Had he in the recent interview, he asked himself, been as kind as he should have been? Had he not been a little harsh? Had he been just a shade lacking in sympathy? Had he played quite the part a father ought to have played?

The answers to the questions, in the order stated, were as follows: No. Yes. Yes. And No.

Waking after a belated sleep and sipping his early tea, Lord Emsworth found himself full of a new resolve. He had changed his mind. It was his intention now to go to this daughter-in-law of his and plead with her as no father-in-law had ever pleaded yet.

A man who has had a disturbed night is not at his best on the following morning. Until after luncheon Lord Emsworth felt much too heavy-headed to do himself justice as a pleader. But a visit to the flowers at Kensington Gardens, followed by a capital chop and half a bottle of claret at the Regent Grill, put him into excellent shape. The heaviness had vanished, and he felt alert and quick-witted.

So much so that, on arriving at the Savoy Hotel, he behaved with a cunning of which he had never hitherto suspected himself capable. On the very verge of giving his name to the desk-clerk, he paused. It might well be, he reflected, that this daughter-in-law of his, including the entire Emsworth family in her feud, would, did she hear that he was waiting below, nip the whole programme in the bud by refusing to see him. Better, he decided, not to risk it. Moving away from the desk, he headed for the lift, and presently found himself outside the door of Suite Sixty-seven.

He tapped on the door. There was no answer. He tapped again, and, once more receiving no reply, felt a little nonplussed. He was not a very farseeing man, and the possibility that his daughter-in-law might not be at home had not occurred to him. He was about to go away when, peering at the door, he perceived that it was ajar. He pushed it open; and, ambling in, found himself in a cosy sitting-room, crowded, as feminine sitting-rooms are apt to be, with flowers of every description.

Flowers were always a magnet to Lord Emsworth, and for some happy minutes he pottered from vase to vase, sniffing.

It was after he had sniffed for perhaps the twentieth time that the impression came to him that the room contained a curious echo. It was almost as though, each time he sniffed, some other person sniffed too. And yet the place was apparently empty. To submit the acoustics to a final test, his lordship sniffed once more. But this time the sound that followed was of a more sinister character. It sounded to Lord Emsworth exactly like a snarl.

It was a snarl. Chancing to glance floorwards, he became immediately aware, in close juxtaposition to his ankles, of what appeared at first sight to be a lady's muff. But, this being one of his bright afternoons, he realized in the next instant that it was no muff but a toy dog of the kind which women are only too prone to leave lying about their sitting-rooms.

'God bless my soul!' exclaimed Lord Emsworth, piously commending his safety to Heaven, as so many of his rugged ancestors had done in rather similar circumstances on the battle-fields of the Middle Ages.

He backed uneasily. The dog followed him. It appeared to have no legs, but to move by faith alone.

'Go away, sir!' said Lord Emsworth.

He hated small dogs. They nipped you. Take your eye off them, and they had you by the ankle before you knew where you were. Discovering that his manoeuvres had brought him to a door, he decided to take cover. He opened the door and slipped through. Blood will tell. An Emsworth had taken cover at Agincourt.

He was now in a bedroom, and, judging by the look of

things, likely to remain there for some time. The woolly dog, foiled by superior intelligence, was now making no attempt to conceal its chagrin. It had cast off all pretence of armed neutrality and was yapping with a hideous intensity and shrillness. And ever and anon it scratched with baffled fury at the lower panels.

'Go away, sir!' thundered his lordship.

'Who's there?'

Lord Emsworth leaped like a jumping bean. So convinced had he been of the emptiness of this suite of rooms that the voice, speaking where no voice should have been, crashed into his nerve centres like a shell.

'Who is there?'

The mystery, which had begun to assume an aspect of the supernatural, was solved. On the other side of the room was a door, and it was from behind this that the voice had spoken. It occurred to Lord Emsworth that it was merely part of the general malignity of Fate that he should have selected for a formal father-in-lawful call the moment when his daughter-in-law was taking a bath.

He approached the door, and spoke soothingly.

'Pray do not be alarmed, my dear.'

'Who are you? What are you doing in my room?'

'There is no cause for alarm —'

He broke off abruptly, for his words had suddenly been proved fundamentally untrue. There was very vital cause for alarm. The door of the bedroom had opened, and the muff-like dog, shrilling hate, was scuttling in its peculiar legless manner straight for his ankles.

Peril brings out unsuspected qualities in every man. Lord Emsworth was not a professional acrobat, but the leap he gave in this crisis would have justified his being mistaken for one. He floated through the air like a homing bird. From where he had been standing the bed was a considerable distance away, but he reached it with inches to spare, and stood there, quivering. Below him, the woolly dog raged like the ocean at the base of a cliff.

It was at this point that his lordship became aware of a

young woman standing in the doorway through which he had just passed.

About this young woman there were many points which would have found little favour in the eyes of a critic of feminine charm. She was too short, too square, and too solid. She had a much too determined chin. And her hair was of an unpleasing gingery hue. But the thing Lord Emsworth liked least about her was the pistol she was pointing at his head.

A plaintive voice filtered through the bathroom door. 'Who's there?'

'It's a man,' said the girl behind the gun.

'I know it's a man. He spoke to me. Who is he?'

'I don't know. A nasty-looking fellow. I saw him hanging about the passage outside your door, and I got my gun and came along. Come on out.'

'I can't. I'm all wet.'

It is not easy for a man who is standing on a bed with his hands up to achieve dignity, but Lord Emsworth did the best he could.

'My dear madam!'

'What are you doing here?'

'I found the door ajar —'

'And walked in to see if there were any jewel-cases ajar, too. I think,' added the young woman, raising her voice so as to make herself audible to the unseen bather, 'it's Dopey Smith.'

'Who?'

'Dopey Smith. The fellow the cops said tried for your jewels in New York. He must have followed you over here.'

'I am not Dopey Smith, madam,' cried his lordship. 'I am the Earl of Emsworth.'

'You are?'

'Yes, I am.'

'Yes, you are!'

'I came to see my daughter-in-law.'

'Well, here she is.'

The bathroom door opened, and there emerged a charming figure draped in a kimono. Even in that tense moment Lord Emsworth was conscious of a bewildered astonishment that such a girl could ever have stooped to mate with his son Frederick.

'Who did you say he was?' she asked, recommending herself still more strongly to his lordship's esteem by scooping up the woolly dog and holding it securely in her arms.

'He says he's the Earl of Emsworth.'

'I am the Earl of Emsworth.'

The girl in the kimono looked keenly at him as he descended from the bed.

'You know, Jane,' she said, a note of uncertainty in her voice, 'it might be. He looks very like Freddie.'

The appalling slur on his personal appearance held Lord Emsworth dumb. Like other men, he had had black moments when his looks had not altogether satisfied him, but he had never supposed that he had a face like Freddie's.

The girl with the pistol uttered a stupefying whoop.

'Jiminy Chistmas!' she cried. 'Don't you see?'

'See what?'

'Why, it *is* Freddie. Disguised. Trying to get at you this way. It's just the sort of movie stunt he would think clever. Take them off, Ralph Vandeleur – I know you!'

She reached out a clutching hand, seized his lordship's beard in a vice-like grip, and tugged with all the force of a modern girl, trained from infancy at hockey, tennis, and Swedish exercises.

It had not occurred to Lord Emsworth a moment before that anything could possibly tend to make his situation more uncomfortable than it already was. He saw now that he had been mistaken in this view. Agony beyond his liveliest dreams flamed through his shrinking frame.

The girl regarded him with a somewhat baffled look.

'H'm!' she said disappointedly. 'It seems to be real. Unless,' she continued, on a more optimistic note, 'he's fixed it on with specially strong fish-glue or something. I'd better try again.'

'No, don't,' said his lordship's daughter-in-law. 'It isn't Freddie. I would have recognized him at once.'

'Then he's a crook, after all. Kindly step into that cupboard, George, while I phone for the constabulary.'

Lord Emsworth danced a few steps.

'I will not step into cupboards. I insist on being heard. I don't know who this woman is —'

'My name's Jane Yorke, if you're curious.'

'Ah! The woman who poisons my son's wife's mind against him! I know all about you.' He turned to the girl in the kimono. 'Yesterday my son Frederick implored me by telegram to come to London. I saw him at my club. Stop that dog barking!'

'Why shouldn't he bark?' said Miss Yorke. 'He's in his own home.'

'He told me,' proceeded Lord Emsworth, raising his voice, 'that there had been a little misunderstanding between you —'

'Little misunderstanding is good,' said Miss Yorke.

'He dined with that woman for a purpose.'

'And directly I saw them', said Miss Yorke, 'I knew what the purpose was.'

The Hon. Mrs Threepwood looked at her friend, wavering.

'I believe it's true,' she said, 'and he really is Lord Emsworth. He seems to know all that happened. How could he know if Freddie hadn't told him?'

'If this fellow is a crook from the other side, of course he would know. The thing was in *Broadway Whispers* and *Town Gossip*, wasn't it?'

'All the same —'

The telephone bell rang sharply.

'I assure you —' began Lord Emsworth.

'Right!' said the unpleasant Miss Yorke, at the receiver. 'Send him right up.' She regarded his lordship with a brightly triumphant eye. 'You're out of luck, my friend,' she said. 'Lord Emsworth has just arrived, and he's on his way up now.'

There are certain situations in which the human brain may be excused for reeling. Lord Emsworth's did not so much reel as perform a kind of dance, as if it were in danger of coming unstuck. Always a dreamy and absent-minded man, unequal to the rough hurly-burly of life, he had passed this afternoon through an ordeal which might well have unsettled the most practical. And this extraordinary announcement, coming on top of all he had been through, was too much for him. He tottered into the sitting-room and sank into a chair. It seemed to him that he was living in a nightmare.

And certainly in the figure that entered a few moments later there was nothing whatever to correct this impression. It might have stepped straight into anybody's nightmare and felt perfectly at home right from the start.

The figure was that of a tall, thin man with white hair and a long and flowing beard of the same venerable hue. Strange as it seemed that a person of such appearance should not have been shot on sight early in his career, he obviously had reached an extremely advanced age. He was either a man of about a hundred and fifty who was rather young for his years or a man of about a hundred and ten who had been aged by trouble.

'My dear child!' piped the figure in a weak, quavering voice.

'Freddie!' cried the girl in the kimono.

'Oh, dash it!' said the figure.

There was a pause, broken by a sort of gasping moan from Lord Emsworth. More and more every minute his lordship was feeling the strain.

'Good God, guv'nor!' said the figure, sighting him.

His wife pointed at Lord Emsworth.

'Freddie, is that your father?'

'Oh, yes. Rather. Of course. Absolutely. But he said he wasn't coming.'

'I changed my mind,' said Lord Emsworth in a low, stricken voice.

'I told you so, Jane,' said the girl. 'I thought he was Lord

Emsworth all the time. Surely you can see the likeness now?'

A kind of wail escaped his lordship.

'Do I look like that?' he said brokenly. He gazed at his son once more and shut his eyes.

'Well,' said Miss Yorke, in her detestable managing way, turning her forceful personality on the newcomer, 'now that you are here, Freddie Threepwood, looking like Father Christmas, what's the idea? Aggie told you never to come near her again.'

A young man of his natural limpness of character might well have retired in disorder before this attack, but Love had apparently made Frederick Threepwood a man of steel. Removing his beard and eyebrows, he directed a withering glance at Miss Yorke.

'I don't want to talk to you,' he said. 'You're a serpent in the bosom. I mean a snake in the grass.'

'Oh, am I?'

'Yes, you are. You poisoned Aggie's mind against me. If it hadn't been for you, I could have got her alone and told her my story as man to man.'

'Well, let's hear it now. You've had plenty of time to rehearse it.'

Freddie turned to his wife with a sweeping gesture.

'I —' He paused. 'I say, Aggie, old thing, you look perfectly topping in that kimono.'

'Stick to the point,' said Miss Yorke.

'That is the point,' said Mrs Freddie, not without a certain softness. 'But if you think I look perfectly topping, why do you go running around with movie-actresses with carroty hair?'

'Red-gold,' suggested Freddie deferentially.

'Carroty!'

'Carroty it is. You're absolutely right. I never liked it all along.'

'Then why were you dining with it?'

'Yes, why?' inquired Miss Yorke.

'I wish you wouldn't butt in,' said Freddie petulantly. 'I'm not talking to you.'

'You might just as well, for all the good it's going to do you.'

'Be quiet, Jane. Well, Freddie?'

'Aggie,' said the Hon. Freddie, 'it was this way.'

'Never believe a man who starts a story like that,' said Miss Yorke.

'Do please be quiet, Jane. Yes, Freddie?'

'I was trying to sell that carroty female a scenario, and I was keeping it from you because I wanted it to be a surprise.'

'Freddie darling! Was that really it?'

'You don't mean to say —' began Miss Yorke incredulously.

'Absolutely it. And, in order to keep in with the woman – whom, I may as well tell you, I disliked rather heartily from the start – I had to lush her up a trifle from time to time.'

'Of course.'

'You have to with these people.'

'Naturally.'

'Makes all the difference in the world if you push a bit of food into them preparatory to talking business.'

'All the difference in the world.'

Miss Yorke, who seemed temporarily to have lost her breath, recovered it.

'You don't mean to tell me,' she cried, turning in a kind of wild despair to the injured wife, 'that you really believe this apple sauce?'

'Of course she does,' said Freddie. 'Don't you, precious?'

'Of course I do, sweetie-pie.'

'And, what's more,' said Freddie, pulling from his breast-pocket a buff-coloured slip of paper with the air of one who draws from his sleeve that extra ace which makes all the difference in a keenly contested game, 'I can prove it. Here's a cable that came this morning from the Super-Ultra-Art Film Company, offering me a thousand solid dollars for the scenario. So another time, you, will you kindly refrain from judging your – er – fellows by the beastly light of your own – ah – foul imagination?'

'Yes,' said his wife, 'I must say, Jane, that you have made as much mischief as anyone ever did. I wish in future you would stop interfering in other people's concerns.'

'Spoken,' said Freddie, 'with vim and not a little terse good sense. And I may add —'

'If you ask me,' said Miss Yorke, 'I think it's a fake.'

'What's a fake?'

'That cable.'

'What do you mean, a fake?' cried Freddie indignantly. 'Read it for yourself.'

'It's quite easy to get cables cabled you by cabling a friend in New York to cable them.'

'I don't get that,' said Freddie, puzzled.

'I do,' said his wife; and there shone in her eyes the light that shines only in the eyes of wives who, having swallowed their husband's story, resent destructive criticism from outsiders. 'And I never want to see you again, Jane Yorke.'

'Same here,' agreed Freddie. 'In Turkey they'd shove a girl like that in a sack and drop her in the Bosphorus.'

'I might as well go,' said Miss Yorke.

'And don't come back,' said Freddie. 'The door is behind you.'

The species of trance which had held Lord Emsworth in its grip during the preceding conversational exchanges was wearing off. And now, perceiving that Miss Yorke was apparently as unpopular with the rest of the company as with himself, he came gradually to life again. His recovery was hastened by the slamming of the door and the spectacle of his son Frederick clasping in his arms a wife who, his lordship had never forgotten, was the daughter of probably the only millionaire in existence who had that delightful willingness to take Freddie off his hands which was, in Lord Emsworth's eyes, the noblest quality a millionaire could possess.

He sat up and blinked feebly. Though much better, he was still weak.

'What was your scenario about, sweetness?' asked Mrs Freddie.

'I'll tell you, angel-face. Or should we stir up the guv'nor? He seems a bit under the weather.'

'Better leave him to rest for awhile. That woman Jane Yorke upset him.'

'She would upset anybody. If there's one person I bar, it's the blister who comes between man and wife. Not right, I mean, coming between man and wife. My scenario's about a man and wife. This fellow, you understand, is a poor cove – no money, if you see what I mean – and he has an accident, and the hospital blokes say they won't operate unless he can chip in with five hundred dollars down in advance. But where to get it? You see the situation?'

'Oh, yes.'

'Strong, what?'

'Awfully strong.'

'Well, it's nothing to how strong it gets later on. The cove's wife gets hold of a millionaire bloke and vamps him and lures him to the flat and gets him to promise he'll cough up the cash. Meanwhile, cutbacks of the doctor at the hospital on the phone. And she laughing merrily so as not to let the millionaire bloke guess that her heart is aching. I forgot to tell you the cove had to be operated on immediately or he would hand in his dinner-pail. Dramatic, eh?'

'Frightfully.'

'Well, then the millionaire bloke demands his price. I thought of calling it "A Woman's Price".'

'Splendid.'

'And now comes the blow-out. They go into the bed-room and — Oh, hullo, guv'nor! Feeling better?'

Lord Emsworth had risen. He was tottering a little as he approached them, but his mind was at rest.

'Much better, thank you.'

'You know my wife, what?'

'Oh, Lord Emsworth,' said Mrs Freddie, 'I'm so dreadfully sorry. I wouldn't have had anything like this happen for the world. But —'

Lord Emsworth patted her hand paternally. Once more he was overcome with astonishment that his son Frederick should have been able to win the heart of a girl so beautiful, so sympathetic, so extraordinarily rich.

'The fault was entirely mine, my dear child. But —' He paused. Something was plainly troubling him. 'Tell me, when Frederick was wearing that beard – when Frederick was – was – when he was wearing that beard, did he really look like me?'

'Oh, yes. Very like.'

'Thank you, my dear. That was all I wanted to know. I will leave you now. You will wish to be alone. You must come down to Blandings, my dear child, at the very earliest opportunity.'

He walked thoughtfully from the room.

'Does this hotel,' he inquired of the man who took him down in the lift, 'contain a barber's shop?'

'Yes, sir.'

'I wonder if you would direct me to it?' said his lordship.

Lord Emsworth sat in his library at Blandings Castle, drinking that last restful whisky and soda of the day. Through the open window came the scent of flowers and the little noises of the summer night.

He should have been completely at rest, for much had happened since his return to sweeten life for him. Angus McAllister had reported that the greenfly were yielding to treatment with whale-oil solution; and the stricken cow had taken a sudden turn for the better, and at last advices was sitting up and taking nourishment with something of the old appetite. Moreover, as he stroked his shaven chin, his lordship felt a better, lighter man, as if some burden had fallen from him.

And yet, as he sat there, a frown was on his forehead.

He rang the bell.

'M'lord?'

Lord Emsworth looked at his faithful butler with appreciation. Deuce of a long time Beach had been at the Castle, and would, no doubt, be there for many a year to come. A good fellow. Lord Emsworth had liked the way the man's eyes had lighted up on his return, as if the sight of his employer had removed a great weight from his mind.

'Oh, Beach,' said his lordship, 'kindly put in a trunk-call to London on the telephone.'

'Very good, m'lord.'

'Get through to Suite Number Sixty-seven at the Savoy Hotel, and speak to Mr Frederick.'

'Yes, your lordship.'

'Say that I particularly wish to know how that scenario of his ended.'

'Scenario, your lordship?'

'Scenario.'

'Very good, m'lord.'

Lord Emsworth returned to his reverie. Time passed. The butler returned.

'I have spoken to Mr Frederick, your lordship.'

'Yes?'

'He instructed me to give your lordship his best wishes, and to tell you that, when the millionaire and Mr Cove's wife entered the bedroom, there was a black jaguar tied to the foot of the bed.'

'A jaguar?'

'A jaguar, your lordship. Mrs Cove stated that it was there to protect her honour, whereupon the millionaire, touched by this, gave her the money, and they sang the Theme Song as a duet. Mr Cove made a satisfactory recovery after his operation, your lordship.'

'Ah!' said Lord Emsworth, expelling a deep breath. 'Thank you, Beach, that is all.'

CHAPTER 3

Pig-hoo-o-o-o-ey!

THANKS to the publicity given to the matter by *The Bridgnorth, Shifnal, and Albrighton Argus* (with which is incorporated *The Wheat-Growers' Intelligencer and Stock Breeders' Gazetteer*), the whole world to-day knows that the silver medal in the Fat Pigs class at the eighty-seventh annual Shropshire Agricultural Show was won by the Earl of Emsworth's black Berkshire sow, Empress of Blandings.

Very few people, however, are aware how near that splendid animal came to missing the coveted honour.

Now it can be told.

This brief chapter of Secret History may be said to have begun on the night of the eighteenth of July, when George Cyril Wellbeloved (twenty-nine), pig-man in the employ of Lord Emsworth, was arrested by Police-Constable Evans of Market Blandings for being drunk and disorderly in the tap-room of the Goat and Feathers. On July the nineteenth, after first offering to apologize, then explaining that it had been his birthday, and finally attempting to prove an alibi, George Cyril was very properly jugged for fourteen days without the option of a fine.

On July the twentieth, Empress of Blandings, always hitherto a hearty and even a boisterous feeder, for the first time on record declined all nourishment. And on the morning of July the twenty-first, the veterinary surgeon called in to diagnose and deal with this strange asceticism, was compelled to confess to Lord Emsworth that the thing was beyond his professional skill.

Let us just see, before proceeding, that we have got these dates correct:

July 18. – Birthday Orgy of Cyril Wellbeloved.

July 19. – Incarceration of Ditto.

July 20. – Pig Lays off the Vitamins.

July 21. – Veterinary Surgeon Baffled.
Right.

The effect of the veterinary surgeon's announcement on Lord Emsworth was overwhelming. As a rule, the wear and tear of our complex modern life left this vague and amiable peer unscathed. So long as he had sunshine, regular meals, and complete freedom from the society of his younger son Frederick, he was placidly happy. But there were chinks in his armour, and one of these had been pierced this morning. Dazed by the news he had received, he stood at the window of the great library of Blandings Castle, looking out with unseeing eyes.

As he stood there, the door opened. Lord Emsworth turned; and having blinked once or twice, as was his habit when confronted suddenly with anything, recognized in the handsome and imperious-looking woman who had entered, his sister, Lady Constance Keeble. Her demeanour, like his own, betrayed the deepest agitation.

'Clarence,' she cried, 'an awful thing has happened!'

Lord Emsworth nodded dully.

'I know. He's just told me.'

'What! Has he been here?'

'Only this moment left.'

'Why did you let him go? You must have known I would want to see him.'

'What good would that have done?'

'I could at least have assured him of my sympathy,' said Lady Constance stiffly.

'Yes, I suppose you could,' said Lord Emsworth, having considered the point. 'Not that he deserves any sympathy. The man's an ass.'

'Nothing of the kind. A most intelligent young man, as young men go.'

'Young? Would you call him young? Fifty, I should have said, if a day.'

'Are you out of your senses? Heacham fifty?'

'Not Heacham. Smithers.'

As frequently happened to her when in conversation with her brother, Lady Constance experienced a swimming sensation in the head.

'Will you kindly tell me, Clarence, in a few simple words, what you imagine we are talking about?'

'I'm talking about Smithers. Empress of Blandings is refusing her food, and Smithers says he can't do anything about it. And he calls himself a vet!'

'Then you haven't heard? Clarence, a dreadful thing has happened. Angela has broken off her engagement to Heacham.'

'And the Agricultural Show on Wednesday week!'

'What on earth has that got to do with it?' demanded Lady Constance, feeling a recurrence of the swimming sensation.

'What has it got to do with it?' said Lord Emsworth warmly. 'My champion sow, with less than ten days to prepare herself for a most searching examination in competition with all the finest pigs in the county, starts refusing her food —'

'Will you stop maundering on about your insufferable pig and give your attention to something that really matters? I tell you that Angela – your niece Angela – has broken off her engagement to Lord Heacham and expresses her intention of marrying that hopeless ne'er-do-well, James Belford.'

'The son of old Belford, the parson?'

'Yes.'

'She can't. He's in America.'

'He is not in America. He is in London.'

'No,' said Lord Emsworth, shaking his head sagely. 'You're wrong. I remember meeting his father two years ago out on the road by Meeker's twenty-acre field, and he distinctly told me the boy was sailing for America next day. He must be there by this time.'

'Can't you understand? He's come back.'

'Oh? Come back? I see. Come *back*?'

'You know there was once a silly sentimental sort of

affair between him and Angela; but a year after he left she became engaged to Heacham and I thought the whole thing was over and done with. And now it seems that she met this young man Belford when she was in London last week, and it has started all over again. She tells me she has written to Heacham and broken the engagement.'

There was a silence. Brother and sister remained for a space plunged in thought. Lord Emsworth was the first to speak.

'We've tried acorns,' he said. 'We've tried skim milk. And we've tried potato-peel. But, no, she won't touch them.'

Conscious of two eyes raising blisters on his sensitive skin, he came to himself with a start.

'Absurd! Ridiculous! Preposterous!' he said, hurriedly. 'Breaking the engagement? Pooh! Tush! What nonsense! I'll have a word with that young man. If he thinks he can go about the place playing fast and loose with my niece and jilting her without so much as a —'

'Clarence!'

Lord Emsworth blinked. Something appeared to be wrong, but he could not imagine what. It seemed to him that in his last speech he had struck just the right note – strong, forceful, dignified.

'Eh?'

'It is Angela who has broken the engagement.'

'Oh, Angela?'

'She is infatuated with this man Belford. And the point is, what are we to do about it?'

Lord Emsworth reflected.

'Take a strong line,' he said firmly. 'Stand no nonsense. Don't send 'em a wedding-present.'

There is no doubt that, given time, Lady Constance would have found and uttered some adequately corrosive comment on this imbecile suggestion; but even as she was swelling preparatory to giving tongue, the door opened and a girl came in.

She was a pretty girl, with fair hair and blue eyes which

in their softer moments probably reminded all sorts of people of twin lagoons slumbering beneath a southern sky. This, however, was not one of those moments. To Lord Emsworth, as they met his, they looked like something out of an oxy-acetylene blow-pipe; and, as far as he was capable of being disturbed by anything that was not his younger son Frederick, he was disturbed. Angela, it seemed to him, was upset about something; and he was sorry. He liked Angela.

To ease a tense situation, he said:

'Angela, my dear, do you know anything about pigs?'

The girl laughed. One of those sharp, bitter laughs which are so unpleasant just after breakfast.

'Yes, I do. You're one.'

'Me?'

'Yes, you. Aunt Constance says that, if I marry Jimmy, you won't let me have my money.'

'Money? Money?' Lord Emsworth was mildly puzzled. 'What money? You never lent me any money.'

Lady Constance's feelings found vent in a sound like an overheated radiator.

'I believe this absent-mindedness of yours is nothing but a ridiculous pose, Clarence. You know perfectly well that when poor Jane died she left you Angela's trustee.'

'And I can't touch my money without your consent till I'm twenty-five.'

'Well, how old are you?'

'Twenty-one.'

'Then what are you worrying about?' asked Lord Emsworth, surprised. 'No need to worry about it for another four years. God bless my soul, the money is quite safe. It is in excellent securities.'

Angela stamped her foot. An unladylike action, no doubt, but how much better than kicking an uncle with it, as her lower nature prompted.

'I have told Angela,' explained Lady Constance, 'that, while we naturally cannot force her to marry Lord Heacham, we can at least keep her money from being squandered by this wastrel on whom she proposes to throw herself away.'

'He isn't a wastrel. He's got quite enough money to marry me on, but he wants some capital to buy a partnership in a —'

'He is a wastrel. Wasn't he sent abroad because —'

'That was two years ago. And since then —'

'My dear Angela, you may argue until —'

'I'm not arguing. I'm simply saying that I'm going to marry Jimmy, if we both have to starve in the gutter.'

'What gutter?' asked his lordship, wrenching his errant mind away from thoughts of acorns.

'Any gutter.'

'Now, please listen to me, Angela.'

It seemed to Lord Emsworth that there was a frightful amount of conversation going on. He had the sensation of having become a mere bit of flotsam upon a tossing sea of female voices. Both his sister and his niece appeared to have much to say, and they were saying it simultaneously and fortissimo. He looked wistfully at the door.

It was smoothly done. A twist of the handle, and he was where beyond those voices there was peace. Galloping gaily down the stairs, he charged out into the sunshine.

His gaiety was not long-lived. Free at last to concentrate itself on the really serious issues of life, his mind grew sombre and grim. Once more there descended upon him the cloud which had been oppressing his soul before all this Heacham-Angela-Belford business began. Each step that took him nearer to the sty where the ailing Empress resided seemed a heavier step than the last. He reached the sty; and, draping himself over the rails, peered moodily at the vast expanse of pig within.

For, even though she had been doing a bit of dieting of late, Empress of Blandings was far from being an ill-nourished animal. She resembled a captive balloon with ears and a tail, and was as nearly circular as a pig can be without bursting. Nevertheless, Lord Emsworth, as he regarded her, mourned and would not be comforted. A few more square meals under her belt, and no pig in all Shropshire could have held its head up in the Empress's presence. And now, just for lack of those few meals, the supreme animal would probably be relegated to the mean obscurity of an 'Honourably Mentioned'. It was bitter, bitter.

He became aware that somebody was speaking to him; and, turning, perceived a solemn young man in riding breeches.

'I say,' said the young man.

Lord Emsworth, though he would have preferred solitude, was relieved to find that the intruder was at least one of his own sex. Women are apt to stray off into side-issues, but men are practical and can be relied on to stick to the fundamentals. Besides, young Heacham probably kept pigs himself and might have a useful hint or two up his sleeve.

'I say, I've just ridden over to see if there was anything I could do about this fearful business.'

'Uncommonly kind and thoughtful of you, my dear fellow,' said Lord Emsworth, touched. 'I fear things look very black.'

'It's an absolute mystery to me.'

'To me, too.'

'I mean to say, she was all right last week.'

'She was all right as late as the day before yesterday.'

'Seemed quite cheery and chirpy and all that.'

'Entirely so.'

'And then this happens – out of a blue sky, as you might say.'

'Exactly. It is insoluble. We have done everything possible to tempt her appetite.'

'Her appetite? Is Angela ill?'

'Angela? No, I fancy not. She seemed perfectly well a few minutes ago.'

'You've seen her this morning, then? Did she say anything about this fearful business?'

'No. She was speaking about some money.'

'It's all so dashed unexpected.'

'Like a bolt from the blue,' agreed Lord Emsworth.

'Such a thing has never happened before. I fear the worst. According to the Wolff-Lehmann feeding standards, a pig, if in health, should consume daily nourishment amounting to fifty-seven thousand eight hundred calories, these to consist of proteins four pounds five ounces, carbohydrates twenty-five pounds —'

'What has that got to do with Angela?'

'Angela?'

'I came to find out why Angela has broken off our engagement.'

Lord Emsworth marshalled his thoughts. He had a misty idea that he had heard something mentioned about that. It came back to him.

'Ah, yes, of course. She has broken off the engagement, hasn't she? I believe it is because she is in love with someone else. Yes, now that I recollect, that was distinctly stated. The whole thing comes back to me quite clearly. Angela has decided to marry someone else. I knew there was some satisfactory explanation. Tell me, my dear fellow, what are your views on linseed meal?'

'What do you mean, linseed meal?'

'Why, linseed meal,' said Lord Emsworth, not being able to find a better definition. 'As a food for pigs.'

'Oh, curse all pigs!'

'What!' There was a sort of astounded horror in Lord Emsworth's voice. He had never been particularly fond of young Heacham, for he was not a man who took much to his juniors, but he had not supposed him capable of anarchistic sentiments like this. 'What did you say?'

'I said, "Curse all pigs!" You keep talking about pigs. I'm not interested in pigs. I don't want to discuss pigs. Blast and damn every pig in existence!'

Lord Emsworth watched him, as he strode away, with an emotion that was partly indignation and partly relief – indignation that a landowner and a fellow son of Shropshire could have brought himself to utter such words, and relief that one capable of such utterance was not going to marry into his family. He had always in his woollen-headed way been very fond of his niece Angela, and it was nice to think that the child had such solid good sense and so much cool discernment. Many girls of her age would have been carried away by the glamour of young Heacham's position and wealth; but she, divining with an intuition beyond her years that he was unsound on the subject of pigs, had drawn back while there was still time and refused to marry him.

A pleasant glow suffused Lord Emsworth's bosom, to be frozen out a few moments later as he perceived his sister Constance bearing down upon him. Lady Constance was a beautiful woman, but there were times when the charm of her face was marred by a rather curious expression; and from nursery days onward his lordship had learned that this expression meant trouble. She was wearing it now.

'Clarence,' she said, 'I have had enough of this nonsense of Angela and young Belford. The thing cannot be allowed to go drifting on. You must catch the two o'clock train to London.'

'What! Why?'

'You must see this man Belford and tell him that, if Angela insists on marrying him, she will not have a penny for four years. I shall be greatly surprised if that piece of information does not put an end to the whole business.'

Lord Emsworth scratched meditatively at the Empress's tank-like back. A mutinous expression was on his mild face.

'Don't see why she shouldn't marry the fellow,' he mumbled.

'Marry James Belford?'

'I don't see why not. Seems fond of him and all that.'

'You never have had a grain of sense in your head, Clarence. Angela is going to marry Heacham.'

'Can't stand that man. All wrong about pigs.'

'Clarence, I don't wish to have any more discussion and argument. You will go to London on the two o'clock train. You will see Mr Belford. And you will tell him about Angela's money. Is that quite clear?'

'Oh, all right,' said his lordship moodily. 'All right, all right, all right.'

The emotions of the Earl of Emsworth, as he sat next day facing his luncheon-guest, James Bartholomew Belford, across a table in the main dining-room of the Senior Conservative Club, were not of the liveliest and most agreeable. It was bad enough to be in London at all on such a day of golden sunshine. To be charged, while there, with the task of blighting the romance of two young people for whom he entertained a warm regard was unpleasant to a degree.

For, now that he had given the matter thought, Lord Emsworth recalled that he had always liked this boy Belford. A pleasant lad, with, he remembered now, a healthy fondness for that rural existence which so appealed to himself. By no means the sort of fellow who, in the very presence and hearing of Empress of Blandings, would have spoken disparagingly and with oaths of pigs as a class. It occurred to Lord Emsworth, as it has occurred to so many people, that the distribution of money in this world is all wrong. Why should a man like pig-despising Heacham have a rent roll that ran into the tens of thousands, while this very deserving youngster had nothing?

These thoughts not only saddened Lord Emsworth – they embarrassed him. He hated unpleasantness, and it was suddenly borne in upon him that, after he had broken the news that Angela's bit of capital was locked up and not likely to get loose, conversation with his young friend during the remainder of lunch would tend to be somewhat difficult.

He made up his mind to postpone the revelation. During the meal, he decided, he would chat pleasantly of this and that; and then, later, while bidding his guest good-bye, he would spring the thing on him suddenly and dive back into the recesses of the club.

Considerably cheered at having solved a delicate problem with such adroitness, he started to prattle.

'The gardens at Blandings,' he said, 'are looking particularly attractive this summer. My head-gardener, Angus McAllister, is a man with whom I do not always find myself seeing eye to eye, notably in the matter of hollyhocks, on which I consider his views subversive to a degree; but there is no denying that he understands roses. The rose garden—'

'How well I remember that rose garden,' said James Belford, sighing slightly and helping himself to brussels sprouts. 'It was there that Angela and I used to meet on summer evenings.'

Lord Emsworth blinked. This was not an encouraging start, but the Emsworths were a fighting clan. He had another try.

'I have seldom seen such a blaze of colour as was to be witnessed there during the month of June. Both McAllister and I adopted a very strong policy with the slugs and plant lice, with the result that the place was a mass of flourishing Damasks and Ayrshires and —'

'Properly to appreciate roses,' said James Belford, 'you want to see them as a setting for a girl like Angela. With her fair hair gleaming against the green leaves she makes a rose garden seem a veritable Paradise.'

'No doubt,' said Lord Emsworth. 'No doubt. I am glad you liked my rose garden. At Blandings, of course, we have the natural advantage of loamy soil, rich in plant food and humus; but, as I often say to McAllister, and on this point we have never had the slightest disagreement, loamy soil by itself is not enough. You must have manure. If every autumn a liberal mulch of stable manure is spread upon the beds and the coarser parts removed in the spring before the annual forking —'

'Angela tells me,' said James Belford, 'that you have forbidden our marriage.'

Lord Emsworth choked dismally over his chicken. Directness of this kind, he told himself with a pang of self-pity, was the sort of thing young Englishmen picked up in America. Diplomatic circumlocution flourished only in a more leisurely civilization, and in those energetic and forceful surroundings you learned to Talk Quick and Do It Now, and all sorts of uncomfortable things.

'Er – well, yes, now you mention it, I believe some informal decision of that nature was arrived at. You see, my dear fellow, my sister Constance feels rather strongly —'

'I understand. I suppose she thinks I'm a sort of prodigal.'

'No, no, my dear fellow. She never said that. Wastrel was the term she employed.'

'Well, perhaps I did start out in business on those lines. But you can take it from me that when you find yourself employed on a farm in Nebraska belonging to an apple-jack-nourished patriarch with strong views on work and a good vocabulary, you soon develop a certain liveliness.'

'Are you employed on a farm?'

'I was employed on a farm.'

'Pigs?' said Lord Emsworth in a low, eager voice.

'Among other things.'

Lord Emsworth gulped. His fingers clutched at the table-cloth.

'Then perhaps, my dear fellow, you can give me some advice. For the last two days my prize sow, Empress of Blandings, has declined all nourishment. And the Agricultural Show is on Wednesday week. I am distracted with anxiety.'

James Belford frowned thoughtfully.

'What does your pig-man say about it?'

'My pig-man was sent to prison two days ago. Two days!' For the first time the significance of the coincidence struck him. 'You don't think that can have anything to do with the animal's loss of appetite?'

'Certainly. I imagine she is missing him and pining away because he isn't there.'

Lord Emsworth was surprised. He had only a distant acquaintance with George Cyril Wellbeloved, but from what he had seen of him he had not credited him with this fatal allure.

'She probably misses his afternoon call.'

Again his lordship found himself perplexed. He had had no notion that pigs were such sticklers for the formalities of social life.

'His call?'

'He must have had some special call that he used when he wanted her to come to dinner. One of the first things you learn on a farm is hog-calling. Pigs are temperamental. Omit to call them, and they'll starve rather than put on the nose-bag. Call them right, and they will follow you to the ends of the earth with their mouths watering.'

'God bless my soul! Fancy that.'

'A fact, I assure you. These calls vary in different parts of America. In Wisconsin, for example, the words "Poig, Poig, Poig" bring home – in both the literal and the figurative sense – the bacon. In Illinois, I believe they call "Burp, Burp, Burp", while in Iowa the phrase "Kus, Kus, Kus" is preferred. Proceeding to Minnesota, we find "Peega, Peega, Peega" or, alternatively, "Oink, Oink, Oink", whereas in Milwaukee, so largely inhabited by those of German descent, you will hear the good old Teuton "Komm Schweine, Komm Schweine". Oh, yes, there are all sorts of pig-calls, from the Massachusetts "Phew, Phew, Phew" to the "Loo-ey, Loo-ey, Loo-ey" of Ohio, not counting various local devices such as beating on tin cans with axes or rattling pebbles in a suit-case. I knew a man out in Nebraska who used to call his pigs by tapping on the edge of the trough with his wooden leg.'

'Did he, indeed?'

'But a most unfortunate thing happened. One evening, hearing a woodpecker at the top of a tree, they started shinning up it; and when the man came out he found them all lying there in a circle with their necks broken.'

'This is no time for joking,' said Lord Emsworth, pained.

'I'm not joking. Solid fact. Ask anybody out there.'

Lord Emsworth placed a hand to his throbbing forehead.

'But if there is this wide variety, we have no means of knowing which call Wellbeloved ...'

'Ah,' said James Belford, 'but wait. I haven't told you all. There is a master-word.'

'A what?'

'Most people don't know it, but I had it straight from the lips of Fred Patzel, the hog-calling champion of the Western States. What a man! I've known him to bring pork chops leaping from their plates. He informed me that, no matter whether an animal has been trained to answer to the Illinois "Burp" or the Minnesota "Oink", it will always give immediate service in response to this magic combination of syllables. It is to the pig world what the Masonic grip is to the human. "Oink" in Illinois or "Burp" in Minnesota, and the animal merely raises its eyebrows and stares coldly. But go to either state and call "Pig-hoo-oo-ey!"...'

The expression on Lord Emsworth's face was that of a drowning man who sees a lifeline.

'It that the master-word of which you spoke?'

'That's it.'

'Pig – !'

'– hoo-oo-ey.'

'Pig-hoo-o-ey!'

'You haven't got it quite right. The first syllable should be short and staccato, the second long and rising into a falsetto, high but true.'

'Pig-hoo-o-o-ey.'

'Pig-hoo-o-o-ey.'

'Pig-hoo-o-o-ey!' yodelled Lord Emsworth, flinging his head back and giving tongue in a high, penetrating tenor which caused ninety-three Senior Conservatives, lunching in the vicinity, to congeal into living statues of alarm and disapproval.

'More body to the "hoo",' advised James Belford.

'Pig-hoo-o-o-ey!'

The Senior Conservative Club is one of the few places in London where lunchers are not accustomed to getting music with their meals. White-whiskered financiers gazed bleakly at bald-headed politicians, as if asking silently what was to be done about this. Bald-headed politicians stared back at white-whiskered financiers, replying in the language of the eye that they did not know. The general sentiment prevailing was a vague determination to write to the Committee about it.

'Pig-hoo-o-o-o-ey!' carolled Lord Emsworth. And, as he did so, his eye fell on the clock over the mantelpiece. Its hands pointed to twenty minutes to two.

He started convulsively. The best train in the day for Market Blandings was the one which left Paddington station at two sharp. After that there was nothing till the five-five.

He was not a man who often thought; but, when he did, to think was with him to act. A moment later he was scudding over the carpet, making for the door that led to the broad staircase.

Throughout the room which he had left, the decision to write in strong terms to the Committee was now universal; but from the mind, such as it was, of Lord Emsworth the past, with the single exception of the word 'Pig-hoo-o-o-o-ey!', had been completely blotted.

Whispering the magic syllables, he sped to the cloak-room and retrieved his hat. Murmuring them over and over again, he sprang into a cab. He was still repeating them as the train moved out of the station; and he would doubtless have gone on repeating them all the way to Market Blandings had he not, as was his invariable practice when travelling by rail, fallen asleep after the first ten minutes of the journey.

The stopping of the train at Swindon Junction woke him with a start. He sat up, wondering, after his usual fashion on these occasions, who and where he was. Memory returned to him, but a memory that was, alas, incomplete. He remembered his name. He remembered that he was on his way home from a visit to London. But what it was that you said to a pig when inviting it to drop in for a bite of dinner he had completely forgotten.

It was the opinion of Lady Constance Keeble, expressed verbally during dinner in the brief intervals when they were alone, and by means of silent telepathy when Beach, the butler, was adding his dignified presence to the proceedings, that her brother Clarence, in his expedition to London to put matters plainly to James Belford, had made an outstanding idiot of himself.

There had been no need whatever to invite the man Belford to lunch; but, having invited him to lunch, to leave him sitting, without having clearly stated that Angela would have no money for four years, was the act of a congenital imbecile. Lady Constance had been aware ever since their childhood days that her brother had about as much sense as a —

Here Beach entered, superintending the bringing-in of the savoury, and she had been obliged to suspend her remarks.

This sort of conversation is never agreeable to a sensitive man, and his lordship had removed himself from the danger zone as soon as he could manage it. He was now seated in the library, sipping port and straining a brain which Nature had never intended for hard exercise in an effort to bring back that word of magic of which his unfortunate habit of sleeping in trains had robbed him.

'Pig —'

He could remember as far as that; but of what avail was a single syllable? Besides, weak as his memory was, he could recall that the whole gist or nub of the thing lay in the syllable that followed. The 'pig' was a mere preliminary.

Lord Emsworth finished his port and got up. He felt restless, stifled. The summer night seemed to call to him like some silver-voiced swineherd calling to his pig. Possibly, he thought, a breath of fresh air might stimulate his brain-cells. He wandered downstairs; and, having dug a shocking old slouch hat out of the cupboard where he hid it to keep his sister Constance from impounding and burning it, he strode heavily out into the garden.

He was pottering aimlessly to and fro in the parts adjacent to the rear of the castle when there appeared in his path a slender female form. He recognized it without pleasure. Any unbiased judge would have said that his niece

Angela, standing there in the soft, pale light, looked like some dainty spirit of the Moon. Lord Emsworth was not an unbiased judge. To him Angela merely looked like Trouble. The march of civilization has given the modern girl a vocabulary and an ability to use it which her grandmother never had. Lord Emsworth would not have minded meeting Angela's grandmother a bit.

'Is that you, my dear?' he said nervously.

'Yes.'

'I didn't see you at dinner.'

'I didn't want any dinner. The food would have choked me. I can't eat.'

'It's precisely the same with my pig,' said his lordship. 'Young Belford tells me —'

Into Angela's queenly disdain there flashed a sudden animation.

'Have you seen Jimmy? What did he say?'

'That's just what I can't remember. It began with the word "Pig" —'

'But after he had finished talking about you, I mean. Didn't he say anything about coming down here?'

'Not that I remember.'

'I expect you weren't listening. You've got a very annoying habit, Uncle Clarence,' said Angela maternally, 'of switching your mind off and just going blah when people are talking to you. It gets you very much disliked on all sides. Didn't Jimmy say anything about me?'

'I fancy so. Yes, I am nearly sure he did.'

'Well, what?'

'I cannot remember.'

There was a sharp clicking noise in the darkness. It was caused by Angela's upper front teeth meeting her lower front teeth; and was followed by a sort of wordless exclamation. It seemed only too plain that the love and respect which a niece should have for an uncle were in the present instance at a very low ebb.

'I wish you wouldn't do that,' said Lord Emsworth plaintively.

'Do what?'

'Make clicking noises at me.'

'I will make clicking noises at you. You know perfectly well, Uncle Clarence, that you are behaving like a bohunkus.'

'A what?'

'A bohunkus,' explained his niece coldly, 'is a very inferior sort of worm. Not the kind of worm that you see on lawns, which you can respect, but a really degraded species.'

'I wish you would go in, my dear,' said Lord Emsworth. 'The night air may give you a chill.'

'I won't go in. I came out here to look at the moon and think of Jimmy. What are you doing out here, if it comes to that?'

'I came here to think. I am greatly exercised about my pig, Empress of Blandings. For two days she has refused her food, and young Belford says she will not eat until she hears the proper call or cry. He very kindly taught it to me, but unfortunately I have forgotten it.'

'I wonder you had the nerve to ask Jimmy to teach you pig-calls, considering the way you're treating him.'

'But —'

'Like a leper, or something. And all I can say is that, if you remember this call of his, and it makes the Empress eat, you ought to be ashamed of yourself if you still refuse to let me marry him.'

'My dear,' said Lord Emsworth earnestly, 'if through young Belford's instrumentality Empress of Blandings is induced to take nourishment once more there is nothing I will refuse him – nothing.'

'Honour bright?'

'I give you my solemn word.'

'You won't let Aunt Constance bully you out of it?'

Lord Emsworth drew himself up.

'Certainly not,' he said proudly. 'I am always ready to listen to your Aunt Constance's views, but there are certain matters where I claim the right to act according to my own judgement.' He paused and stood musing. 'It began with the word "Pig —" '

From somewhere near at hand music made itself heard. The servants' hall, its day's labours ended, was refreshing itself with the housekeeper's gramophone. To Lord Emsworth the strains were merely an additional annoyance. He was not fond of music. It reminded him of his younger son Frederick, a flat but persevering songster both in and out of the bath.

'Yes, I can distinctly recall as much as that. Pig – Pig —'

'WHO —'

Lord Emsworth leaped in the air. It was as if an electric shock had been applied to his person.

'WHO stole my heart away?' howled the gramophone. 'WHO —?'

The peace of the summer night was shattered by a triumphant shout.

'Pig-HOO-o-o-o-ey!'

A window opened. A large, bald head appeared. A dignified voice spoke.

'Who is there? Who is making that noise?'

'Beach!' cried Lord Emsworth. 'Come out here at once.'

'Very good, your lordship.'

And presently the beautiful night was made still more lovely by the added attraction of the butler's presence.

'Beach, listen to this.'

'Very good, your lordship.'

'Pig-hoo-o-o-o-ey!'

'Very good, your lordship.'

'Now you do it.'

'I, your lordship?'

'Yes. It's a way you call pigs.'

'I do not call pigs, your lordship,' said the butler coldly.

'What do you want Beach to do it for?' asked Angela.

'Two heads are better than one. If we both learn it, it will not matter should I forget it again.'

'By Jove, yes! Come on, Beach. Push it over the thorax,' urged the girl eagerly. 'You don't know it, but this is a matter of life and death. At-a-boy, Beach! Inflate the lungs and go to it.'

It had been the butler's intention, prefacing his remarks with the statement that he had been in service at the castle for eighteen years, to explain frigidly to Lord Emsworth that it was not his place to stand in the moonlight practising pig-calls. If, he would have gone on to add, his lordship saw the matter from a different angle, then it was his, Beach's, painful duty to tender his resignation, to become effective one month from that day.

But the intervention of Angela made this impossible to a man of chivalry and heart. A paternal fondness for the girl, dating from the days when he had stooped to enacting – and very convincingly, too, for his was a figure that lent itself to the impersonation – the role of a hippopotamus for her childish amusement, checked the words he would have uttered. She was looking at him with bright eyes, and even the rendering of pig-noises seemed a small sacrifice to make for her sake.

'Very good, your lordship,' he said in a low voice, his face pale and set in the moonlight. 'I shall endeavour to give satisfaction. I would merely advance the suggestion, your lordship, that we move a few steps farther away from the vicinity of the servants' hall. If I were to be overheard by any of the lower domestics, it would weaken my position as a disciplinary force.'

'What chumps we are!' cried Angela, inspired. 'The place to do it is outside the Empress's sty. Then, if it works, we'll see it working.'

Lord Emsworth found this a little abstruse, but after a moment he got it.

'Angela,' he said, 'you are a very intelligent girl. Where you get your brains from, I don't know. Not from my side of the family.'

The bijou residence of the Empress of Blandings looked very snug and attractive in the moonlight. But beneath even the beautiful things of life there is always an underlying sadness. This was supplied in the present instance by

a long, low trough, only too plainly full to the brim of suc-
culent mash and acorns. The fast, obviously, was still in
progress.

The sty stood some considerable distance from the castle
walls, so that there had been ample opportunity for Lord
Emsworth to rehearse his little company during the
journey. By the time they had ranged themselves against
the rails, his two assistants were letter-perfect.

'Now,' said his lordship.

There floated out upon the summer night a strange com-
posite sound that sent the birds roosting in the trees above
shooting off their perches like rockets. Angela's clear
soprano rang out like the voice of the village blacksmith's
daughter. Lord Emsworth contributed a reedy tenor. And
the bass notes of Beach probably did more to startle the
birds than any other one item in the programme.

They paused and listened. Inside the Empress's boudoir
there sounded the movement of a heavy body. There was
an inquiring grunt. The next moment the sacking that
covered the doorway was pushed aside, and the noble
animal emerged.

'Now!' said Lord Emsworth again.

Once more that musical cry shattered the silence of the
night. But it brought no responsive movement from Empress of Blandings. She stood there motionless, her nose
elevated, her ears hanging down, her eyes everywhere but
on the trough where, by rights, she should now have been
digging in and getting hers. A chill disappointment crept
over Lord Emsworth, to be succeeded by a gust of petulant
anger.

'I might have known it,' he said bitterly. 'That young
scoundrel was deceiving me. He was playing a joke on me.'

'He wasn't,' cried Angela indignantly. 'Was he, Beach?'

'Not knowing the circumstances, miss, I cannot venture
an opinion.'

'Well, why has it no effect, then?' demanded Lord Emsworth.

'You can't expect it to work right away. We've got her

stirred up, haven't we? She's thinking it over, isn't she? Once more will do the trick. Ready, Beach?'

'Quite ready, miss.'

'Then when I say three. And this time, Uncle Clarence, do please for goodness' sake not yowl like you did before. It was enough to put any pig off. Let it come out quite easily and gracefully. Now, then. One, two – three!'

The echoes died away. And as they did so a voice spoke.

'Community singing?'

'Jimmy!' cried Angela, whisking round.

'Hullo, Angela. Hullo, Lord Emsworth. Hullo, Beach.'

'Good evening, sir. Happy to see you once more.'

'Thanks. I'm spending a few days at the Vicarage with my father. I got down here by the five-five.'

Lord Emsworth cut peevishly in upon these civilities.

'Young man,' he said, 'what do you mean by telling me that my pig would respond to that cry? It does nothing of the kind.'

'You can't have done it right.'

'I did it precisely as you instructed me. I have had, moreover, the assistance of Beach here and my niece Angela —'

'Let's hear a sample.'

Lord Emsworth cleared his throat.

'Pig-hoo-o-o-o-ey!'

James Belford shook his head.

'Nothing like it,' he said. "You want to begin the "Hoo" in a low minor of two quarter notes in four-four time. From this build gradually to a higher note, until at last the voice is soaring in full crescendo, reaching F sharp on the natural scale and dwelling for two retarded half-notes, then breaking into a shower of accidental grace-notes.'

'God bless my soul!' said Lord Emsworth, appalled. 'I shall never be able to do it.'

'Jimmy will do it for you,' said Angela. 'Now that he's engaged to me, he'll be one of the family and always popping about here. He can do it every day till the show is over.'

James Belford nodded.

'I think that would be the wisest plan. It is doubtful if an

amateur could ever produce real results. You need a voice
that has been trained on the open prairie and that has
gathered richness and strength from competing with tor-
nadoes. You need a manly, sunburned, wind-scorched voice
with a suggestion in it of the crackling of corn husks and
the whisper of evening breezes in the fodder. Like this!'

Resting his hands on the rail before him, James Belford
swelled before their eyes like a young balloon. The muscles
on his cheekbones stood out, his forehead became corrugated, his ears seemed to shimmer. Then, at the very
height of the tension, he let it go like, as the poet beauti-
fully puts it, the sound of a great Amen.

'Pig-HOOOOO-OOO-OOO-O-O-ey!'

They looked at him, awed. Slowly, fading off across hill
and dale, the vast bellow died away. And suddenly, as it
died, another, softer sound succeeded it. A sort of gulpy,
gurgly, plobby, squishy, wofflesome sound, like a thousand eager men drinking soup in a foreign restaurant. And,
as he heard it, Lord Emsworth uttered a cry of rapture.

The Empress was feeding.

CHAPTER 4

Company for Gertrude

THE Hon. Freddie Threepwood, married to the charming daughter of Donaldson's Dog-Biscuits of Long
Island City, N.Y., and sent home by his father-in-law to
stimulate the sale of the firm's products in England,
naturally thought right away of his aunt Georgiana. There,
he reasoned, was a woman who positively ate dog-biscuits.
She had owned, when he was last in the country, a matter
of four Pekes, two Poms, a Yorkshire terrier, five Sealyhams, a Borzoi, and an Airedale: and if that didn't consti-
tute a promising market for Donaldson's Dog-Joy ('Get
your dog thinking the Donaldson way'), he would like to

know what did. The Alcester connexion ought, he considered, to be good for at least ten of the half-crown cellophane-sealed packets a week.

A day or so after his arrival, accordingly, he hastened round to Upper Brook Street to make a sales-talk: and it was as he was coming rather pensively out of the house at the conclusion of the interview that he ran into Beefy Bingham, who had been up at Oxford with him. Several years had passed since the other, then a third-year Blood and Trial Eights man, had bicycled along tow-paths saying rude things through a megaphone about Freddie's stomach, but he recognized him instantly. And this in spite of the fact that the passage of time appeared to have turned old Beefers into a clergyman. For the colossal frame of this Bingham was now clad in sober black, and he was wearing one of those collars which are kept in position without studs, purely by the exercise of will-power.

'Beefers!' cried Freddie, his slight gloom vanishing in the pleasure of this happy reunion.

The Rev. Rupert Bingham, though he returned his greeting with cordiality, was far from exuberant. He seemed subdued, gloomy, as if he had discovered schism among his flock. His voice, when he spoke, was the voice of a man with a secret sorrow.

'Oh, hullo, Freddie. I haven't seen you for years. Keeping pretty fit!'

'As a fiddle, Beefers, old man, as a fiddle. And you?'

'Oh, I'm all right,' said the Rev. Rupert, still with that same strange gloom. 'What were you doing in that house?'

'Trying to sell dog-biscuits.'

'Do you sell dog-biscuits?'

'I do when people have sense enough to see that Donaldson's Dog-Joy stands alone. But could I make my fat-headed aunt see that? No, Beefers, not though I talked for an hour and sprayed her with printed matter like a —'

'Your aunt? I didn't know Lady Alcester was your aunt.'

'Didn't you, Beefers? I thought it was all over London.'

'Did she tell you about me?'

'What about you? Great Scott! Are you the impoverished bloke who wants to marry Gertrude?'

'Yes.'

'Well, I'm dashed.'

'I love her, Freddie,' said the Rev. Rupert Bingham. 'I love her as no man ...'

'Rather. Quite. Absolutely. I know. All the usual stuff. And she loves you, what?'

'Yes. And now they've gone and sent her off to Blandings, to be out of my way.'

'Low. Very low. But why are you impoverished? What about tithes? I always understood you birds made a pot out of tithes.'

'There aren't any tithes where I am.'

'No tithes?'

'None.'

'H'm. Not so hot. Well, what are you going to do about it, Beefers?'

'I thought of calling on your aunt, and trying to reason with her.'

Freddie took his old friend's arm sympathetically and drew him away.

'No earthly good, old man. If a woman won't buy Donaldson's Dog-Joy, it means she has some sort of mental kink and it's no use trying to reason with her. We must think of some other procedure. So Gertrude is at Blandings, is she? She would be. The family seem to look on the place as a sort of Bastille. Whenever the young of the species make a floater like falling in love with the wrong man, they are always shot off to Blandings to recover. The guv'nor has often complained about it bitterly. Now, let me think.'

They passed into Park Street. Some workmen were busy tearing up the paving with pneumatic drills, but the whirring of Freddie's brain made the sound almost inaudible.

'I've got it,' he said at length, his features relaxing from the terrific strain. 'And it's a dashed lucky thing for you, my lad, that I went last night to see that super-film, "Young Hearts Adrift", featuring Rosalie Norton and Otto Byng. Beefers, old man, you're legging it straight down to Blandings this very afternoon.'

'What!'

'By the first train after lunch. I've got the whole thing planned out. In this super-film, "Young Hearts Adrift", a poor but deserving young man was in love with the daughter of rich and haughty parents, and they took her away to the country so that she could forget, and a few days later a mysterious stranger turned up at the place and ingratiated himself with the parents and said he wanted to marry their daughter, and they gave their consent, and the wedding took place, and then he tore off his whiskers and it was Jim!'

'Yes, but ...'

'Don't argue. The thing's settled. My aunt needs a sharp lesson. You would think a woman would be only too glad to put business in the way of her nearest and dearest, especially when shown samples and offered a fortnight's free trial. But no! She insists on sticking to Peterson's Pup-Food, a wholly inferior product – lacking, I happen to know, in many of the essential vitamins – and from now on, old boy, I am heart and soul in your cause.'

'Whiskers?' said the Rev. Rupert doubtfully.

'You won't have to wear any whiskers. My guv'nor's never seen you. Or has he?'

'No, I've not met Lord Emsworth.'

'Very well, then.'

'But what good will it do me, ingratiating myself, as you call it, with your father? He's only Gertrude's uncle.'

'What good? My dear chap, are you aware that the guv'nor owns the country-side for miles around? He has all sorts of livings up his sleeve – livings simply dripping with tithes – and can distribute them to whoever he likes. I know, because at one time there was an idea of making me a parson. But I would have none of it.'

The Rev. Rupert's face cleared.

'Freddie, there's something in this.'

'You bet there's something in it.'

'But how can I ingratiate myself with your father?'

'Perfectly easy. Cluster round him. Hang on his every word. Interest yourself in his pursuits. Do him little services. Help him out of chairs.... Why, great Scott, I'd undertake to ingratiate myself with Stalin if I gave my mind to it. Pop off and pack the old toothbrush, and I'll go and get the guv'nor on the phone.'

At about the time when this pregnant conversation was taking place in London, W.1, far away in distant Shropshire Clarence, ninth Earl of Emsworth, sat brooding in the library of Blandings Castle. Fate, usually indulgent to this dreamy peer, had suddenly turned nasty and smitten him a grievous blow beneath the belt.

They say Great Britain is still a first-class power, doing well and winning respect from the nations: and, if so, it is, of course, extremely gratifying. But what of the future? That was what Lord Emsworth was asking himself. Could this happy state of things last? He thought not. Without wishing to be pessimistic, he was dashed if he saw how a country containing men like Sir Gregory Parsloe-Parsloe of Matchingham Hall could hope to survive.

Strong? No doubt. Bitter? Granted. But not, we think, too strong, not – in the circumstances – unduly bitter. Consider the facts.

When, shortly after the triumph of Lord Emsworth's pre-eminent sow, Empress of Blandings, in the Fat Pigs Class at the eighty-seventh annual Shropshire Agricultural Show, George Cyril Wellbeloved, his lordship's pig-man, had expressed a desire to hand in his portfolio and seek employment elsewhere, the amiable peer, though naturally grieved, felt no sense of outrage. He put the thing down to the old roving spirit of the Wellbeloveds. George Cyril, he assumed, wearying of Shropshire, wished to try a change of air in some southern or eastern county. A nuisance, undoubtedly, for the man, when sober, was beyond question a force in the piggery. He had charm and personality. Pigs liked him. Still, if he wanted to resign office, there was nothing to be done about it.

But when, not a week later, word was brought to Lord Emsworth that, so far from having migrated to Sussex or Norfolk or Kent or somewhere, the fellow was actually just round the corner in the neighbouring village of Much Matchingham, serving under the banner of Sir Gregory Parsloe-Parsloe of Matchingham Hall, the scales fell from his eyes. He realized that black treachery had been at work. George Cyril Wellbeloved had sold himself for gold, and Sir Gregory Parsloe-Parsloe, hitherto looked upon as a high-minded friend and fellow Justice of the Peace, stood revealed as that lowest of created things, a lurer-away of other people's pig-men.

And there was nothing one could do about it.

Monstrous!

But true.

So deeply was Lord Emsworth occupied with the consideration of this appalling state of affairs that it was only when the knock upon the door was repeated that it reached his consciousness.

'Come in,' he said hollowly.

He hoped it was not his niece Gertrude. A gloomy young woman. He could hardly stand Gertrude's society just now.

It was not Gertrude. It was Beach, the butler.

'Mr Frederick wishes to speak to your lordship on the telephone.'

An additional layer of greyness fell over Lord Emsworth's spirit as he toddled down the great staircase to the telephone closet in the hall. It was his experience that almost any communication from Freddie indicated trouble.

But there was nothing in his son's voice as it floated over the wire to suggest that all was not well.

'Hullo, guv'nor.'

'Well, Frederick?'

'How's everything at Blandings?'

Lord Emsworth was not the man to exhibit the vultures

gnawing at his heart to a babbler like the Hon. Freddie. He replied, though it hurt him to do so, that everything at Blandings was excellent.

'Good-oh!' said Freddie. 'Is the old dosshouse very full up at the moment?'

'If,' replied his lordship, 'you are alluding to Blandings Castle, there is nobody at present staying here except myself and your cousin Gertrude. Why?' he added in quick alarm. 'Were you thinking of coming down?'

'Good God, no!' cried his son with equal horror. 'I mean to say, I'd love it, of course, but just now I'm too busy with Dog-Joy.'

'Who is Popjoy?'

'Popjoy? Popjoy? Oh, ah, yes. He's a pal of mine and, as you've plenty of room, I want you to put him up for a bit. Nice chap. You'll like him. Right-ho, then, I'll ship him off on the three-fifteen.'

Lord Emsworth's face had assumed an expression which made it fortunate for his son that television was not yet in operation on the telephone systems of England: and he had just recovered enough breath for the delivery of a blistering refusal to have any friend of Freddie's within fifty miles of the place when the other spoke again.

'He'll be company for Gertrude.'

And at these words a remarkable change came over Lord Emsworth. His face untwisted itself. The basilisk glare died out of his eyes.

'God bless my soul! That's true!' he exclaimed. 'That's certainly true. So he will. The three-fifteen, did you say? I will send the car to Market Blandings to meet it.'

Company for Gertrude? A pleasing thought. A fragrant, refreshing, stimulating thought. Somebody to take Gertrude off his hands occasionally was what he had been praying for ever since his sister Georgiana had dumped her down on him.

One of the chief drawbacks to entertaining in your home a girl who has been crossed in love is that she is extremely apt to go about the place doing good. All that life holds for her now is the opportunity of being kind to others, and she intends to be kind if it chokes them. For two weeks Lord Emsworth's beautiful young niece had been moving to and fro through the castle with a drawn face, doing good right and left: and his lordship, being handiest, had had to bear the brunt of it. It was with the first real smile he had smiled that day that he came out of the telephone-cupboard and found the object of his thoughts entering the hall in front of him.

'Well, well, well, my dear,' he said cheerily. 'And what have you been doing?'

There was no answering smile on his niece's face. Indeed, looking at her, you could see that this was a girl who had forgotten how to smile. She suggested something symbolic out of Maeterlinck.

'I have been tidying your study, Uncle Clarence,' she replied listlessly. 'It was in a dreadful mess.'

Lord Emsworth winced as a man of set habits will who has been remiss enough to let a Little Mother get at his study while his back is turned, but he continued bravely on the cheerful note.

'I have been talking to Frederick on the telephone.'

'Yes?' Gertrude sighed, and a bleak wind seemed to blow through the hall. 'Your tie's crooked, Uncle Clarence.'

'I like it crooked,' said his lordship, backing. 'I have a piece of news for you. A friend of Frederick's is coming down here to-night for a visit. His name, I understand, is Popjoy. So you will have some young society at last.'

'I don't want young society.'

'Oh, come, my dear.'

She looked at him thoughtfully with large, sombre eyes. Another sigh escaped her.

'It must be wonderful to be as old as you are, Uncle Clarence.'

'Eh?' said his lordship, starting.

'To feel that there is such a short, short step to the quiet tomb, to the ineffable peace of the grave. To me, life seems to stretch out endlessly, like a long, dusty desert. Twenty-three! That's all I am. Only twenty-three. And all our family live to sixty.'

'What do you mean, sixty?' demanded his lordship, with the warmth of a man who would be that next birthday. 'My poor father was seventy-seven when he was killed in the hunting-field. My uncle Robert lived till nearly ninety. My cousin Claude was eighty-four when he broke his neck trying to jump a five-barred gate. My mother's brother, Alistair ...'

'Don't!' said the girl with a little shudder. 'Don't! It makes it all seem so awful and hopeless.'

Yes, that was Gertrude: and in Lord Emsworth's opinion she needed company.

The reactions of Lord Emsworth to the young man Popjoy, when he encountered him for the first time in the drawing-room shortly before dinner, were in the beginning wholly favourable. His son's friend was an extraordinarily large and powerful person with a frank, open, ingenuous face about the colour of the inside of a salmon, and he seemed a little nervous. That, however, was in his favour. It was, his lordship felt, a pleasant surprise to find in one of the younger generation so novel an emotion as diffidence.

He condoned, therefore, the other's trick of laughing hysterically even when the subject under discussion was the not irresistibly ludicrous one of greenfly in the rose-garden. He excused him for appearing to find something outstandingly comic in the statement that the glass was going up. And when, springing to his feet at the entrance of Gertrude, the young man performed some complicated steps in conjunction with a table covered with china and photograph-frames, he joined in the mirth which the feat provoked not only from the visitor but actually from Gertrude herself.

Yes, amazing though it might seem, his niece Gertrude, on seeing this young Popjoy, had suddenly burst into a peal of happy laughter. The gloom of the last two weeks appeared to be gone. She laughed. The young man laughed.

They proceeded down to dinner in a perfect gale of merriment, rather like a chorus of revellers exiting after a concerted number in an old-fashioned comic opera.

And at dinner the young man had spilt his soup, broken a wine-glass and almost taken another spectacular toss when leaping up at the end of the meal to open the door. At which Gertrude had laughed, and the young man had laughed, and his lordship had laughed – though not, perhaps, quite so heartily as the young folks, for that wine-glass had been one of a set which he valued.

However, weighing profit and loss as he sipped his port, Lord Emsworth considered that the ledger worked out on the right side. True, he had taken into his home what appeared to be a half-witted acrobat: but then any friend of his son Frederick was bound to be weak in the head, and, after all, the great thing was that Gertrude seemed to appreciate the newcomer's society. He looked forward contentedly to a succession of sunshine days of peace, perfect peace with loved ones far away; days when he would be able to work in his garden without the fear, which had been haunting him for the last two weeks, of finding his niece drooping wanly at his side and asking him if he was wise to stand about in the hot sun. She had company now that would occupy her elsewhere.

His lordship's opinion of his guest's mental deficiencies was strengthened late that night when, hearing footsteps on the terrace, he poked his head out and found him standing beneath his window, blowing kisses at it.

At the sight of his host he appeared somewhat confused.

'Lovely evening,' he said, with his usual hyenaesque laugh. 'I – er – thought ... or, rather ... that is to say. ... Ha, ha, ha!'

'Is anything the matter?'

'No, no! No! No, thanks, no! No! No, no! I – er – ho, ho, ho! – just came out for a stroll, ha, ha!'

Lord Emsworth returned to his bed a little thoughtfully. Perhaps some premonition of what was to come afflicted his subconscious mind, for, as he slipped between the sheets, he shivered. But gradually, as he dozed off, his equanimity became restored.

Looking at the thing in the right spirit, it might have been worse. After all, he felt, the mists of sleep beginning to exert their usual beneficent influence, he might have been entertaining at Blandings Castle one of his nephews, or one of his sisters, or even – though this was morbid – his younger son Frederick.

In matters where shades of feeling are involved, it is not always easy for the historian to be as definite as he could wish. He wants to keep the record straight, and yet he cannot take any one particular moment of time, pin it down for the scrutiny of Posterity and say, 'This was the moment when Lord Emsworth for the first time found himself wishing that his guest would tumble out of an upper window and break his neck.' To his lordship it seemed that this had been from the beginning his constant day-dream, but such was not the case. When, on the second morning of the other's visit, the luncheon-gong had found them chatting in the library and the young man, bounding up, had extended a hand like a ham and, placing it beneath his host's arm, gently helped him to rise, Lord Emsworth had been quite pleased by the courteous attention.

But when the fellow did the same thing day after day, night after night, every time he caught him sitting; when he offered him an arm to help him across floors; when he assisted him up stairs, along corridors, down paths, out of rooms and into raincoats; when he snatched objects from his hands to carry them himself; when he came galloping out of the house on dewy evenings laden down with rugs, mufflers, hats and, on one occasion, positively a blasted respirator ... why, then Lord Emsworth's proud spirit rebelled. He was a tough old gentleman and, like most tough old gentlemen, did not enjoy having his juniors look on him as something pathetically helpless that crawled the earth waiting for the end.

It had been bad enough when Gertrude was being the

Little Mother. This was infinitely worse. Apparently having conceived for him one of those unreasoning, overwhelming devotions, this young Popjoy stuck closer than a brother; and for the first time Lord Emsworth began to appreciate what must have been the feelings of that Mary who aroused a similar attachment in the bosom of her lamb. It was as if he had been an Oldest Inhabitant fallen into the midst of a troop of Boy Scouts, all doing Good Deeds simultaneously, and he resented it with an indescribable bitterness. One can best illustrate his frame of mind by saying that, during the last phase, if he had been called upon to choose between his guest and Sir Gregory Parsloe-Parsloe as a companion for a summer ramble through the woods, he would have chosen Sir Gregory.

And then, on top of all this, there occurred the episode of the step-ladder.

The Hon. Freddie Threepwood, who had decided to run down and see how matters were developing, learned the details of this rather unfortunate occurrence from his cousin Gertrude. She met him at Market Blandings Station, and he could see there was something on her mind. She had not become positively Maeterlinckian again, but there was sorrow in her beautiful eyes: and Freddie, rightly holding that with a brainy egg like himself directing her destinies they should have contained only joy and sunshine, was disturbed by this.

'Don't tell me the binge has sprung a leak,' he said anxiously.

Gertrude sighed.

'Well, yes and no.'

'What do you mean, yes and no? Properly worked, the thing can't fail. This points to negligence somewhere. Has old Beefers been ingratiating himself?'

'Yes.'

'Hanging on the guv'nor's every word? Interesting himself in his pursuits? Doing him little services? And been at it two weeks? Good heavens! By now the guv'nor should be looking on him as a prize pig. Why isn't he?'

'I didn't say he wasn't. Till this afternoon I rather think he was. At any rate, Rupert says he often found Uncle Clarence staring at him in a sort of lingering, rather yearning way. But when that thing happened this afternoon, I'm afraid he wasn't very pleased.'

'What thing?'

'That step-ladder business. It was like this. Rupert and I sort of went for a walk after lunch, and by the time I had persuaded him that he ought to go and find Uncle Clarence and ingratiate himself with him, Uncle Clarence had disappeared. So Rupert hunted about for a long time and at last heard a snipping noise and found him miles away standing on a step-ladder, sort of pruning some kind of tree with a pair of shears. So Rupert said, "Oh, there you are!" And Uncle Clarence said, Yes, there he was, and Rupert said, "Ought you to tire yourself? Won't you let me do that for you?"'

'The right note,' said Freddie approvingly. 'Assiduity. Zeal. Well?'

'Well, Uncle Clarence said, "No, thank you!" – Rupert thinks it was "Thank you" – and Rupert stood there for a bit, sort of talking, and then he suddenly remembered and told Uncle Clarence that you had just phoned that you were coming down this evening, and I think Uncle Clarence must have got a touch of cramp or something, because he gave a kind of sudden sharp groan, Rupert says, and sort of quivered all over. This made the steps wobble, of course, so Rupert dashed forward to steady them, and he doesn't know how it happened, but they suddenly seemed to sort of shut up like a pair of scissors, and the next thing he knew Uncle Clarence was sitting on the grass, not seeming to like it much, Rupert says. He had ricked his ankle a bit and shaken himself up a bit, and altogether, Rupert says, he wasn't fearfully sunny. Rupert says he thinks he may have lost ground a little.'

Freddie pondered with knit brows. He was feeling something of the chagrin of a general who, after sweating himself to a shadow planning a great campaign, finds his troops unequal to carrying it out.

'It's such a pity it should have happened. One of the vicars near here has just been told by the doctor that he's got to go off to the south of France, and the living is in Uncle Clarence's gift. If only Rupert could have had that, we could have got married. However, he's bought Uncle Clarence some lotion.'

Freddie started. A more cheerful expression came into his sternly careworn face.

'Lotion?'

'For his ankle.'

'He couldn't have done better,' said Freddie warmly. 'Apart from showing the contrite heart, he has given the guv'nor medicine, and medicine to the guv'nor is what catnip is to the cat. Above all things he dearly loves a little bit of amateur doctoring. As a rule he tries it on somebody else – two years ago he gave one of the housemaids some patent ointment for chilblains and she went screaming about the house – but, no doubt, now that the emergency has occurred, he will be equally agreeable to treating himself. Old Beefers has made the right move.'

In predicting that Lord Emsworth would appreciate the gift of lotion, Freddie had spoken with an unerring knowledge of his father's character. The master of Blandings was one of those fluffy-minded old gentlemen who are happiest when experimenting with strange drugs. In a less censorious age he would have been a Borgia. It was not until he had retired to bed that he discovered the paper-wrapped bottle on the table by his side. Then he remembered that the pest Popjoy had mumbled something at dinner about buying him something or other for his injured ankle. He tore off the paper and examined the contents of the bottle with a lively satisfaction. The liquid was a dingy grey and sloshed pleasantly when you shook it. The name on the label – Blake's Balsam – was new to him, and that in itself was a recommendation.

His ankle had long since ceased to pain him, and to some men this might have seemed an argument against smearing it with balsam; but not to Lord Emsworth. He decanted a liberal dose into the palm of his hand. He sniffed it. It had a strong, robust, bracing sort of smell. He spent the next five minutes thoughtfully rubbing it in. Then he put the light out and went to sleep.

It is a truism to say that in the world as it is at present constituted few things have more far-reaching consequences than the accident of birth. Lord Emsworth had probably suspected this. He was now to receive direct proof. If he had been born a horse instead of the heir to an earldom, that lotion would have been just right for him. It was for horses, though the Rev. Rupert Bingham had omitted to note the fact, that Blake had planned his balsam; and anyone enjoying even a superficial acquaintance with horses and earls knows that an important difference between them is that the latter have the more sensitive skins. Waking at a quarter to two from dreams of being burned at the stake by Red Indians, Lord Emsworth found himself suffering acute pain in the right leg.

He was a little surprised. He had not supposed that that fall from the ladder had injured him so badly. However, being a good amateur doctor, he bore up bravely and took immediate steps to cope with the trouble. Having shaken the bottle till it foamed at the mouth, he rubbed in some more lotion. It occurred to him that the previous application might have been too sketchy, so this time he did it thoroughly. He rubbed and kneaded for some twenty minutes. Then he tried to go to sleep.

Nature has made some men quicker thinkers than others. Lord Emsworth's was one of those leisurely brains. It was not till nearly four o'clock that the truth came home to him. When it did, he was just on the point of applying a fifth coating of the balsam to his leg. He stopped abruptly, replaced the cork, and, jumping out of bed, hobbled to the cold-water tap and put as much of himself under it as he could manage.

The relief was perceptible, but transitory. At five he was out again, and once more at half-past. At a quarter to six, succeeding in falling asleep, he enjoyed a slumber, somewhat disturbed by the intermittent biting of sharks, which lasted till a few minutes past eight. Then he woke as if an alarm clock had rung, and realized that further sleep was out of the question.

He rose from his bed and peered out of the window. It was a beautiful morning. There had been rain in the night and a world that looked as if it had just come back from the cleaner's sparkled under a beaming sun. Cedars cast long shadows over the smooth green lawns. Rooks cawed soothingly: thrushes bubbled in their liquid and musical way: and the air was full of a summer humming. Among those present of the insect world, Lord Emsworth noticed several prominent gnats.

Beyond the terrace, glittering through the trees, gleamed the waters of the lake. They seemed to call to him like a bugle. Although he had neglected the practice of late, there was nothing Lord Emsworth enjoyed more than a before-breakfast dip: and to-day anything in the nature of water had a particularly powerful appeal for him. The pain in his ankle had subsided by now to a dull throbbing, and it seemed to him that a swim might remove it altogether. Putting on a dressing-gown and slippers, he took his bathing-suit from its drawer and went downstairs.

The beauties of a really fine English summer day are so numerous that it is excusable in a man if he fails immediately to notice them all. Only when the sharp agony of the first plunge had passed and he was floating out in mid-water did Lord Emsworth realize that in some extraordinary way he had overlooked what was beyond dispute the best thing that this perfect morning had to offer him. Gazing from his bedroom window, he had observed the sun, the shadows, the birds, the trees, and the insects, but he had omitted to appreciate the fact that nowhere in this magic world that stretched before him was there a trace of his young guest,

Popjoy. For the first time in two weeks he appeared to be utterly alone and free from him.

Floating on his back and gazing up into the turquoise sky, Lord Emsworth thrilled at the thought He kicked sportively in a spasm of pure happiness. But this, he felt, was not enough. It failed to express his full happiness. To the ecstasy of this golden moment only music – that mystic language of the soul – could really do justice. The next instant there had cut quiveringly into the summer stillness that hung over the gardens of Blandings Castle a sudden sharp wail that seemed to tell of a human being in mortal distress. It was the voice of Lord Emsworth, raised in song.

It was a gruesome sound, calculated to startle the stoutest: and two bees, buzzing among the lavender, stopped as one bee and looked at each other with raised eyebrows. Nor were they alone affected. Snails withdrew into their shells: a squirrel doing calisthenics on the cedar nearly fell off its branch: and – moving a step up in the animal kingdom – the Rev. Rupert Bingham, standing behind the rhododendron bushes and wondering how long it would be before the girl he loved came to keep her tryst, started violently, dropped his cigarette and, tearing off his coat, rushed to the water's edge.

Out in the middle of the lake, Lord Emsworth's transports continued undiminished. His dancing feet kicked up a flurry of foam. His short-sighted, but sparkling, eyes stared into the blue. His voice rose to a pulsing scream.

'Love me,' sang Lord Emsworth, 'and the wo-o-o-o-rld is – ah – mi-yun!'

'It's all right,' said a voice in his ear. 'Keep cool. Keep quite cool.'

The effect of a voice speaking suddenly, as it were out of the void, is always, even in these days of wireless, disconcerting to a man. Had he been on dry land Lord Emsworth would have jumped. Being in ten feet of water, he went under as if a hand had pushed him. He experienced a momentary feeling of suffocation, and then a hand gripped him painfully by the fleshy part of the arm and he was on the surface again, spluttering.

'Keep quite cool,' murmured the voice. 'There's no danger.'

And now he recognized whose voice it was.

There is a point beyond which the human brain loses its kinship with the Infinite and becomes a mere seething mass of deleterious passions. Malays, when pushed past this point, take down the old *kris* from its hook and go out and start carving up the neighbours. Women have hysterics. Earls, if Lord Emsworth may be taken as a sample, haul back their right fists and swing them as violently as their age and physique will permit. For two long weeks Lord Emsworth had been enduring this pestilential young man with outward nonchalance, but the strain had told. Suppressed emotions are always the most dangerous. Little by little, day by day, he had been slowly turning into a human volcano, and this final outrage blew the lid off him.

He raged with a sense of intolerable injury. Was it not enough that this porous plaster of a young man should adhere to him on shore? Must he even pursue him out into the waste of waters and come fooling about and pawing at him when he was enjoying the best swim he had had that summer? In all their long and honourable history no member of his ancient family had ever so far forgotten the sacred obligations of hospitality as to plug a guest in the eye. But then they had never had guests like this. With a sharp, passionate snort, Lord Emsworth extracted his right hand from the foam, clenched it, drew it back and let it go.

He could have made no more imprudent move. If there was one thing the Rev. Rupert Bingham, who in his time had swum for Oxford, knew, it was what to do when drowning men struggled. Something that might have been a very hard and knobbly leg of mutton smote Lord Emsworth violently behind the ear: the sun was turned off at the main: the stars came out, many of them of a singular brightness: there was a sound of rushing waters: and he knew no more.

When Lord Emsworth came to himself, he was lying in bed. And, as it seemed a very good place to be, he remained there. His head ached abominably, but he scarcely noticed this, so occupied was he with the thoughts which surged inside it. He mused on the young man Popjoy: he meditated on Sir Gregory Parsloe-Parsloe: and wondered from time to time which he disliked the more. It was a problem almost too nice for human solution. Here, on the one hand, you had a man who pestered you for two weeks and wound up by nearly murdering you as you bathed, but who did not steal pig-men: there, on the other, one who stole pig-men but stopped short of actual assault on the person. Who could hope to hold the scales between such a pair?

He had just remembered the lotion and was wondering if this might not be considered the deciding factor in this contest for the position of the world's premier blot, when the door opened and the Hon. Freddie Threepwood insinuated himself into the room.

'Hullo, guv'nor.'

'Well, Frederick?'

'How are you feeling?'

'Extremely ill.'

'Might have been worse, you know.'

'Bah!'

'Watery grave and all that.'

'Tchah!' said Lord Emsworth.

There was a pause. Freddie, wandering about the room, picked up and fidgeted with a chair, a vase, a hair-brush, a comb, and a box of matches: then, retracing his steps, fidgeted with them all over again in the reverse order. Finally he came to the foot of his father's bed and dropped over it like, it seemed to that sufferer's prejudiced eye, some hideous animal gaping over a fence.

'I say, guv'nor.'

'Well, Frederick?'

'Narrow squeak, that, you know.'

'Pah!'

'Do you wish to thank your brave preserver?'

Lord Emsworth plucked at the coverlet.

'If that young man comes near me,' he said, 'I will not be answerable for the consequences.'

'Eh?' Freddie stared. 'Don't you like him?'

'Like him! I think he is the most appalling young man I ever met.'

It is customary when making statements of this kind to except present company, but so deeply did Lord Emsworth feel on the subject that he omitted to do so. Freddie, having announced that he was dashed, removed himself from the bed-rail and, wandering once more about the room, fidgeted with a toothbrush, a soap-dish, a shoe, a volume on spring bulbs, and a collar-stud.

'I say, guv'nor.'

'Well, Frederick?'

'That's all very well, you know, guv'nor,' said the Hon. Freddie, returning to his post and seeming to draw moral support from the feel of the bed-rail, 'but after what's happened it looks to me as if you were jolly well bound to lend your countenance to the union, if you know what I mean.'

'Union? What are you talking about? What union?'

'Gertrude and old Beefers.'

'Who the devil is old Beefers?'

'Oh, I forgot to tell you about that. This bird Popjoy's name isn't Popjoy. It's Bingham. Old Beefy Bingham. You know, the fellow Aunt Georgie doesn't want to marry Gertrude.'

'Eh?'

'Throw your mind back. They pushed her off to Blandings to keep her out of his way. And I had the idea of sending him down here *incog.* to ingratiate himself with you. The scheme being that, when you had learned to love him, you would slip him a vacant vicarage, thus enabling them to get married. Beefers is a parson, you know.'

Lord Emsworth did not speak. It was not so much the shock of this revelation that kept him dumb as the astounding discovery that any man could really want to marry Gertrude, and any girl this Popjoy. Like many a thinker before him, he was feeling that there is really no limit to the eccentricity of human tastes. The thing made his head swim.

But when it had ceased swimming he perceived that this was but one aspect of the affair. Before him stood the man who had inflicted Popjoy on him, and with something of King Lear in his demeanour Lord Emsworth rose slowly from the pillows. Words trembled on his lips, but he rejected them as not strong enough and sought in his mind for others.

'You know, guv'nor,' proceeded Freddie, 'there's nothing to prevent you doing the square thing and linking two young hearts in the bonds of the Love God, if you want to. I mean to say, old Braithwaite at Much Matchingham has been ordered to the south of France by his doctor, so there's a living going that you've got to slip to somebody.'

Lord Emsworth sank back on the pillows.

'Much Matchingham!'

'Oh, dash it, you must know Much Matchingham, guv'nor. It's just round the corner. Where old Parsloe lives.'

'Much Matchingham!'

Lord Emsworth was blinking, as if his eyes had seen a dazzling light. How wrong, he felt, how wickedly mistaken and lacking in faith he had been when he had said to himself in his folly that Providence offers no method of retaliation to the just whose pig-men have been persuaded by Humanity's dregs to leave their employment and seek advanced wages elsewhere. Conscience could not bring remorse to Sir Gregory Parsloe-Parsloe, and the law, in its present imperfect state, was powerless to punish. But there was still a way. With this young man Popjoy – or Bingham – or whatever his name was, permanently established not a hundred yards from his park gates, would Sir Gregory Parsloe-Parsloe ever draw another really care-free breath? From his brief, but sufficient, acquaintance with the young man Bingham – or Popjoy – Lord Emsworth thought not.

The punishment was severe, but who could say that Sir Gregory had not earned it?

'A most admirable idea,' said Lord Emsworth cordially. 'Certainly I will give your friend the living of Much Matchingham.'

'You will?'

'Most decidedly.'

'At-a-boy, guv'nor!' said Freddie. 'Came the Dawn!'

CHAPTER 5

The Go-getter

ON the usually unruffled brow of the Hon. Freddie Threepwood, as he paced the gardens of Blandings Castle, there was the slight but well-marked frown of one whose mind is not at rest. It was high summer and the gardens were at their loveliest, but he appeared to find no solace in their splendour. Calceolarias, which would have drawn senile yips of ecstasy from his father, Lord Emsworth, left him cold. He eyed the lobelias with an unseeing stare, as if he were cutting an undesirable acquaintance in the paddock at Ascot.

What was troubling this young man was the continued sales-resistance of his Aunt Georgiana. Ever since his marriage to the only daughter of Donaldson's Dog-Biscuits, of Long Island City, N.Y., Freddie Threepwood had thrown himself heart and soul into the promotion of the firm's wares. And, sent home to England to look about for likely prospects, he had seen in Georgiana, Lady Alcester, as has been already related, a customer who approximated to the ideal. The owner of four Pekingese, two Poms, a Yorkshire terrier, five Sealyhams, a Borzoi and an Airedale, she was a woman who stood for something in dog-loving circles. To secure her patronage would be a big thing for him. It would stamp him as a live wire and a go-getter. It would please his father-in-law hugely. And the proprietor of Donaldson's Dog-Joy was a man who, when even slightly pleased, had a habit of spraying five thousand dollar cheques like a geyser.

And so far, despite all his eloquence, callously oblivious of the ties of kinship and the sacred obligations they involve, Lady Alcester had refused to sign on the dotted line, preferring to poison her menagerie with some degraded garbage called, if he recollected rightly, Peterson's Pup-Food.

A bitter snort escaped Freddie. It was still echoing through the gardens, when he found that he was no longer alone. He had been joined by his cousin Gertrude.

'What ho!' said Freddie amiably. He was fond of Gertrude, and did not hold it against her that she had a mother who was incapable of spotting a good dog-biscuit when she saw one. Between him and Gertrude there had long existed a firm alliance. It was to him that Gertrude had turned for assistance when the family were trying to stop her getting engaged to good old Beefy Bingham: and he had supplied assistance in such good measure that the engagement was now an accepted fact and running along nicely.

'Freddie,' said Gertrude, 'may I borrow your car?'

'Certainly. Most decidedly. Going over to see old Beefers?'

'No,' said Gertrude, and a closer observer than her cousin might have noted in her manner a touch of awkwardness. 'Mr Watkins wants me to drive him to Shrewsbury.'

'Oh? Well, carry on, as far as I'm concerned. You haven't seen your mother anywhere, have you?'

'I think she's sitting on the lawn.'

'Ah! Is she? Right ho. Thanks.'

Freddie moved off in the direction indicated, and presently came in sight of his relative, seated as described. The Airedale was lying at her feet. One of the Pekes occupied her lap. And she was gazing into the middle distance in a preoccupied manner, as if she, like her nephew, had a weight on her mind.

Nor would one who drew this inference from her demeanour have been mistaken. Lady Alcester was feeling disturbed.

A woman who stands *in loco parentis* to fourteen dogs must of necessity have her cares, but it was not the dumb friends that were worrying Lady Alcester now. What was troubling her was the disquieting behaviour of her daughter Gertrude.

Engaged to the Rev. Rupert Bingham, Gertrude seemed to her of late to have become infatuated with Orlo Watkins, the Crooning Tenor, one of those gifted young men whom Lady Constance Keeble, the châtelaine of Blandings, was so fond of inviting down for lengthy visits in the summertime.

On the subject of the Rev. Rupert Bingham, Lady Alcester's views had recently undergone a complete change. In the beginning, the prospect of having him for a son-in-law had saddened and distressed her. Then, suddenly discovering that he was the nephew and heir of as opulent a shipping magnate as ever broke bread at the Adelphi Hotel, Liverpool, she had soared from the depths to the heights. She was now strongly pro-Bingham. She smiled upon him freely. Upon his appointment to the vacant Vicarage of Much Matchingham, the village nearest to Market Blandings, she had brought Gertrude to the Castle so that the young people should see one another frequently.

And, instead of seeing her betrothed frequently, Gertrude seemed to prefer to moon about with this Orlo Watkins, this Crooning Tenor. For days they had been inseparable.

Now, everybody knows what Crooning Tenors are. Dangerous devils. They sit at the piano and gaze into a girl's eyes and sing in a voice that sounds like gas escaping from a pipe about Love and the Moonlight and You: and, before you know where you are, the girl has scrapped the deserving young clergyman with prospects to whom she is affianced and is off and away with a man whose only means of livelihood consists of intermittent engagements with the British Broadcasting Corporation.

If a mother is not entitled to shudder at a prospect like that, it would be interesting to know what she is entitled to shudder at.

Lady Alcester, then, proceeded to shudder: and was still shuddering when the drowsy summer peace was broken by a hideous uproar. The Peke and the Airedale had given tongue simultaneously, and, glancing up, Lady Alcester perceived her nephew Frederick approaching.

And what made her shudder again was the fact that in Freddie's eye she noted with concern the familiar go-getter gleam, the old dog-biscuit glitter.

However, as it had sometimes been her experience, when cornered by her nephew, that she could stem the flood by talking promptly on other subjects, she made a gallant effort to do so now.

'Have you seen Gertrude, Freddie?' she asked.

'Yes. She borrowed my car to go to Shrewsbury.'

'Alone?'

'No. Accompanied by Watkins. The Yowler.'

A further spasm shook Lady Alcester.

'Freddie,' she said, 'I'm terribly worried.'

'Worried?'

'About Gertrude.'

Freddie dismissed Gertrude with a gesture.

'No need to worry about her,' he said. 'What you want to worry about is these dogs of yours. Notice how they barked at me? Nerves. They're a mass of nerves. And why? Improper feeding. As long as you mistakenly insist on giving them Peterson's Pup-Food – lacking, as it is, in many of the essential vitamins – so long will they continue to fly off the handle every time they see a human being on the horizon. Now, pursuant on what we were talking about this morning, Aunt Georgiana, there is a little demonstration I would like ...'

'Can't you give her a hint, Freddie?'

'Who?'

'Gertrude.'

'Yes, I suppose I could give her a hint. What about?'

'She is seeing far too much of this man Watkins.'

'Well, so am I, for the matter of that. So is everybody who sees him more than once.'

'She seems quite to have forgotten that she is engaged to Rupert Bingham.'

'Rupert Bingham, did you say?' said Freddie with sudden animation. 'I'll tell you something about Rupert Bingham. He has a dog named Bottles who has been fed from early youth on Donaldson's Dog-Joy, and I wish you could see him. Thanks to the bone-forming properties of Donaldson's Dog-Joy, he glows with health. A fine, upstanding dog, with eyes sparkling with the joy of living and both feet on the ground. A credit to his master.'

'Never mind about Rupert's dog!'

'You've got to mind about Rupert's dog. You can't afford to ignore him. He is a dog to be reckoned with. A dog that counts. And all through Donaldson's Dog-Joy.'

'I don't want to talk about Donaldson's Dog-Joy.'

'I do. I want to give you a demonstration. You may not know it, Aunt Georgiana, but over in America the way we advertise this product, so rich in bone-forming vitamins, is as follows: We instruct our demonstrator to stand out in plain view before the many-headed and, when the audience is of sufficient size, to take a biscuit and break off a piece and chew it. By this means we prove that Donaldson's Dog-Joy is so superbly wholesome as actually to be fit for human consumption. Our demonstrator not only eats the biscuit – he enjoys it. He rolls it round his tongue. He chews it and mixes it with his saliva ..."

'Freddie, please!'

'With his saliva,' repeated Freddie firmly. 'And so does the dog. He masticates the biscuit. He enjoys it. He becomes a bigger and better dog. I will now eat a Donaldson's Dog-Biscuit.'

And before his aunt's nauseated gaze he proceeded to attempt this gruesome feat.

It was an impressive demonstration, but it failed in one particular. To have rendered it perfect, he should not have choked. Want of experience caused the disaster. Long years of training go to the making of the seasoned demonstrators of Donaldson's Dog-Joy. They start in a small way with carpet-tacks and work up through the flat-irons and patent breakfast cereals till they are ready for the big effort. Freddie was a novice. Endeavouring to roll the morsel round his tongue, he allowed it to escape into his windpipe.

The sensation of having swallowed a mixture of bricks and sawdust was succeeded by a long and painful coughing fit. And when at length the sufferer's eyes cleared, no human form met their gaze. There was the Castle. There was the lawn. There were the gardens. But Lady Alcester had disappeared.

However, it is a well-established fact that good men, like Donaldson's Dog-Biscuits, are hard to keep down. Some fifty minutes later, as the Rev. Rupert Bingham sat in his study at Matchingham Vicarage, the parlourmaid announced a visitor. The Hon. Freddie Threepwood limped in, looking shop-soiled.

'What ho, Beefers,' he said. 'I just came to ask if I could borrow Bottles.'

He bent to where the animal lay on the hearth-rug and prodded it civilly in the lower ribs. Bottles waved a long tail in brief acknowledgement. He was a fine dog, though of uncertain breed. His mother had been a popular local belle with a good deal of sex-appeal, and the question of his paternity was one that would have set a Genealogical College pursing its lips perplexedly.

'Oh, hullo, Freddie,' said the Rev. Rupert.

The young Pastor of Souls spoke in an absent voice. He was frowning. It is a singular fact – and one that just goes to show what sort of a world this is – that of the four foreheads introduced so far to the reader of this chronicle, three

have been corrugated with care. And, if girls had con-
sciences, Gertrude's would have been corrugated, too –
giving us a full hand.

'Take a chair,' said the Rev. Rupert.

'I'll take a sofa,' said Freddie, doing so. 'Feeling a bit
used up. I had to hoof it all the way over.'

'What's happened to your car?'

'Gertrude took it to drive Watkins to Shrewsbury.'

The Rev. Rupert sat for a while in thought. His face,
which was large and red, had a drawn look. Even the massive body which had so nearly won him a Rowing Blue at
Oxford gave the illusion of having shrunk. So marked was
his distress that even Freddie noticed it.

'Something up, Beefers?' he inquired.

For answer the Rev. Rupert Bingham extended a ham-
like hand which held a letter. It was written in a sprawling,
girlish handwriting.

'Read that.'

'From Gertrude?'

'Yes. It came this morning. Well?'

Freddie completed his perusal and handed the document
back. He was concerned.

'I think it's the bird,' he said.

'So do I.'

'It's long,' said Freddie, 'and it's rambling. It is full of
stuff about "Are we sure?" and "Do we know our own
minds?" and "Wouldn't it be better, perhaps?" But I think
it is the bird.'

'I can't understand it.'

Freddie sat up.

'I can,' he said. 'Now I see what Aunt Georgiana was
drooling about. Her fears were well founded. The snake
Watkins has stolen Gertrude from you.'

'You think Gertrude's in love with Watkins?'

'I do. And I'll tell you why. He's a yowler, and girls always fall for yowlers. They have a glamour.'

'I've never noticed Watkins's glamour. He has always
struck me as a bit of a weed.'

'Weed he may be, Beefers, but, none the less, he knows how to do his stuff. I don't know why it should be, but there is a certain type of tenor voice which acts on girls like catnip on a cat.'

The Rev. Rupert breathed heavily.

'I see,' he said.

'The whole trouble is, Beefers,' proceeded Freddie, 'that Watkins is romantic and you're not. Your best friend couldn't call you romantic. Solid worth, yes. Romance, no.'

'So it doesn't seem as if there was much to be done about it?'

Freddie reflected.

'Couldn't you manage to show yourself in a romantic light?'

'How?'

'Well – stop a runaway horse.'

'Where's the horse?'

'M'yes,' said Freddie. 'That's by way of being the difficulty, isn't it? The horse – where is it?'

There was silence for some moments.

'Well, be that as it may,' said Freddie. 'Can I borrow Bottles?'

'What for?'

'Purposes of demonstration. I wish to exhibit him to my Aunt Georgiana, so that she may see for herself to what heights of robustness a dog can rise when fed sedulously on Donaldson's Dog-Joy. I'm having a lot of trouble with that woman, Beefers. I try all the artifices which win to success in salesmanship, and they don't. But I have a feeling that if she could see Bottles and poke him in the ribs and note the firm, muscular flesh, she might drop. At any rate, it's worth trying. I'll take him along, may I?'

'All right.'

'Thanks. And, in regard to your little trouble, I'll be giving it my best attention. You're looking in after dinner to-night?'

'I suppose so,' said the Rev. Rupert moodily.

The information that her impressionable daughter had gone off to roam the country-side in a two-seater car with the perilous Watkins had come as a grievous blow to Lady Alcester. As she sat on the terrace, an hour after Freddie had begun the weary homeward trek from Matchingham Vicarage, her heart was sorely laden.

The Airedale had wandered away upon some private ends, but the Peke lay slumbering in her lap. She envied it its calm detachment. To her the future looked black and the air seemed heavy with doom.

Only one thing mitigated her depression. Her nephew Frederick had disappeared. Other prominent local pests were present, such as flies and gnats, but not Frederick. The grounds of Blandings Castle appeared to be quite free from him.

And then even this poor consolation was taken from the stricken woman. Limping a little, as if his shoes hurt him, the Hon. Freddie came round the corner of the shrubbery, headed in her direction. He was accompanied by something having the outward aspect of a dog.

'What ho, Aunt Georgiana!'

'Well, Freddie?' sighed Lady Alcester resignedly.

The Peke, opening one eye, surveyed the young man for a moment, seemed to be debating within itself the advisability of barking, came apparently to the conclusion that it was too hot, and went to sleep again.

'This is Bottles,' said Freddie.

'Who?'

'Bottles. The animal I touched on some little time back. Note the well-muscled frame.'

'I never saw such a mongrel in my life.'

'Kind hearts are more than coronets,' said Freddie. 'The point at issue is not this dog's pedigree, which, I concede, is not all Burke and Debrett, but his physique. Reared exclusively on a diet of Donaldson's Dog-Joy, he goes his way with his chin up, frank and fearless. I should like you, if you don't mind, to come along to the stables and watch him among the rats. It will give you some idea.'

He would have spoken further, but at this point something occurred, as had happened during his previous sales-talk, to mar the effect of Freddie's oratory.

The dog Bottles, during this conversation, had been roaming to and fro in the inquisitive manner customary with dogs who find themselves in strange territory. He had sniffed at trees. He had rolled on the turf. Now, returning to the centre of things, he observed for the first time that on the lap of the woman seated in the chair there lay a peculiar something.

What it was Bottles did not know. It appeared to be alive. A keen desire came upon him to solve this mystery. To keep the records straight, he advanced to the chair, thrust an inquiring nose against the object, and inhaled sharply.

The next moment, to his intense surprise, the thing had gone off like a bomb, had sprung to the ground, and was moving rapidly towards him.

Bottles did not hesitate. A rough-and-tumble with one of his peers he enjoyed. He, as it were, rolled it round his tongue and mixed it with his saliva. But this was different. He had never met a Pekingese before, and no one would have been more surprised than himself if he had been informed that this curious, fluffy thing was a dog. Himself he regarded it as an Act of God, and, thoroughly unnerved, he raced three times round the lawn and tried to climb a tree. Failing in this endeavour, he fitted his ample tail if possible more firmly into its groove and vanished from the scene.

The astonishment of the Hon. Freddie Threepwood was only equalled by his chagrin. Lady Alcester had begun now to express her opinion of the incident, and her sneers, her jeers, her unveiled innuendoes were hard to bear. If, she said, the patrons of Donaldson's Dog-Joy allowed themselves to be chased off the map in this fashion by Pekingese, she was glad she had never been weak enough to be persuaded to try it.

'It's lucky,' said Lady Alcester in her hard, scoffing way, 'that Susan wasn't a rat. I suppose a rat would have given that mongrel of yours heart failure.'

'Bottles,' said Freddie stiffly, 'is particularly sound on rats. I think, in common fairness, you ought to step to the stables and give him a chance of showing himself in a true light.'

'I have seen quite enough, thank you.'

'You won't come to the stables and watch him dealing with rats?'

'I will not.'

'In that case,' said Freddie sombrely, 'there is nothing more to be said. I suppose I may as well take him back to the Vicarage.'

'What Vicarage?'

'Matchingham Vicarage.'

'Was that Rupert's dog?'

'Of course it was.'

'Then have you seen Rupert?'

'Of course I have.'

'Did you warn him? About Mr Watkins?'

'It was too late to warn him. He had had a letter from Gertrude, giving him the raspberry.'

'What!'

'Well, she said Was he sure and Did they know their own minds, but you can take it from me that it was tantamount to the raspberry. Returning, however, to the topic of Bottles, Aunt Georgiana, I think you ought to take into consideration the fact that, in his recent encounter with the above Peke, he was undergoing a totally new experience and naturally did not appear at his best. I repeat once more that you should see him among the rats.'

'Oh, Freddie!'

'Hullo?'

'How can you babble about this wretched dog when Gertrude's whole future is at stake? It is simply vital that somehow she be cured of this dreadful infatuation. . . .'

'Well, I'll have a word with her if you like, but, if you ask me, I think the evil has spread too far. Watkins has yowled himself into her very soul. However, I'll do my best. Excuse me, Aunt Georgiana.'

From a neighbouring bush the honest face of Bottles was protruding. He seemed to be seeking assurance that the All Clear had been blown.

It was at the hour of the ante-dinner cocktail that Freddie found his first opportunity of having the promised word with Gertrude. Your true salesman and go-getter is never beaten, and a sudden and brilliant idea for accomplishing the conversion of his Aunt Georgiana had come to him as he brushed his hair. He descended to the drawing-room with a certain jauntiness, and was reminded by the sight of Gertrude of his mission. The girl was seated at the piano, playing dreamy chords.

'I say,' said Freddie, 'a word with you, young Gertrude. What is all this bilge I hear about you and Beefers?'

The girl flushed.

'Have you seen Rupert?'

'I was closeted with him this afternoon. He told me all.'

'Oh?'

'He's feeling pretty low.'

'Oh?'

'Yes,' said Freddie, 'pretty low the poor old chap is feeling, and I don't blame him with the girl he's engaged to rushing about the place getting infatuated with tenors. I never heard of such a thing, dash it! What do you see in this Watkins? Wherein lies his attraction? Certainly not in his ties. They're awful. And the same applies to his entire outfit. He looks as if he had bought his clothes off the peg at a second-hand gents' costumiers. And, as if that were not enough, he wears short, but distinct, side-whiskers. You aren't going to tell me that you're seriously considering chucking a sterling egg like old Beefers in favour of a whiskered warbler?'

There was a pause. Gertrude played more dreamy chords.

'I'm not going to discuss it,' she said. 'It's nothing to do with you.'

'Pardon me!' said Freddie. 'Excuse me! If you will throw your mind back to the time when Beefers was conducting his wooing, you may remember that I was the fellow who worked the whole thing. But for my resource and ingenuity you and the old bounder would never have got engaged. I regard myself, therefore, in the light of a guardian angel or something; and as such am entitled to probe the matter to its depths. Of course,' said Freddie, 'I know exactly how you're feeling. I see where you have made your fatal bloomer. This Watkins has cast his glamorous spell about you, and you're looking on Beefers as a piece of unromantic cheese. But mark this, girl ...'

'I wish you wouldn't call me "girl".'

'Mark this, old prune,' amended Freddie. 'And mark it well. Beefers is tried, true and trusted. A man to be relied on. Whereas Watkins, if I have read those whiskers aright, is the sort of fellow who will jolly well let you down in a crisis. And then, when it's too late, you'll come moaning to me, weeping salt tears and saying, "Ah, why did I not know in time?" And I shall reply, "You unhappy little fathead ...!"'

'Oh, go and sell your dog-biscuits, Freddie!'

Gertrude resumed her playing. Her mouth was set in an obstinate line. Freddie eyed her with disapproval.

'It's some taint in the blood,' he said. 'Inherited from female parent. Like your bally mother, you are constitutionally incapable of seeing reason. Pig-headed, both of you. Sell my dog-biscuits, you say? Ha! As if I hadn't boosted them to Aunt Georgiana till my lips cracked. And with what result? So far, none. But wait till to-night.'

'It is to-night.'

'I mean, wait till later on to-night. Watch my little experiment.'

'What little experiment?'

'Ah!'

'What do you mean, "Ah"?'

'Just "Ah!"' said Freddie.

The hour of the after-dinner coffee found Blandings Castle apparently an abode of peace. The superficial observer, peeping into the amber drawing-room through the french windows that led to the terrace, would have said that all was well with the inmates of this stately home of England. Lord Emsworth sat in a corner absorbed in a volume dealing with the treatment of pigs in sickness and in health. His sister, Lady Constance Keeble, was sewing. His other sister, Lady Alcester, was gazing at Gertrude. Gertrude was gazing at Orlo Watkins. And Orlo Watkins was gazing at the ceiling and singing in that crooning voice of his a song of Roses.

The Hon. Freddie Threepwood was not present. And that fact alone, if one may go by the views of his father, Lord Emsworth, should have been enough to make a success of any party.

And yet beneath this surface of cosy peace troubled currents were running. Lady Alcester, gazing at Gertrude, found herself a prey to gloom. She did not like the way Gertrude was gazing at Orlo Watkins. Gertrude, for her part, as the result of her recent conversation with the Hon. Freddie, was experiencing twinges of remorse and doubt. Lady Constance was still ruffled from the effect of Lady Alcester's sisterly frankness that evening on the subject of the imbecility of hostesses who deliberately let Crooning Tenors loose in castles. And Lord Emsworth was in that state of peevish exasperation which comes to dreamy old gentlemen who, wishing to read of Pigs, find their concentration impaired by voices singing of Roses.

Only Orlo Watkins was happy. And presently he, too, was to join the ranks of gloom. For just as he started to let himself go and handle this song as a song should be handled, there came from the other side of the door the sound of eager barking. A dog seemed to be without. And, apart from the fact that he disliked and feared all dogs, a tenor resents competition.

The next moment the door had opened, and the Hon. Freddie Threepwood appeared. He carried a small sack, and was accompanied by Bottles, the latter's manner noticeably lacking in repose.

On the face of the Hon. Freddie, as he advanced into the

room, there was that set, grim expression which is always seen on the faces of those who are about to put their fortune to the test, to win or lose it all. The Old Guard at Waterloo looked much the same. For Freddie had decided to stake all on a single throw.

Many young men in his position, thwarted by an aunt who resolutely declined to amble across to the stables and watch a dog redeem himself among the rats, would have resigned themselves sullenly to defeat. But Freddie was made of finer stuff.

'Aunt Georgiana,' he said, holding up the sack, at which Bottles was making agitated leaps, 'you refused to come to the stables this afternoon to watch this Donaldson's Dog-Joy-fed animal in action, so you have left me no alternative but to play the fixture on your own ground.'

Lord Emsworth glanced up from his book.

'Frederick, stop gibbering. And take that dog out of here.'

Lady Constance glanced up from her sewing.

'Frederick, if you are coming in, come in and sit down. And take that dog out of here.'

Lady Alcester, glancing up from Gertrude, exhibited in even smaller degree the kindly cordiality which might have been expected from an aunt.

'Oh, do go away, Freddie! You're a perfect nuisance. And take that dog out of here.'

The Hon. Freddie, with a noble look of disdain, ignored them all.

'I have here, Aunt Georgiana,' he said, 'a few simple rats. If you will kindly step out on to the terrace I shall be delighted to give a demonstration which should, I think, convince even your stubborn mind.'

The announcement was variously received by the various members of the company. Lady Alcester screamed. Lady Constance sprang for the bell. Lord Emsworth snorted. Orlo Watkins blanched and retired behind Gertrude. And Gertrude, watching him blench, seeing him retire, tightened her lips. A country-bred girl, she was on terms of easy familiarity with rats, and this evidence of alarm in one whom she had set on a pedestal disquieted her.

The door opened and Beach entered. He had come in pursuance of his regular duties to remove the coffee cups, but arriving, found other tasks assigned to him.

'Beach!' The voice was that of Lady Constance. 'Take away those rats.'

'Rats, m'lady?'

'Take that sack away from Mr Frederick!'

Beach understood. If he was surprised at the presence of the younger son of the house in the amber drawing-room with a sack of rats in his hand, he gave no indication of the fact. With a murmured apology, he secured the sack and started to withdraw. It was not, strictly, his place to carry rats, but a good butler is always ready to give and take. Only so can the amenities of a large country house be preserved.

'And don't drop the dashed things,' urged Lord Emsworth.

'Very good, m'lord.'

The Hon. Freddie had flung himself into a chair, and was sitting with his chin cupped in his hands, a bleak look on his face. To an ardent young go-getter these tyrannous actions in restraint of trade are hard to bear.

Lord Emsworth returned to his book.

Lady Constance returned to her sewing.

Lady Alcester returned to her thoughts.

At the piano Orlo Watkins was endeavouring to justify the motives which had led him a few moments before to retire prudently behind Gertrude.

'I hate rats,' he said. 'They jar upon me.'

'Oh?' said Gertrude.

'I'm not afraid of them, of course, but they give me the creeps.'

'Oh?' said Gertrude.

There was an odd look in her eyes. Of what was she thinking, this idealistic girl? Was it of the evening, a few short weeks before, when, suddenly encountering a beastly bat in the gloaming, she had found in the Rev. Rupert Bingham a sturdy and intrepid protector? Was she picturing the Rev. Rupert as she had seen him then – gallant, fearless, cleaving the air with long sweeps of his clerical hat, encouraging her the while with word and gesture?

Apparently so, for a moment later she spoke.

'How are you on bats?'

'Rats?'

'Bats.'

'Oh, bats?'

'Are you afraid of bats?'

'I don't like bats,' admitted Orlo Watkins.

Then, dismissing the subject, he reseated himself at the piano and sang of June and the scent of unseen flowers.

Of all the little group in the amber drawing-room, only one member has now been left unaccounted for.

An animal of slow thought-processes, the dog Bottles had not at first observed what was happening to the sack. At the moment of its transference from the custody of Freddie to that of Beach, he had been engaged in sniffing at the leg of a chair. It was only as the door began to close that he became aware of the bereavement that threatened him. He bounded forward with a passionate cry, but it was too late. He found himself faced by unyielding wood. And when he started to scratch vehemently on this wood, a sharp pain assailed him. A book on the treatment of Pigs in sickness and in health, superbly aimed, had struck him in the small of the back. Then, for a space, he, like the Hon. Freddie Threepwood, his social sponsor, sat down and mourned.

'Take that beastly, blasted, infernal dog out of here,' cried Lord Emsworth.

Freddie rose listlessly.

'It's old Beefers' dog,' he said. 'Beefers will be here at any moment. We can hand the whole conduct of the affair over to him.'

Gertrude started.

'Is Rupert coming here to-night?'

'Said he would,' responded Freddie, and passed from the scene. He had had sufficient of his flesh and blood and was indisposed to linger. It was his intention to pop down to Market Blandings in his two-seater, soothe his wounded sensibilities, so far as they were capable of being soothed, with a visit to the local motion-picture house, look in at the Emsworth Arms for a spot of beer, and then home to bed, to forget.

Gertrude had fallen into a reverie. Her fair young face was overcast. A feeling of embarrassment had come upon her. When she had written that letter and posted it on the previous night, she had not foreseen that the Rev. Rupert would be calling so soon.

'I didn't know Rupert was coming to-night,' she said.

'Oh, yes,' said Lady Alcester brightly.

'Like a lingering tune, my whole life through, 'twill haunt me for EV-ah, that night in June with you-oo,' sang Orlo Watkins.

And Gertrude, looking at him, was aware for the first time of a curious sensation of not being completely in harmony with this young whiskered man. She wished he would stop singing. He prevented her thinking.

Bottles, meanwhile, had resumed his explorations. Dogs are philosophers. They soon forget. They do not waste time regretting the might-have-beens. Adjusting himself with composure to the changed conditions, Bottles moved to and fro in a spirit of affable inquiry. He looked at Lord Emsworth, considered the idea of seeing how he smelt, thought better of it, and advanced towards the French windows. Something was rustling in the bushes outside, and it seemed to him that this might as well be looked into before he went and breathed on Lady Constance's leg.

He had almost reached his objective, when Lady Alcester's Airedale, who had absented himself from the room some time before in order to do a bit of bone-burying, came bustling in, ready, his business completed, to resume the social whirl.

Seeing Bottles, he stopped abruptly.

Both then began a slow and cautious forward movement, of a crab-like kind. Arriving at close quarters, they stopped again. Their nostrils twitched a little. They rolled their eyes. And to the ears of those present there came, faintly at first, a low, throaty sound, like the far-off gargling of an octogenarian with bronchial trouble.

This rose to a sudden crescendo. And the next moment hostilities had begun.

In underrating Bottles's qualities and scoffing at him as a fighting force, Lady Alcester had made an error. Capable though he was of pusillanimity in the presence of female Pekingese, there was nothing of the weakling about this sterling animal. He had cleaned up every dog in Much Matchingham and was spoken of on all sides – from the Blue Boar in the High Street to the distant Cow and Caterpillar on the Shrewsbury Road – as an ornament to the Vicarage and a credit to his master's Cloth.

On the present occasion, moreover, he was strengthened by the fact that he felt he had right on his side. In spite of a certain coldness on the part of the Castle circle and a soreness about the ribs where the book on Pigs and their treatment had found its billet, there seems to be no doubt that Bottles had by this time become thoroughly convinced that this drawing-room was his official home. And, feeling that all these delightful people were relying on him to look after their interests and keep alien and subversive influences at a distance, he advanced with a bright willingness to the task of ejecting this intruder.

Nor was the Airedale disposed to hold back. He, too, was no stranger to the ring. In Hyde Park, where, when at his London residence, he took his daily airing, he had met all comers and acquitted himself well. Dogs from Mayfair, dogs from Bayswater, dogs from as far afield as the Brompton Road and West Kensington had had experience of the stuff of which he was made. Bottles reminded him a little of an animal from Pont Street, over whom he had once obtained a decision on the banks of the Serpentine; and he joined battle with an easy confidence.

The reactions of a country-house party to an after-dinner dog-fight in the drawing-room always vary considerably according to the individual natures of its members. Lady Alcester, whose long association with the species had made her a sort of honorary dog herself, remained tranquil. She surveyed the proceedings with unruffled equanimity through a tortoiseshell-rimmed lorgnette. Her chief emotion was one of surprise at the fact that Bottles was unquestionably getting the better of the exchanges. She liked his footwork. Impressed, she was obliged to admit that, if this was the sort of battler it turned out, there must be something in Donaldson's Dog-Joy after all.

The rest of the audience were unable to imitate her nonchalance. The two principals were giving that odd illusion, customary on these occasions, of being all over the place at the same time: and the demeanour of those in the ring-side seats was frankly alarmed. Lady Constance had backed against the wall, from which position she threw a futile cushion. Lord Emsworth, in his corner, was hunting feebly for ammunition and wishing that he had not dropped the pince-nez, without which he was no sort of use in a crisis.

And Gertrude? Gertrude was staring at Orlo Watkins, who, with a resource and presence of mind unusual in one so young, had just climbed on top of a high cabinet containing china.

His feet were on a level with her eyes, and she saw that they were feet of clay.

And it was at this moment, when a girl stood face to face with her soul, that the door opened.

'Mr Bingham,' announced Beach.

Men of the physique of the Rev. Rupert Bingham are not as a rule quick thinkers. From earliest youth, the Rev. Rupert had run to brawn rather than brain. But even the dullest-witted person could have told, on crossing that threshold, that there was a dog-fight going on. Beefy Bingham saw it in a flash, and he acted promptly.

There are numerous methods of stopping these painful

affairs. Some advocate squirting water, others prefer to sprinkle pepper. Good results may be obtained, so one school of thought claims, by holding a lighted match under the nearest nose. Beefy Bingham was impatient of these subtleties.

To Beefy all this was old stuff. Ever since he had been given his Cure of Souls, half his time, it sometimes seemed to him, had been spent in hauling Bottles away from the throats of the dogs of his little flock. Experience had given him a technique. He placed one massive hand on the neck of the Airedale, the other on the neck of Bottles, and pulled. There was a rending sound, and they came apart.

'Rupert!' cried Gertrude.

Gazing at him, she was reminded of the heroes of old. And few could have denied that he made a strangely impressive figure, this large young man, standing there with bulging eyes and a gyrating dog in each hand. He looked like a statue of Right triumphing over Wrong. You couldn't place it exactly, because it was so long since you had read the book, but he reminded you of something out of *Pilgrim's Progress*.

So, at least, thought Gertrude. To Gertrude it was as if the scales had fallen from her eyes and she had wakened from some fevered dream. Could it be she, she was asking herself, who had turned from this noble youth and strayed towards one who, though on the evidence he seemed to have a future before him as an Alpine climber, was otherwise so contemptible?

'Rupert!' said Gertrude.

Beefy Bingham had now completed his masterly campaign. He had thrown Bottles out of the window and shut it behind him. He had dropped the Airedale to the carpet, where it now sat, licking itself in a ruminative way. He had produced a handkerchief and was passing it over his vermilion brow.

'Oh, Rupert!' said Gertrude, and flung herself into his arms.

The Rev. Rupert said nothing. On such occasions your

knowledgeable Vicar does not waste words.

Nor did Orlo Watkins speak. He had melted away. Perhaps, perched on his eyrie, he had seen in Gertrude's eyes the look which, when seen in the eyes of a girl by any interested party, automatically induces the latter to go to his room and start packing, in readiness for the telegram which he will receive on the morrow, summoning him back to London on urgent business. At any rate, he had melted.

It was late that night when the Hon. Freddie Threepwood returned to the home of his fathers. Moodily undressing, he was surprised to hear a knock on the door.

His Aunt Georgiana entered. On her face was the unmistakable look of a mother whose daughter has seen the light and will shortly be marrying a deserving young clergyman with a bachelor uncle high up in the shipping business.

'Freddie,' said Lady Alcester, 'you know that stuff you're always babbling about – I've forgotten its name ...'

'Donaldson's Dog-Joy,' said Freddie. 'It may be obtained either in the small (or one-and-threepenny) packets or in the half-crown (or large) size. A guarantee goes with each purchase. Unique in its health-giving properties ...'

'I'll take two tons to start with,' said Lady Alcester.

CHAPTER 6

Lord Emsworth and the Girl Friend

THE day was so warm, so fair, so magically a thing of sunshine and blue skies and bird-song that anyone acquainted with Clarence, ninth Earl of Emsworth, and aware of his liking for fine weather, would have pictured him going about the place on this summer morning with a beaming smile and an uplifted heart. Instead of which, humped over the breakfast table, he was directing at a blameless kippered herring a look of such intense bitterness that the fish seemed to sizzle beneath it. For it was August Bank Holiday, and Blandings Castle on August Bank Holiday became, in his lordship's opinion, a miniature Inferno.

This was the day when his park and grounds broke out into a noisome rash of swings, roundabouts, marquees, toy balloons and paper bags; when a tidal wave of the peasantry and its squealing young engulfed those haunts of immemorial peace. On August Bank Holiday he was not allowed to potter pleasantly about his gardens in an old coat: forces beyond his control shoved him into a stiff collar and a top hat and told him to go out and be genial. And in the cool of the quiet evenfall they put him on a platform and made him make a speech. To a man with a day like that in front of him fine weather was a mockery.

His sister, Lady Constance Keeble, looked brightly at him over the coffee-pot.

'What a lovely morning!' she said.

Lord Emsworth's gloom deepened. He chafed at being called upon – by this woman of all others – to behave as if everything was for the jolliest in the jolliest of all possible worlds. But for his sister Constance and her hawk-like vigilance, he might, he thought, have been able at least to dodge the top hat.

'Have you got your speech ready?'

'Yes.'

'Well, mind you learn it by heart this time and don't stammer and dodder as you did last year.'

Lord Emsworth pushed plate and kipper away. He had lost his desire for food.

'And don't forget you have to go to the village this morning to judge the cottage gardens.'

'All right, all right, all right,' said his lordship testily. 'I've not forgotten.'

'I think I will come to the village with you. There are a number of those Fresh Air London children staying there now, and I must warn them to behave properly when they come to the Fête this afternoon. You know what London children are. McAllister says he found one of them in the gardens the other day, picking his flowers.'

At any other time the news of this outrage would, no doubt, have affected Lord Emsworth profoundly. But now, so intense was his self-pity, he did not even shudder. He drank coffee with the air of a man who regretted that it was not hemlock.

'By the way, McAllister was speaking to me again last night about that gravel path through the yew alley. He seems very keen on it.'

'Glug!' said Lord Emsworth – which, as any philologist will tell you, is the sound which peers of the realm make when stricken to the soul while drinking coffee.

Concerning Glasgow, that great commercial and manufacturing city in the county of Lanarkshire in Scotland, much has been written. So lyrically does the *Encyclopaedia Britannica* deal with the place that it covers twenty-seven pages before it can tear itself away and go on to Glass, Glastonbury, Glatz, and Glauber. The only aspect of it, however, which immediately concerns the present historian is the fact that the citizens it breeds are apt to be grim, dour, persevering, tenacious men; men with red whiskers who know what they want and mean to get it. Such a one was Angus McAllister, head-gardener at Blandings Castle.

For years Angus McAllister had set before himself as his earthly goal the construction of a gravel path through the Castle's famous yew alley. For years he had been bringing the project to the notice of his employer, though in anyone less whiskered the latter's unconcealed loathing would have caused embarrassment. And now, it seemed, he was at it again.

'Gravel path!' Lord Emsworth stiffened through the whole length of his stringy body. Nature, he had always maintained, intended a yew alley to be carpeted with a mossy growth. And, whatever Nature felt about it, he personally was dashed if he was going to have men with

Clydeside accents and faces like dissipated potatoes coming along and mutilating that lovely expanse of green velvet. 'Gravel path, indeed! Why not asphalt? Why not a few hoardings with advertisements of liver pills and a filling-station? That's what the man would really like.'

Lord Emsworth felt bitter, and when he felt bitter he could be terribly sarcastic.

'Well, I think it is a very good idea,' said his sister. 'One could walk there in wet weather then. Damp moss is ruinous to shoes.'

Lord Emsworth rose. He could bear no more of this. He left the table, the room and the house and, reaching the yew alley some minutes later, was revolted to find it infested by Angus McAllister in person. The head-gardener was standing gazing at the moss like a high priest of some ancient religion about to stick the gaff into the human sacrifice.

'Morning, McAllister,' said Lord Emsworth coldly.

'Good morrrrning, your lorrudsheep.'

There was a pause. Angus McAllister, extending a foot that looked like a violin-case, pressed it on the moss. The meaning of the gesture was plain. It expressed contempt, dislike, a generally anti-moss spirit: and Lord Emsworth, wincing, surveyed the man unpleasantly through his pince-nez. Though not often given to theological speculation, he was wondering why Providence, if obliged to make head-gardeners, had found it necessary to make them so Scotch. In the case of Angus McAllister, why, going a step farther, have made him a human being at all? All the ingredients of a first-class mule simply thrown away. He felt that he might have liked Angus McAllister if he had been a mule.

'I was speaking to her leddyship yesterday.'

'Oh?'

'About the gravel path I was speaking to her leddyship.'

'Oh?'

'Her leddyship likes the notion fine.'

'Indeed! Well ...'

Lord Emsworth's face had turned a lively pink, and he

was about to release the blistering words which were form-
ing themselves in his mind when suddenly he caught the
head-gardener's eye and paused. Angus McAllister was
looking at him in a peculiar manner, and he knew what that
look meant. Just one crack, his eye was saying – in Scotch,
of course – just one crack out of you and I tender my
resignation. And with a sickening shock it came home to
Lord Emsworth how completely he was in this man's
clutches.

He shuffled miserably. Yes, he was helpless. Except for
that kink about gravel paths, Angus McAllister was a head-
gardener in a thousand, and he needed him. He could not
do without him. That, unfortunately, had been proved by
experiment. Once before, at the time when they were
grooming for the Agricultural Show that pumpkin which
had subsequently romped home so gallant a winner, he had
dared to flout Angus McAllister. And Angus had resigned,
and he had been forced to plead – yes, plead – with him to
come back. An employer cannot hope to do this sort of
thing and still rule with an iron hand. Filled with the
coward rage that dares to burn but does not dare to blaze,
Lord Emsworth coughed a cough that was undisguisedly
a bronchial white flag.

'I'll – er – I'll think it over, McAllister.'
'Mphm.'
'I have to go to the village now. I will see you later.'
'Mphm.'
'Meanwhile, I will – er – think it over.'
'Mphm.'

The task of judging the floral displays in the cottage gardens of the little village of Blandings Parva was one to
which Lord Emsworth had looked forward with pleasurable
anticipation. It was the sort of job he liked. But now, even
though he had managed to give his sister Constance the
slip and was free from her threatened society, he approached
the task with a downcast spirit. It is always unpleasant for
a proud man to realize that he is no longer captain of his

soul; that he is to all intents and purposes ground beneath the number twelve heel of a Glaswegian head-gardener; and, brooding on this, he judged the cottage gardens with a distrait eye. It was only when he came to the last on his list that anything like animation crept into his demeanour.

This, he perceived, peering over its rickety fence, was not at all a bad little garden. It demanded closer inspection. He unlatched the gate and pottered in. And a dog, dozing behind a water-butt, opened one eye and looked at him. It was one of those hairy, nondescript dogs, and its gaze was cold, wary and suspicious, like that of a stockbroker who thinks someone is going to play the confidence trick on him.

Lord Emsworth did not observe the animal. He had pottered to a bed of wallflowers and now, stooping, he took a sniff at them.

As sniffs go, it was an innocent sniff, but the dog for some reason appeared to read into it criminality of a high order. All the indignant householder in him woke in a flash. The next moment the world had become full of hideous noises, and Lord Emsworth's preoccupation was swept away in a passionate desire to save his ankles from harm.

As these chronicles of Blandings Castle have already shown, he was not at his best with strange dogs. Beyond saying 'Go away, sir!' and leaping to and fro with an agility surprising in one of his years, he had accomplished little in the direction of a reasoned plan of defence when the cottage door opened and a girl came out.

'Hoy!' cried the girl.

And on the instant, at the mere sound of her voice, the mongrel, suspending hostilities, bounded at the new-comer and writhed on his back at her feet with all four legs in the air. The spectacle reminded Lord Emsworth irresistibly of his own behaviour when in the presence of Angus McAllister.

He blinked at his preserver. She was a small girl, of uncertain age – possibly twelve or thirteen, though a combination of London fogs and early cares had given her face a sort of wizened motherliness which in some odd way caused his lordship from the first to look on her as belonging to his own generation. She was the type of girl you see in back streets carrying a baby nearly as large as herself and still retaining sufficient energy to lead one little brother by the hand and shout recrimination at another in the distance. Her cheeks shone from recent soaping, and she was dressed in a velveteen frock which was obviously the pick of her wardrobe. Her hair, in defiance of the prevailing mode, she wore drawn tightly back into a short pigtail.

'Er – thank you,' said Lord Emsworth.

'Thank you, sir,' said the girl.

For what she was thanking him, his lordship was not able to gather. Later, as their acquaintance ripened, he was to discover that this strange gratitude was a habit with his new friend. She thanked everybody for everything. At the moment, the mannerism surprised him. He continued to blink at her through his pince-nez.

Lack of practice had rendered Lord Emsworth a little rusty in the art of making conversation to members of the other sex. He sought in his mind for topics.

'Fine day.'

'Yes, sir. Thank you, sir.'

'Are you' – Lord Emsworth furtively consulted his list – 'are you the daughter of – ah – Ebenezer Sprockett?' he asked, thinking, as he had often thought before, what ghastly names some of his tenantry possessed.

'No, sir. I'm from London, sir.'

'Ah? London, eh? Pretty warm it must be there.' He paused. Then, remembering a formula of his youth: 'Er – been out much this Season?'

'No, sir.'

'Everybody out of town now, I suppose? What part of London?'

'Drury Line, sir.'

'What's your name? Eh, what?'

'Gladys, sir. Thank you, sir. This is Ern.'

A small boy had wandered out of the cottage, a rather

hard-boiled specimen with freckles, bearing surprisingly in his hand a large and beautiful bunch of flowers. Lord Emsworth bowed courteously and with the addition of this third party to the *tête-à-tête*, felt more at his ease.

'How do you do?' he said. 'What pretty flowers.'

With her brother's advent Gladys, also, had lost diffidence and gained conversational aplomb.

'A treat, ain't they? ' she agreed eagerly. 'I got 'em for 'im up at the big 'ahse. Coo! The old josser the plice belongs to didn't arf chase me. 'E found me picking 'em and 'e sharted somefin at me and come runnin' after me, but I copped 'im on the shin wiv a stone and 'e stopped to rub it and I come away.'

Lord Emsworth might have corrected her impression that Blandings Castle and its gardens belonged to Angus McAllister, but his mind was so filled with admiration and gratitude that he refrained from doing so. He looked at the girl almost reverently. Not content with controlling savage dogs with a mere word, this super-woman actually threw stones at Angus McAllister – a thing which he had never been able to nerve himself to do in an association which had lasted nine years – and, what was more, copped him on the shin with them. What nonsense, Lord Emsworth felt, the papers talked about the Modern Girl. If this was a specimen, the Modern Girl was the highest point the sex had yet reached.

'Ern,' said Gladys, changing the subject, 'is wearin' 'air-oil todiy.'

Lord Emsworth had already observed this and had, indeed, been moving to windward as she spoke.

'For the Feet,' explained Gladys.

'For the feet?' It seemed unusual.

'For the Feet in the pork this afternoon.'

'Oh, you are going to the Fête?'

'Yes, sir, thank you, sir.'

For the first time, Lord Emsworth found himself regarding that grisly social event with something approaching favour.

'We must look out for one another there,' he said cordially. 'You will remember me again? I shall be wearing' – he gulped – 'a top hat.'

'Ern's going to wear a stror penamaw that's been give 'im.'

Lord Emsworth regarded the lucky young devil with frank envy. He rather fancied he knew that panama. It had been his constant companion for some six years and then had been torn from him by his sister Constance and handed over to the vicar's wife for her rummage-sale.

He sighed.

'Well, good-bye.'

'Good-bye, sir. Thank you, sir.'

Lord Emsworth walked pensively out of the garden and, turning into the little street, encountered Lady Constance.

'Oh, there you are, Clarence.'

'Yes,' said Lord Emsworth, for such was the case.

'Have you finished judging the gardens?'

'Yes.'

'I am just going into this end cottage here. The vicar tells me there is a little girl from London staying there. I want to warn her to behave this afternoon. I have spoken to the others.'

Lord Emsworth drew himself up. His pince-nez were slightly askew, but despite this his gaze was commanding and impressive.

'Well, mind what you say,' he said authoritatively. 'None of your district-visiting stuff, Constance.'

'What do you mean?'

'You know what I mean. I have the greatest respect for the young lady to whom you refer. She behaved on a certain recent occasion – on two recent occasions – with notable gallantry and resource, and I won't have her bally-ragged. Understand that!'

The technical title of the orgy which broke out annually on the first Monday in August in the park of Blandings Castle was the Blandings Parva School Treat, and it seemed to Lord Emsworth, wanly watching the proceedings from under the shadow of his top hat, that if this was the sort of thing schools looked on as pleasure he and they were mentally poles apart. A function like the Blandings Parva School Treat blurred his conception of Man as Nature's Final Word.

The decent sheep and cattle to whom this park normally belonged had been hustled away into regions unknown, leaving the smooth expanse of turf to children whose vivacity scared Lord Emsworth and adults who appeared to him to have cast aside all dignity and every other noble quality which goes to make a one hundred per cent British citizen. Look at Mrs Rossiter over there, for instance, the wife of Jno. Rossiter, Provisions, Groceries and Home-made Jams. On any other day of the year, when you met her, Mrs Rossiter was a nice, quiet, docile woman who gave at the knees respectfully as you passed. To-day, flushed in the face and with her bonnet on one side, she seemed to have gone completely native. She was wandering to and fro drinking lemonade out of a bottle and employing her mouth, when not so occupied, to make a devastating noise with what he believed was termed a squeaker.

The injustice of the thing stung Lord Emsworth. This park was his own private park. What right had people to come and blow squeakers in it? How would Mrs Rossiter like it if one afternoon he suddenly invaded her neat little garden in the High Street and rushed about over her lawn, blowing a squeaker?

And it was always on these occasions so infernally hot. July might have ended in a flurry of snow, but directly the first Monday in August arrived and he had to put on a stiff collar, out came the sun, blazing with tropic fury.

Of course, admitted Lord Emsworth, for he was a fair-minded man, this cut both ways. The hotter the day, the more quickly his collar lost its starch and ceased to spike him like a javelin. This afternoon, for instance, it had resolved itself almost immediately into something which felt like a wet compress. Severe as were his sufferings, he was compelled to recognize that he was that much ahead of the game.

A masterful figure loomed at his side.

'Clarence!'

Lord Emsworth's mental and spiritual state was now such that not even the advent of his sister Constance could add noticeably to his discomfort.

'Clarence, you look a perfect sight.'

'I know I do. Who wouldn't in a rig-out like this? Why in the name of goodness you always insist ...'

'Please don't be childish, Clarence. I cannot understand the fuss you make about dressing for once in your life like a reasonable English gentleman and not like a tramp.'

'It's this top hat. It's exciting the children.'

'What on earth do you mean, exciting the children?'

'Well, all I can tell you is that just now, as I was passing the place where they're playing football – Football! In weather like this! – a small boy called out something derogatory and threw a portion of a coco-nut at it.'

'If you will identify the child,' said Lady Constance warmly, 'I will have him severely punished.'

'How the dickens,' replied his lordship with equal warmth, 'can I identify the child? They all look alike to me. And if I did identify him, I would shake him by the hand. A boy who throws coco-nuts at top hats is fundamentally sound in his views. And stiff collars ...'

'Stiff! That's what I came to speak to you about. Are you aware that your collar looks like a rag? Go in and change it at once.'

'But, my dear Constance ...'

'At once, Clarence. I simply cannot understand a man having so little pride in his appearance. But all your life you have been like that. I remember when we were childen ...'

Lord Emsworth's past was not of such a purity that he was prepared to stand and listen to it being lectured on by a sister with a good memory.

'Oh, all right, all right, all right,' he said. 'I'll change it, I'll change it.'

'Well, hurry. They are just starting tea.'

Lord Emsworth quivered.

'Have I got to go into that tea-tent?'

'Of course you have. Don't be so ridiculous. I do wish you would realize your position. As master of Blandings Castle ...'

A bitter, mirthless laugh from the poor peon thus ludicrously described drowned the rest of the sentence.

It always seemed to Lord Emsworth, in analysing these entertainments, that the August Bank Holiday Saturnalia at Blandings Castle reached a peak of repulsiveness when tea was served in the big marquee. Tea over, the agony abated, to become acute once more at the moment when he stepped to the edge of the platform and cleared his throat and tried to recollect what the deuce he had planned to say to the goggling audience beneath him. After that, it subsided again and passed until the following August.

Conditions during the tea hour, the marquee having stood all day under a blazing sun, were generally such that Shadrach, Meshach and Abednego, had they been there, could have learned something new about burning fiery furnaces. Lord Emsworth, delayed by the revision of his toilet, made his entry when the meal was half over and was pleased to find that his second collar almost instantaneously began to relax its iron grip. That, however, was the only gleam of happiness which was to be vouchsafed him. Once in the tent, it took his experienced eye but a moment to discern that the present feast was eclipsing in frightfulness all its predecessors.

Young Blandings Parva, in its normal form, tended rather to the stolidly bovine than the riotous. In all villages, of course, there must of necessity be an occasional tough egg – in the case of Blandings Parva the names of Willie Drake and Thomas (Rat-Face) Blenkiron spring to the mind – but it was seldom that the local infants offered anything beyond the power of a curate to control. What was giving the present gathering its striking resemblance to a reunion of *sans-culottes* at the height of the French Revolution was the admixture of the Fresh Air London visitors.

About the London child, reared among the tin cans and cabbage stalks of Drury Lane and Clare Market, there is a breezy insouciance which his country cousin lacks. Years of back-chat with annoyed parents and relatives have cured him of any tendency he may have had towards shyness, with the result that when he requires anything he grabs for it, and when he is amused by any slight peculiarity in the personal appearance of members of the governing classes he finds no difficulty in translating his thoughts into speech. Already, up and down the long tables, the curate's unfortunate squint was coming in for hearty comment, and the front teeth of one of the school-teachers ran it a close second for popularity. Lord Emsworth was not, as a rule, a man of swift inspirations, but it occurred to him at this juncture that it would be a prudent move to take off his top hat before his little guests observed it and appreciated its humorous possibilities.

The action was not, however, necessary. Even as he raised his hand a rock cake, singing through the air like a shell, took it off for him.

Lord Emsworth had had sufficient. Even Constance, unreasonable woman though she was, could hardly expect him to stay and beam genially under conditions like this. All civilized laws had obviously gone by the board and Anarchy reigned in the marquee. The curate was doing his best to form a provisional government consisting of himself and the two school-teachers, but there was only one man who could have coped adequately with the situation and that was King Herod, who – regrettably – was not among those present. Feeling like some aristocrat of the old *régime* sneaking away from the tumbril, Lord Emsworth edged to the exit and withdrew.

Outside the marquee the world was quieter, but only comparatively so. What Lord Emsworth craved was solitude, and in all the broad park there seemed to be but one spot where it was to be had. This was a red-tiled shed, standing beside a small pond, used at happier times as a lounge or retiring-room for cattle. Hurrying thither, his lordship had begun to revel in the cool, cow-scented dimness of its interior when from one of the dark corners, causing him to start and bite his tongue, there came the sound of a subdued sniff.

He turned. This was persecution. With the whole park to mess about in, why should an infernal child invade this one sanctuary of his? He spoke with angry sharpness. He came of a line of warrior ancestors and his fighting blood was up.

'Who's that?'

'Me, sir. Thank you, sir.'

Only one person of Lord Emsworth's acquaintance was capable of expressing gratitude for having been barked at in such a tone. His wrath died away and remorse took its place. He felt like a man who in error has kicked a favourite dog.

'God bless my soul!' he exclaimed. 'What in the world are you doing in a cow-shed?'

'Please, sir, I was put.'

'Put? How do you mean, put? Why?'

'For pinching things, sir.'

'Eh? What? Pinching things? Most extraordinary. What did you – er – pinch?'

'Two buns, two jem-sengwiches, two apples and a slicer cake.'

The girl had come out of her corner and was standing correctly at attention. Force of habit had caused her to intone the list of the purloined articles in the sing-song voice in which she was wont to recite the multiplication-table at school, but Lord Emsworth could see that she was deeply moved. Tear-stains glistened on her face, and no Emsworth had ever been able to watch unstirred a woman's tears. The ninth Earl was visibly affected.

'Blow your nose,' he said, hospitably extending his handkerchief.

'Yes, sir. Thank you, sir.'

'What, did you say you had pinched? Two buns ...'

'... Two jem-sengwiches, two apples and a slicer cake.'

'Did you eat them?'

'No, sir. They wasn't for me. They was for Ern.'

'Ern? Oh, ah, yes. Yes, to be sure. For Ern, eh?'

'Yes, sir.'

'But why the dooce couldn't Ern have – er – pinched them for himself? Strong, able-bodied young feller, I mean.'

Lord Emsworth, a member of the old school, did not like this disposition on the part of the modern young man to shirk the dirty work and let the woman pay.

'Ern wasn't allowed to come to the treat, sir.'

'What! Not allowed? Who said he mustn't?'

'The lidy, sir.'

'What lidy?'

'The one that come in just after you'd gorn this morning.'

A fierce snort escaped Lord Emsworth. Constance! What the devil did Constance mean by taking it upon herself to revise his list of guests without so much as a ... Constance, eh? He snorted again. One of these days Constance would go too far.

'Monstrous!' he cried.

'Yes, sir.'

'High-handed tyranny, by Gad. Did she give any reason?'

'The lidy didn't like Ern biting 'er in the leg, sir.'

'Ern bit her in the leg?'

'Yes, sir. Pliying 'e was a dorg. And the lidy was cross and Ern wasn't allowed to come to the treat, and I told 'im I'd bring 'im back somefing nice.'

Lord Emsworth breathed heavily. He had not supposed that in these degenerate days a family like this existed. The sister copped Angus McAllister on the shin with stones, the brother bit Constance in the leg ... It was like listening to some grand old saga of the exploits of heroes and demigods.

'I thought if I didn't 'ave nothing myself it would make it all right.'

'Nothing?' Lord Emsworth started. 'Do you mean to tell me you have not had tea?'

'No, sir. Thank you, sir. I thought if I didn't 'ave none, then it would be all right Ern 'aving what I would 'ave 'ad if I 'ad 'ave 'ad.'

His lordship's head, never strong, swam a little. Then it resumed its equilibrium. He caught her drift.

'God bless my soul!' said Lord Emsworth. 'I never heard anything so monstrous and appalling in my life. Come with me immediately.'

'The lidy said I was to stop 'ere, sir.'

Lord Emsworth gave vent to his loudest snort of the afternoon.

'Confound the lidy!'

'Yes, sir. Thank you, sir.'

Five minutes later Beach, the butler, enjoying a siesta in the housekeeper's room, was roused from his slumbers by the unexpected ringing of a bell. Answering its summons, he found his employer in the library, and with him a surprising young person in a velveteen frock, at the sight of whom his eyebrows quivered and, but for his iron self-restraint, would have risen.

'Beach!'

'Your lordship?'

'This young lady would like some tea.'

'Very good, your lordship.'

'Buns, you know. And apples, and jem – I mean jam-sandwiches, and cake, and that sort of thing.'

'Very good, your lordship.'

'And she has a brother, Beach.'

'Indeed, your lordship?'

'She will want to take some stuff away for him.' Lord Emsworth turned to his guest. 'Ernest would like a little chicken, perhaps?'

'Coo!'

'I beg your pardon?'

'Yes, sir. Thank you, sir.'

'And a slice or two of ham?'

'Yes, sir. Thank you, sir.'

'And – he has no gouty tendency?'

'No, sir. Thank you, sir.'

'Capital! Then a bottle of that new lot of port, Beach. It's some stuff they've sent me down to try,' explained his lordship. 'Nothing special, you understand,' he added apologetically, 'but quite drinkable. I should like your brother's opinion of it. See that all that is put together in a parcel, Beach, and leave it on the table in the hall. We will pick it up as we go out.'

A welcome coolness had crept into the evening air by the time Lord Emsworth and his guest came out of the great door of the castle. Gladys, holding her host's hand and clutching the parcel, sighed contentedly. She had done herself well at the tea-table. Life seemed to have nothing more to offer.

Lord Emsworth did not share this view. His spacious mood had not yet exhausted itself.

'Now, is there anything else you can think of that Ernest would like?' he asked. 'If so, do not hesitate to mention it. Beach, can you think of anything?'

The butler, hovering respectfully, was unable to do so.

'No, your lordship. I ventured to add – on my own responsibility, your lordship – some hard-boiled eggs and a pot of jam to the parcel.'

'Excellent! You are sure there is nothing else?'

A wistful look came into Gladys's eyes.

'Could he 'ave some flarze?'

'Certainly,' said Lord Emsworth. 'Certainly, certainly, certainly. By all means. Just what I was about to suggest my – er – what *is* flarze?'

Beach, the linguist, interpreted.

'I think the young lady means flowers, your lordship.'

'Yes, sir. Thank you, sir. Flarze.'

'Oh?' said Lord Emsworth. 'Oh? Flarze?' he said slowly. 'Oh, ah, yes. Yes. I see. H'm!'

He removed his pince-nez, wiped them thoughtfully, replaced them, and gazed with wrinkling forehead at the gardens that stretched gaily out before him. Flarze! It would be idle to deny that those gardens contained flarze in full measure. They were bright with Achillea, Bignonia Radicans, Campanula, Digitalis, Euphorbia, Funkia, Gypsophila, Helianthus, Iris, Liatris, Monarda, Phlox Drummondi, Salvia, Thalictrum, Vinca and Yucca. But the devil of it was that Angus McAllister would have a fit if they were picked. Across the threshold of this Eden the ginger whiskers of Angus McAllister lay like a flaming sword.

As a general rule, the procedure for getting flowers out of Angus McAllister was as follows. You waited till he was in one of his rare moods of complaisance, then you led the conversation gently round to the subject of interior decoration, and then, choosing your moment, you asked if he could possibly spare a few to be put in vases. The last thing you thought of doing was to charge in and start helping yourself.

'I – er ...' said Lord Emsworth.

He stopped. In a sudden blinding flash of clear vision he had seen himself for what he was – the spineless, unspeakably unworthy descendant of ancestors who, though they may have had their faults, had certainly known how to handle employees. It was 'How now, varlet!' and 'Marry come up, thou malapert knave!' in the days of previous Earls of Emsworth. Of course, they had possessed certain advantages which he lacked. It undoubtedly helped a man in his dealings with the domestic staff to have, as they had had, the rights of the high, the middle and the low justice – which meant, broadly, that if you got annoyed with your head-gardener you could immediately divide him into four head-gardeners with a battle-axe and no questions asked – but even so, he realized that they were better men than he was and that, if he allowed craven fear of Angus McAllister to stand in the way of this delightful girl and her charming brother getting all the flowers they required, he was not worthy to be the last of their line.

Lord Emsworth wrestled with his tremors.

'Certainly, certainly, certainly,' he said, though not without a qualm. 'Take as many as you want.'

And so it came about that Angus McAllister, crouched in his potting-shed like some dangerous beast in its den, beheld a sight which first froze his blood and then sent it boiling through his veins. Flitting to and fro through his sacred gardens, picking his sacred flowers, was a small girl in a velveteen frock. And – which brought apoplexy a step closer – it was the same small girl who two days before had copped him on the shin with a stone. The stillness of the summer evening was shattered by a roar that sounded like boilers exploding, and Angus McAllister came out of the potting-shed at forty-five miles per hour.

Gladys did not linger. She was a London child, trained from infancy to bear herself gallantly in the presence of alarms and excursions, but this excursion had been so sudden that it momentarily broke her nerve. With a horrified yelp she scuttled to where Lord Emsworth stood and, hiding behind him, clutched the tails of his morning-coat.

'Oo-er!' said Gladys.

Lord Emsworth was not feeling so frightfully good himself. We have pictured him a few moments back drawing inspiration from the nobility of his ancestors and saying, in effect, 'That for McAllister!', but truth now compels us to admit that this hardy attitude was largely due to the fact that he believed the head-gardener to be a safe quarter of a mile away among the swings and roundabouts of the Fête. The spectacle of the man charging vengefully down on him with gleaming eyes and bristling whiskers made him feel like a nervous English infantryman at the Battle of Bannockburn. His knees shook and the soul within him quivered.

And then something happened, and the whole aspect of the situation changed.

It was, in itself, quite a trivial thing, but it had an astoundingly stimulating effect on Lord Emsworth's morale. What happened was that Gladys, seeking further protection, slipped at this moment a small, hot hand into his.

It was a mute vote of confidence, and Lord Emsworth intended to be worthy of it.

'He's coming,' whispered his lordship's Inferiority Complex agitatedly.

'What of it?' replied Lord Emsworth stoutly.

'Tick him off,' breathed his lordship's ancestors in his other ear.

'Leave it to me,' replied Lord Emsworth.

He drew himself up and adjusted his pince-nez. He felt filled with a cool masterfulness. If the man tendered his resignation, let him tender his damned resignation.

'Well, McAllister?' said Lord Emsworth coldly.

He removed his top hat and brushed it against his sleeve.

'What is the matter, McAllister?'

He replaced his top hat.

'You appear agitated, McAllister.'

He jerked his head militantly. The hat fell off. He let it lie. Freed from its loathsome weight he felt more masterful than ever. It had just needed that to bring him to the top of his form.

'This young lady,' said Lord Emsworth, 'has my full permission to pick all the flowers she wants, McAllister. If you do not see eye to eye with me in this matter, McAllister, say so and we will discuss what you are going to do about it, McAllister. These gardens, McAllister, belong to me, and if you do not – er – appreciate that fact you will, no doubt, be able to find another employer – ah – more in tune with your views. I value your services highly, McAllister, but I will not be dictated to in my own garden, McAllister. Er – dash it,' added his lordship, spoiling the whole effect.

A long moment followed in which Nature stood still, breathless. The Achillea stood still. So did the Bignonia Radicans. So did the Campanula, the Digitalis, the Euphorbia, the Funkia, the Gypsophila, the Helianthus, the Iris, the Liatris, the Monarda, the Phlox Drummondi, the Salvia, the Thalictrum, the Vinca and the Yucca. From far off in the direction of the park there sounded the happy howls of children who were probably breaking things, but even these seemed hushed. The evening breeze had died away.

Angus McAllister stood glowering. His attitude was that of one sorely perplexed. So might the early bird have looked if the worm ear-marked for its breakfast had suddenly turned and snapped at it. It had never occurred to him that his employer would voluntarily suggest that he sought another position, and now that he had suggested it, Angus McAllister disliked the idea very much. Blandings Castle was in his bones. Elsewhere, he would feel an exile. He fingered his whiskers, but they gave him no comfort.

He made his decision. Better to cease to be a Napoleon than be a Napoleon in exile.

'Mphm,' said Angus McAllister.

'Oh, and by the way, McAllister,' said Lord Emsworth, 'that matter of the gravel path through the yew alley. I've been thinking it over, and I won't have it. Not on any account. Mutilate my beautiful moss with a beastly gravel path? Make an eyesore of the loveliest spot in one of the finest and oldest gardens in the United Kingdom? Certainly not. Most decidedly not. Try to remember, McAllister, as you work in the gardens of Blandings Castle, that you are not back in Glasgow, laying out recreation grounds. That is all, McAllister. Er – dash it – that is all.'

'Mphm,' said Angus McAllister.

He turned. He walked away. The potting-shed swallowed him up. Nature resumed its breathing. The breeze began to blow again. And all over the gardens birds who had stopped on their high note carried on according to plan.

Lord Emsworth took out his handkerchief and dabbed with it at his forehead. He was shaken, but a novel sense of being a man among men thrilled him. It might seem bravado, but he almost wished – yes, dash it, he almost wished – that his sister Constance would come along and start something while he felt like this.

He had his wish.

'Clarence!'

Yes, there she was, hurrying towards him up the garden path. She, like McAllister, seemed agitated. Something was on her mind.

'Clarence!'

'Don't keep saying "Clarence!" as if you were a dashed parrot,' said Lord Emsworth haughtily. 'What the dickens is the matter, Constance?'

'Matter? Do you know what the time is? Do you know that everybody is waiting down there for you to make your speech?'

Lord Emsworth met her eye sternly.

'I do not,' he said. 'And I don't care. I'm not going to make any dashed speech. If you want a speech, let the vicar make it. Or make it yourself. Speech! I never heard such dashed nonsense in my life.' He turned to Gladys. 'Now, my dear,' he said, 'if you will just give me time to get out of these infernal clothes and this ghastly collar and put on something human, we'll go down to the village and have a chat with Ern.'

CHAPTER 7

Mr Potter Takes a Rest Cure

MR JOHN HAMILTON POTTER, founder and proprietor of the well-known New York publishing house of J. H. Potter, Inc., laid down the typescript which had been engaging his leisurely attention, and from the depths of his basket-chair gazed dreamily across the green lawns and gleaming flower-beds to where Skeldings Hall basked in the pleasant June sunshine. He was feeling quietly happy. The waters of the moat glittered like liquid silver; a gentle breeze brought to his nostrils the scent of newly-cut grass; the doves in the immemorial elms cooed with precisely the right gentlemanly intonation; and he had not seen Clifford Gandle since luncheon. God, it seemed to Mr Potter, was in His heaven and all was right with the world.

And how near, he reflected, he had come to missing all this delightful old-world peace. When, shortly after his arrival in England, he had met Lady Wickham at a Pen and Ink Club dinner and she had invited him to pay a visit to Skeldings, his first impulse had been to decline. His hostess was a woman of rather markedly overwhelming personality; and, inasmuch as he had only recently recovered from a nervous breakdown and had been ordered by his doctor complete rest and tranquillity, it had seemed to him that at close range and over an extended period of time she might be a little too much for the old system. Furthermore, she wrote novels: and that instinct of self-preservation which lurks in every publisher had suggested to him that behind her invitation lay a sinister desire to read these to him one by one with a view to getting him to produce them in America. Only the fact that he was a lover of the old and picturesque, coupled with the fact that Skeldings Hall dated back to the time of the Tudors, had caused him to accept.

Not once, however – not even when Clifford Gandle was expressing to him with a politician's trained verbosity his views on the Gold Standard and other weighty matters – had he regretted his decision. When he looked back on his life of the past eighteen months – a life spent in an inferno of shrilling telephones and authors, many of them female, popping in to abuse him for not advertising their books better – he could almost fancy that he had been translated to Paradise.

A Paradise, moreover, which was not without its Peri. For at this moment there approached Mr Potter across the lawn, walking springily as if she were constructed of whalebone and india-rubber, a girl. She was a boyish-looking girl, slim and graceful, and the red hair on her bare head glowed pleasingly in the sun.

'Hullo, Mr Potter!' she said.

The publisher beamed upon her. This was Roberta Wickham, his hostess's daughter, who had returned to her ancestral home two days ago from a visit to friends in the North. A friendly young thing, she had appealed to Mr Potter from the first.

'Well, well, well!' said Mr Potter.

'Don't get up. What are you reading?' Bobbie Wickham picked up the manuscript. '*Ethics of Suicide*,' she read. 'Cheery!'

Mr Potter laughed indulgently.

'No doubt it seems an odd thing to be reading on such a day and in such surroundings. But a publisher is never free. This was sent over for my decision from my New York office. They won't leave me alone, you see, even when I am on vacation.'

Bobbie Wickham's hazel eyes clouded pensively.

'There's a lot to be said for suicide,' she murmured. 'If I had to see much of Clifford Gandle, I'd commit suicide myself.'

Mr Potter started. He had always liked this child, but he never dreamed that she was such a completely kindred soul.

'Don't you like Mr Gandle?'

'No.'

'Nor do I.'

'Nor does anyone,' said Bobbie, 'except mother.' Her eyes clouded again. 'Mother thinks he's wonderful.'

'She does?'

'Yes.'

'Well, well!' said Mr Potter.

Bobbie brooded.

'He's a Member of Parliament, you know.'

'Yes.'

'And they say he may be in the Cabinet any day.'

'So he gave me to understand.'

'And all that sort of thing is very bad for a man, don't you think? I mean, it seems to make him so starchy.'

'The very word.'

'And pompous.'

'The exact adjective I would have selected,' agreed Mr Potter. 'In our frequent conversations, before you arrived, he addressed me as if I were a half-witted deputation of his constituents.'

'Did you see much of him before I came?'

'A great deal, though I did my best to avoid him.'

'He's a difficult man to avoid.'

'Yes.' Mr Potter chuckled sheepishly. 'Shall I tell you something that happened a day or two ago? You must not let it go any farther, of course. I was coming out of the smoking-room one morning, and I saw him approaching me along the passage. So – so I jumped back and – ha, ha! – hid in a small cupboard.'

'Jolly sensible.'

'Yes. But unfortunately he opened the cupboard door and discovered me. It was exceedingly embarrassing.'

'What did you say?'

'There was nothing much I could say. I'm afraid he must have thought me out of my senses.'

'Well, I — All right, mother. Coming.'

The rich contralto of a female novelist calling to its young had broken the stillness of the summer afternoon. Mr Potter looked up with a start. Lady Wickham was standing on the lawn. It seemed to Mr Potter that, as his little friend moved towards her, something of the springiness had gone out of her walk. It was as if she moved reluctantly.

'Where have you been, Roberta?' asked Lady Wickham, as her daughter came within earshot of the normal tone of voice. 'I have been looking everywhere for you.'

'Anything special, mother?'

'Mr Gandle wants to go to Hertford. He has to get some books. I think you had better drive him in your car.'

'Oh, mother!'

Mr Potter, watching from his chair, observed a peculiar expression flit into Lady Wickham's face. Had he been her English publisher, instead of merely her prospective American publisher, he would have been familiar with that look. It meant that Lady Wickham was preparing to exercise her celebrated will-power.

'Roberta,' she said, with dangerous quiet, 'I particularly wish you to drive Mr Gandle to Hertford.'

'But I had promised to go over and play tennis at the Crufts'.'

'Mr Gandle is a much better companion for you than a young waster like Algy Crufts. You must run over and tell him that you cannot play to-day.'

A few minutes later a natty two-seater drew up at the front door of the Crufts' residence down the road; and Bobbie Wickham, seated at the wheel, gave tongue.

'Algy!'

The flannel-clad form of Mr Algernon Crufts appeared at a window.

'Hullo! Down in a jiffy.'

There was an interval. Then Mr Crufts joined her on the drive.

'Hullo! I say, you haven't brought your racket, you poor chump,' he said.

'Tennis is off,' announced Bobbie briefly. 'I've got to drive Clifford Gandle in to Hertford.' She paused. 'I say, Algy, shall I tell you something?'

'What?'

'Between ourselves.'

'Absolutely.'

'Mother wants me to marry Clifford Gandle.'

Algy Crufts uttered a strangled exclamation. Such was his emotion that he nearly swallowed the first eight inches of his cigarette-holder.

'Marry Clifford Gandle!'

'Yes. She's all for it. She says he would have a steadying influence on me.'

'Ghastly! Take my advice and give the project the most absolute go-by. I was up at Oxford with the man. A blighter, if ever there was one. He was President of the Union and all sorts of frightful things.'

'It's all very awkward. I don't know what to do.'

'Kick him in the eye and tell him to go to blazes. That's the procedure.'

'But it's so hard not to do anything mother wants you to do. You know mother.'

'I do,' said Mr Crufts, who did.

'Oh, well,' said Bobbie, 'you never know. There's always the chance that she may take a sudden dislike to him for some reason or other. She does take sudden dislikes to people.'

'She does,' said Mr Crufts. Lady Wickham had disliked him at first sight.

'Well, let's hope she will suddenly dislike Clifford Gandle. But I don't mind telling you, Algy, that at the moment things are looking pretty black.'

'Keep smiling,' urged Mr Crufts.

'What's the good of smiling, you fathead?' said Bobbie morosely.

Night had fallen on Skeldings Hall. Lady Wickham was in her study, thinking those great thoughts which would subsequently be copyrighted in all languages, including the Scandinavian. Bobbie was strolling somewhere in the grounds, having eluded Mr Gandle after dinner. And Mr Gandle, baffled but not defeated, had donned a light overcoat and gone out to try to find Bobbie.

As for Mr Potter, he was luxuriating in restful solitude in a punt under a willow by the bank of the moat.

From the first moment he had set eyes on it, Hamilton Potter had loved the moat at Skeldings Hall. Here, by the willow, it broadened out almost into the dimensions of a lake; and there was in the glitter of stars on its surface and sleepy rustling of birds in the trees along its bank something infinitely soothing. The healing darkness wrapped the publisher about like a blanket; the cool night-wind fanned caressingly a forehead a little heated by Lady Wickham's fine old port; and gradually, lulled by the beauty of the scene, Mr Potter allowed himself to float into one of those reveries which come to publishers at moments such as this.

He mused on jackets and remainders and modes of distribution; on royalties and advertisements and spring lists and booksellers' discounts. And his random thoughts, like fleeting thistledown, had just drifted to the question of the growing price of pulp-paper, when from somewhere near by there came the sound of a voice, jerking him back to the world again.

'Oh, let the solid ground not fail beneath my feet before that I have found what some have found so sweet,' said the voice.

A moderate request, one would have supposed; and yet it irritated Mr Potter like the bite of a mosquito. For the voice was the voice of Clifford Gandle.

'Robertah,' proceeded the voice, and Mr Potter breathed again. He had taken it for granted that the man had perceived and was addressing himself. He gathered now that his presence had not been discovered.

'Robertah,' said Mr Gandle, 'surely you cannot have been blind to the na-chah of my feelings? Surely you must have guessed that it was love that —'

Hamilton Potter congealed into a solid mass of frozen horror. He was listening-in on a proposal of marriage.

The emotions of any delicate-minded man who finds himself in such a position cannot fail to be uncomfortable; and the greater his delicacy of mind the more acute must the discomfort be. Mr Potter, being, as are all publishers, more like a shrinking violet than anything else in the world, nearly swooned. His scalp tingled; his jaw fell; and his toes began to open and shut like poppet-valves.

'Heart of my heart —' said Mr Gandle.

Mr Potter gave a convulsive shudder. And the punt-pole which had been resting on the edge of the boat, clattered down with a noise like a machine-gun.

There was a throbbing silence. Then Mr Gandle spoke sharply.

'Is anybody they-ah?'

There are situations in which a publisher can do only one thing. Raising himself noiselessly, Mr Potter wriggled to the side of the punt and lowered himself into the water.

'Who is they-ah?'

Mr Potter with a strong effort shut his mouth, which was trying to emit a howl of anguish. He had never supposed that water could be so cold. Silently he waded out towards the opposite bank. The only thing that offered any balm in this black moment was the recollection that his hostess had informed him that the moat was not more than four feet deep.

But what Lady Wickham had omitted to inform him was that in one or two places there were ten-foot holes. It came, therefore, as a surprise to Mr Potter, when, after he had travelled some six yards, there happened to him that precise disaster which Mr Gandle, in his recent remarks, had expressed himself as so desirous of avoiding. As the publisher took his next step forward, the solid ground failed beneath his feet.

'Oosh!' ejaculated Mr Potter.

Clifford Gandle was a man of swift intuition. Hearing the cry and becoming aware at the same time of loud splashing noises, he guessed in one masterly flash of inductive reasoning that someone had fallen in. He charged down the bank and perceived the punt. He got into the punt. Bobbie Wickham got into the punt. Mr Gandle seized the pole and propelled the punt out into the waste of waters.

'Are you they-ah?' inquired Mr Gandle.

'Glub!' exclaimed Mr Potter.

'I see him,' said Bobbie. 'More to the left.'

Clifford Gandle drove the rescuing craft more to the left, and was just digging the pole into the water when Mr Potter, coming up for the third time, found it within his reach. The partiality of drowning men for straws is proverbial; but, as a class, they are broad-minded and will clutch at punt-poles with equal readiness. Mr Potter seized the pole and pulled strongly; and Clifford Gandle, who happened to be leaning his whole weight on it at the moment, was not proof against what practically amounted to a formal invitation. A moment later he had joined Mr Potter in the depths.

Bobbie Wickham rescued the punt-pole, which was floating away on the tide, and peered down through the darkness. Stirring things were happening below. Clifford Gandle had grasped Mr Potter. Mr Potter had grasped Clifford Gandle. And Bobbie, watching from above, was irresistibly reminded of a picture she had seen in her childhood of alligators fighting in the River Hooghly. She raised the pole, and, with the best intentions, prodded at the tangled mass.

The treatment proved effective. The pole, taking Clifford Gandle shrewdly in the stomach, caused him to release his grip on Mr Potter; and Mr Potter, suddenly discovering that he was in shallow water again, did not hesitate. By the time Clifford Gandle had scrambled into the punt he was on dry land, squelching rapidly towards the house.

A silence followed his departure. Then Mr Gandle, expelling the last pint of water from his mouth, gave judgement.

'The man must be mad!'

He found some more water which he had overlooked, and replaced it.

'Stark, staring mad!' he repeated. 'He must have deliberately flung himself in.'

Bobbie Wickham was gazing out into the night; and, had the visibility been better, her companion might have observed in her expression the raptness of inspiration.

'There is no other explanation. The punt was they-ah, by the bank, and he was hee-yah, right out in the middle of the moat. I've suspected for days that he was unbalanced. Once I found him hiding in a cupboard. Crouching there with a wild gleam in his eyes. And that brooding look of his. That strange brooding look. I've noticed it every time I've been talking to him.'

Bobbie broke the silence, speaking in a low, grave voice.

'Didn't you know about poor Mr Potter?'

'Eh?'

'That he has suicidal mania?'

Clifford Gandle drew in his breath sharply.

'You can't blame him,' said Bobbie. 'How would you feel if you came home one day and found your wife and your two brothers and a cousin sitting round the dinner-table stone dead?'

'What!'

'Poisoned. Something in the curry.' She shivered. 'This morning I found him in the garden gloating over a book called *Ethics of Suicide*.'

Clifford Gandle ran his fingers through his dripping hair.

'Something ought to be done!'

'What can you do? The thing isn't supposed to be known. If you mention it to him, he will simply go away; and then mother will be furious, because she wants him to publish her books in America.'

'I shall keep the closest watch on the man.'

'Yes, that's the thing to do,' agreed Bobbie.

She pushed the punt to the shore. Mr Gandle, who had begun to feel chilly, leaped out and sped to the house to change his clothes. Bobbie, following at a more leisurely pace, found her mother standing the passage outside her study. Lady Wickham's manner was perturbed.

'Roberta!'

'Yes, mother?'

'What in the world has been happening? A few moments ago Mr Potter ran past my door, dripping wet. And now Clifford Gandle has just gone by, also soaked to the skin. What have they been doing?'

'Fighting in the moat, mother.'

'Fighting in the moat? What do you mean?'

'Mr Potter jumped in to try and get away from Mr Gandle, and then Mr Gandle went in after him and seized him round the neck, and they grappled together for quite a long time, struggling furiously. I think they must have had a quarrel.'

'What on earth would they quarrel about?'

'Well, you know what a violent man Clifford Gandle is.'

This was an aspect of Mr Gandle's character which Lady Wickham had not perceived. She opened her penetrating eyes.

'Clifford Gandle violent?'

'I think he's the sort of man who takes sudden dislikes to people.'

'Nonsense!'

'Well, it all seems very queer to me,' said Bobbie.

She passed on her way upstairs; and, reaching the first landing, turned down the corridor till she came to the principal guest-room. She knocked delicately. There were movements inside, and presently the door opened, revealing Hamilton Potter in a flowered dressing-gown.

'Thank Heaven you're safe!' said Bobbie.

The fervour of her tone touched Mr Potter. His heart warmed to the child.

'If I hadn't been there when Mr Gandle was trying to drown you —'

Mr Potter started violently.

'Trying to drown me?' he gasped.

Bobbie's eyebrows rose.

'Hasn't anybody told you about Mr Gandle – warned you? Didn't you know he was one of the mad Gandles?'

'The – the —'

'Mad Gandles. You know what some of these very old English families are like. All the Gandles have been mad for generations back.'

'You don't mean – you can't mean —' Mr Potter gulped. 'You can't mean that Mr Gandle is homicidal?'

'Not normally. But he takes sudden dislikes to people.'

'I think he likes me,' said Mr Potter, with a certain nervous satisfaction. 'He has made a point of seeking me out and giving me his views on – er – various matters.'

'Did you ever yawn while he was doing it?'

Mr Potter blenched.

'Would – would he mind that very much?'

'Mind it! You lock your door at night, don't you, Mr Potter?'

'But this is terrible.'

'He sleeps in this corridor.'

'But why is the man at large?'

'He hasn't done anything yet. You can't shut a man up till he has done something.'

'Does Lady Wickham know of this?'

'For goodness' sake don't say a word to mother. It would only make her nervous. Everything will be quite all right, if you're only careful. You had better try not to let him get you alone.'

'Yes,' said Mr Potter.

The last of the mad Gandles, meanwhile, having peeled off the dress-clothes moistened during the recent water-carnival, had draped his bony form in a suit of orange-coloured pyjamas, and was now devoting the full force of a legislator's mind to the situation which had arisen.

He was a long, thin young man with a curved nose

which even in his lighter moments gave him the appearance of disapproving things in general; and there had been nothing in the events of the last hour to cause any diminution of this look of disapproval. For we cannot in fairness but admit that, if ever a mad Gandle had good reason to be mad, Clifford Gandle had at this juncture. He had been interrupted at the crucial point of proposal of marriage. He had been plunged into water and prodded with a puntpole. He had sown the seeds of a cold in the head. And he rather fancied that he had swallowed a newt. These things do not conduce to sunniness in a man.

Nor did an inspection of the future do anything to remove his gloom. He had come to Skeldings for rest and recuperation after the labours of an exhausting Session, and now it seemed that, instead of passing his time pleasantly in the society of Roberta Wickham, he would be compelled to devote himself to acting as a guardian to a misguided publisher.

It was not as if he liked publishers, either. His relations with Prodder and Wiggs, who had sold forty-three copies of his book of political essays – *Watchman, What of the Night?* – had not been agreeable.

Nevertheless, this last of the Gandles was a conscientious man. He had no intention of shirking the call of duty. The question of whether it was worth while preventing a publisher committing suicide did not present itself to him.

That was why Bobbie's note, when he read it, produced such immediate results.

Exactly when the missive had been delivered, Clifford Gandle could not say. Much thought had rendered him distrait, and the rustle of the paper as it was thrust under his door did not reach his consciousness. It was only when, after a considerable time, he rose with the intention of going to bed that he perceived lying on the floor an envelope.

He stooped and picked it up. He examined it with a thoughtful stare. He opened it.

The letter was brief. It ran as follows:

'*What about his razors?*'

A thrill of dismay shot through him.

Razors!

He had forgotten them.

Clifford Gandle did not delay. Already it might be that he was too late. He hurried down the passage and tapped at Mr Potter's door.

'Who's there?'

Clifford Gandle was relieved. He was in time.

'Can I come in?'

'Who is that?'

'Gandle.'

'What do you want?'

'Can you – er – lend me a razah?'

'A what?'

'A razah.'

There followed a complete silence from within. Mr Gandle tapped again.

'Are you they-ah?'

The silence was broken by an odd rumbling sound. Something heavy knocked against the woodwork. But that the explanation seemed so improbable, Mr Gandle would have said that this peculiar publisher had pushed a chest of drawers against the door.

'Mr Pottah!'

More silence.

'Are you they-ah, Mr Pottah!'

Additional stillness. Mr Gandle, wearying of a profitless vigil, gave the thing up and returned to his room.

The task that lay before him, he now realized, was to wait awhile and then make his way along the balcony which joined the windows of the two rooms; enter while the other slept, and abstract his weapon or weapons.

He looked at his watch. The hour was close on midnight. He decided to give Mr Potter till two o'clock.

Clifford Gandle sat down to wait.

Mr Potter's first action, after the retreating footsteps had told him that his visitor had gone, was to extract a couple of nerve pills from the box by his bed and swallow them. This was a rite which, by the orders of his medical adviser, he had performed thrice a day since leaving America – once half an hour before breakfast, once an hour before luncheon, and again on retiring to rest.

In spite of the fact that he now consumed these pills, it seemed to Mr Potter that he could scarcely be described as retiring to rest. After the recent ghastly proof of Clifford Gandle's insane malevolence, he could not bring himself to hope that even the most fitful slumber would come to him this night. The horror of the thought of that awful man padding softly to his door and asking for razors chilled Hamilton Potter to the bone.

Nevertheless, he did his best. He switched off the light and, closing his eyes, began to repeat in a soft undertone a formula which he had often found efficacious.

'Day by day,' murmured Mr Potter, 'in every way, I am getting better and better. Day by day, in every way, I am getting better and better.'

It would have astonished Clifford Gandle, yawning in his room down the corridor, if he could have heard such optimistic sentiments proceeding from those lips.

'Day by day, in every way, I am getting better and better.'

Mr Potter's mind performed an unfortunate sideslip. He lay there tingling. Suppose he *was* getting better and better, what of it? What was the use of getting better and better if at any moment a mad Gandle might spring out with a razor and end it all?

He forced his thoughts away from these uncomfortable channels. He clenched his teeth and whispered through them with a touch of defiance.

'Day by day, in every way, I am getting better and better. Day by day, in every way —'

A pleasant drowsiness stole over Mr Potter.

'Day by day, in every way,' he murmured, 'I am getting better and better. Day by day, in every way, I am betting getter and getter. Bay by day, in every way, I am betting getter and wetter. Way by day —'

Mr Potter slept.

Over the stables the clock chimed the hour of two, and Clifford Gandle stepped out on to the balcony.

It has been well said by many thinkers that in human affairs you can never be certain that some little trifling obstacle will not undo the best-laid of schemes. It was the sunken road at Hougoumont that undid the French cavalry at Waterloo, and it was something very similar that caused Clifford Gandle's plan of action to go wrong now – a jug of water, to wit, which the maid who had brought Mr Potter's hot-water-can before dinner had placed immediately beneath the window.

Clifford Gandle, insinuating himself with the extreme of caution through the window and finding his foot resting on something hard, assumed that he was touching the floor, and permitted his full weight to rest upon that foot. Almost immediately afterwards the world collapsed with a crash and a deluge of water; and light, flooding the room, showed Mr Potter sitting up in bed, blinking.

Mr Potter stared at Clifford Gandle. Clifford Gandle stared at Mr Potter.

'Er – hullo!' said Clifford Gandle.

Mr Potter uttered a low, curious sound like a cat with a fish-bone in its throat.

'I – er – just looked in,' said Clifford Gandle.

Mr Potter made a noise like a second and slightly larger cat with another fish-bone in its throat.

'I've come for the razah,' said Clifford Gandle. 'Ah, there it is,' he said, and, moving towards the dressing-table, secured it.

Mr Potter leaped from his bed. He looked about him for a weapon. The only one in sight appeared to be the type-script of *Ethics of Suicide*, and that, while it would have made an admirable instrument for swatting flies, was far too flimsy for the present crisis. All in all, it began to look to Mr Potter like a sticky evening.

'Good night,' said Clifford Gandle.

Mr Potter was amazed to see that his visitor was withdrawing towards the window. It seemed incredible. For a moment he wondered whether Bobbie Wickham had not made some mistake about this man. Nothing could be more temperate than his behaviour at the moment.

And then, as he reached the window, Clifford Gandle smiled, and all Mr Potter's fears leaped into being again.

The opinion of Clifford Gandle regarding this smile was that it was one of those kindly, reassuring smiles – the sort of smile to put the most nervous melancholiac at his ease. To Mr Potter it seemed precisely the kind of maniac grin which he would have expected from such a source.

'Good night,' said Clifford Gandle.

He smiled again, and was gone. And Mr Potter, having stood rooted to the spot for some minutes, crossed the floor and closed the window. He then bolted the window. He perceived a pair of shutters, and shut them. He moved the washhand-stand till it rested against the shutters. He placed two chairs and a small bookcase against the washhand-stand. Then he went to bed, leaving the light burning.

'Day by day, in every way,' said Mr Potter, 'I am getting better and better.'

But his voice lacked the ring of true conviction.

Sunshine filtering in through the shutters, and the song of birds busy in the ivy outside his window, woke Mr Potter at an early hour next morning; but it was some time before he could bring himself to spring from his bed to greet another day. His disturbed night had left him heavy and lethargic. When finally he had summoned up the energy to rise and remove the zariba in front of the window and open the shutters, he became aware that a glorious morning was upon the world. The samples of sunlight that had crept into the room had indicated only feebly the golden wealth without.

But there was no corresponding sunshine in Mr Potter's heart. Spiritually as well as physically he was at a low ebb. The more he examined the position of affairs, the less he liked it. He went down to breakfast in pensive mood.

Breakfast at Skeldings was an informal meal, and visitors were expected to take it when they pleased, irrespective of the movements of their hostess, who was a late riser. In the dining-room, when Mr Potter entered it, only the daughter of the house was present.

Bobbie was reading the morning paper. She nodded cheerfully to him over its top.

'Good morning, Mr Potter. I hope you slept well.'

Mr Potter winced.

'Miss Wickham,' he said, 'last night an appalling thing occurred.'

A startled look came into Bobbie's eyes.

'You don't mean – Mr Gandle?'

'Yes.'

'Oh, Mr Potter, what?'

'Just as I was going to bed, the man knocked at my door and asked if he could borrow my razah – I mean my razor.'

'You didn't lend it to him?'

'No, I did not,' replied Mr Potter, with a touch of asperity. 'I barricaded the door.'

'How wise of you!'

'And at two in the morning he came in through the window!'

'How horrible!'

'He took my razor. Why he did not attack me, I cannot say. But, having obtained it, he grinned at me in a ghastly way and went out.'

There was a silence.

'Have an egg or something,' said Bobbie, in a hushed voice.

'Thank you, I will take a little ham,' whispered Mr Potter.

There was another silence.

'I'm afraid,' said Bobbie at length, 'you will have to go.'

'That is what I think.'

'It is quite evident that Mr Gandle has taken one of his uncontrollable dislikes to you.'

'Yes.'

'What I think you ought to do is to leave quite quietly, without saying good-bye or anything, so that he won't know where you've gone and won't be able to follow you. Then you could write mother a letter, saying that you had to go because of Mr Gandle's persecution.'

'Exactly.'

'You needn't say anything about his being mad. She knows that. Just say that he ducked you in the moat and then came into your room at two in the morning and made faces at you. She will understand.'

'Yes. I – '

'Hush!'

Clifford Gandle came into the room.

'Good morning,' said Bobbie.

'Good morning,' said Mr Gandle.

He helped himself to poached egg; and, glancing across the table at the publisher, was concerned to note how wan and sombre was his aspect. If ever a man looked as if he were on the verge of putting an end to everything, that man was John Hamilton Potter.

Clifford Gandle was not feeling particularly festive himself at the moment, for he was a man who depended greatly for his well-being on a placid eight hours of sleep; but he exerted himself to be bright and optimistic.

'What a lovely morning!' he trilled.

'Yes,' said Mr Potter.

'Surely such weather is enough to make any man happy and satisfied with life.'

'Yes,' said Mr Potter doubtfully.

'Who, with all Na-chah smiling, could seriously contemplate removing himself from so bright a world?'

'George Philibert, of 32 Acacia Road, Cricklewood,

did,' said Bobbie, who had resumed her study of the paper.

'Eh? said Mr Gandle.

'George Philibert, of 32 Acacia Road, Cricklewood, was had up before the beak yesterday, charged with attempted suicide. He stated that —'

Mr Gandle cast a reproachful look at her. He had always supposed Roberta Wickham to be a girl of fair intelligence, as women go; and it seemed to him that he had over-estimated her good sense. He did his best to cover up her blunder.

'Possibly,' he said, 'with some really definite and serious reason —'

'I can never understand,' said Mr Potter, coming out of what had all the outward appearance of a trance, 'why the idea arose that suicide is wrong.'

He spoke with a curious intensity. The author of *Ethics of Suicide* had wielded a plausible pen, and the subject was one on which he now held strong views. And, even if he had not already held them, his mood this morning was of a kind to breed them in his bosom.

'The author of a very interesting book which I intend to publish shortly,' he said, 'points out that none but the votaries of the monotheistic religions look upon suicide as a crime.'

'Yes,' said Mr Gandle, 'but —'

'If, he goes on to say, the criminal law forbids suicide, that is not an argument valid in the Church. And, besides, the prohibition is ridiculous, for what penalty can frighten a man who is not afraid of death itself?'

'George Philibert got fourteen days,' said Bobbie.

'Yes, but —' said Mr Gandle.

'The ancients were very far from regarding the matter in the modern light. Indeed, in Massilia and on the island of Cos, the man who could give valid reasons for relinquishing his life was handed the cup of hemlock by the magistrate, and that, too, in public.'

'Yes, but —'

'And why,' said Mr Potter, 'suicide should be regarded

as cowardly is beyond me. Surely no man who had not an iron nerve —'

He broke off. The last two words had tapped a chord in his memory. Abruptly it occurred to him that here he was, half-way through breakfast, and he had not taken those iron nerve-pills which his doctor had so strictly ordered him to swallow thirty minutes before the morning meal.

'Yes,' said Mr Gandle. He lowered his cup, and looked across the table. 'But —'

His voice died away. He sat staring before him in horror-struck silence. Mr Potter, with a strange, wild look in his eyes, was in the very act of raising to his lips a sinister-looking white pellet. And, even as Mr Gandle gazed, the wretched man's lips closed over the horrid thing and a movement of his Adam's apple showed that the deed was done.

'Surely,' said Mr Potter, 'no man who —'

It seemed that Fate was inflexibly bent on preventing him from finishing that particular sentence this morning. For he had got thus far when Clifford Gandle, seizing the mustard-pot, rose with a maniac screech and bounded, wild-eyed, round the table at him.

Lady Wickham came downstairs and made her way like a stately galleon under sail towards the dining-room. Unlike others of the household, she was feeling particularly cheerful this morning. She liked fine weather, and the day was unusually fine. Also, she had resolved that after breakfast she would take Mr Potter aside and use the full force of her commanding personality to extract from him something in the nature of an informal contract.

She would not, she decided, demand too much at first. If he would consent to undertake the American publication of *Agatha's Vow*, *A Strong Man's Love*, and – possibly – *A Man for A' That*, she would be willing to postpone discussion of *Meadowsweet*, *Fetters of Fate*, and the rest of her works. But if he thought he could eat her bread and salt and sidestep *Agatha's Vow*, he had grievously under-estimated the power of her cold grey eye when it came to subduing such members of the animal kingdom as publishers.

There was a happy smile, therefore, on Lady Wickham's face as she entered the room. She was not actually singing, but she stopped only just short of it.

She was surprised to find that, except for her daughter Roberta, the dining-room was empty.

'Good morning, mother,' said Bobbie.

'Good morning. Has Mr Potter finished his breakfast?'

Bobbie considered the question.

'I don't know if he had actually finished,' she said. 'But he didn't seem to want any more.'

'Where is he?'

'I don't know, mother.'

'When did he go?'

'He's only just left.'

'I didn't meet him.'

'He went out of the window.'

The sunshine faded from Lady Wickham's face.

'Out of the window? Why?'

'I think it was because Clifford Gandle was between him and the door.'

'What do you mean? Where is Clifford Gandle?'

'I don't know, mother. He went out of the window, too. They were both running down the drive when I last saw them.' Bobbie's face grew pensive. 'Mother, I've been thinking,' she said. 'Are you really sure that Clifford Gandle would be such a steadying influence for me? He seems to me rather eccentric.'

'I cannot understand a word of what you are saying.'

'Well, he is eccentric. At two o'clock this morning, Mr Potter told me, he climbed in through Mr Potter's window, made faces at him, and climbed out again. And just now—'

'Made faces at Mr Potter?'

'Yes, mother. And just now Mr Potter was peacefully eating his breakfast, when Clifford Gandle suddenly uttered a loud cry and sprang at him. Mr Potter jumped out of the window and Clifford Gandle jumped out after him and chased him down the drive. I thought Mr Potter ran awfully well for an elderly man, but that sort of thing can't be good for him in the middle of breakfast.'

Lady Wickham subsided into a chair.

'Is everybody mad?'

'I think Clifford Gandle must be. You know, these men who do wonderful things at the University often do crack up suddenly. I was reading a case only yesterday about a man in America. He took every possible prize at Harvard or wherever it was, and then, just as everybody was predicting the most splendid future for him, he bit his aunt. He —'

'Go and find Mr Potter,' cried Lady Wickham. 'I must speak to him.'

'I'll try. But I don't believe it will be easy. I think he's gone for good.'

Lady Wickham uttered a bereaved cry, such as a tigress might who sees its prey snatched from it.

'Gone!'

'He told me he was thinking of going. He said he couldn't stand Clifford Gandle's persecution any longer. And that was before breakfast, so I don't suppose he has changed his mind. I think he means to go on running.'

A sigh like the whistling of the wind through the cracks in a broken heart escaped Lady Wickham.

'Mother,' said Bobbie, 'I've something to tell you. Last night Clifford Gandle asked me to marry him. I hadn't time to answer one way or the other, because just after he had proposed he jumped into the moat and tried to drown Mr Potter; but if you really think he would be a steadying influence for me —'

Lady Wickham uttered a snort of agony.

'I forbid you to dream of marrying this man!'

'Very well, mother,' said Bobbie dutifully. She rose and moved to the sideboard. 'Would you like an egg, mother?'

'No!'

'Some ham?'

'No!'

'Very well.' Bobbie paused at the door. 'Don't you think it would be a good idea,' she said, 'if I were to go and find Clifford Gandle and tell him to pack up and go away? I'm sure you won't like having him about after this.'

Lady Wickham's eyes flashed fire.

'If that man dares to come back, I'll – I'll — Yes. Tell him to go. Tell him to go away and never let me set eyes on him again.'

'Very well, mother,' said Bobbie.

‹‹‹›››‹‹‹›››‹‹‹›››‹‹‹›››‹‹‹›››‹‹‹›››‹‹‹›››‹‹‹›››

CHAPTER 8

Monkey Business

A TANKARD of Stout had just squashed a wasp as it crawled on the arm of Miss Postlethwaite, our popular barmaid, and the conversation in the bar-parlour of the Angler's Rest had turned to the subject of physical courage.

The Tankard himself was inclined to make light of the whole affair, urging modestly that his profession, that of a fruit-farmer, gave him perhaps a certain advantage over his fellow-men when it came to dealing with wasps.

'Why, sometimes in the picking season,' said the Tankard, 'I've had as many as six standing on each individual plum, rolling their eyes at me and daring me to come on.'

Mr Mulliner looked up from his hot Scotch and lemon.

'Suppose they had been gorillas?' he said.

The Tankard considered this.

'There wouldn't be room,' he argued, 'not on an ordinary-sized plum.'

'Gorillas?' said a Small Bass, puzzled.

'And I'm sure if it had been a gorilla Mr Bunyan would have squashed it just the same,' said Miss Postlethwaite, and she gazed at the Tankard with wholehearted admiration in her eyes.

Mr Mulliner smiled gently.

'Strange,' he said, 'how even in these orderly civilized days women still worship heroism in the male. Offer them wealth, brains, looks, amiability, skill at card-tricks or at playing the ukelele ... unless these are accompanied by physical courage they will turn away in scorn.'

'Why gorillas?' asked the Small Bass, who liked to get these things settled.

'I was thinking of a distant cousin of mine whose life became for a time considerably complicated owing to one of these animals. Indeed, it was the fact that this gorilla's path crossed his that nearly lost Montrose Mulliner the hand of Rosalie Beamish.'

The Small Bass still appeared mystified.

'I shouldn't have thought anybody's path *would* have crossed a gorilla's. I'm forty-five next birthday, and I've never so much as seen a gorilla.'

'Possibly Mr Mulliner's cousin was a big-game hunter,' said a Gin Fizz.

'No,' said Mr Mulliner. 'He was an assistant-director in the employment of the Perfecto-Zizzbaum Motion Picture Corporation of Hollywood: and the gorilla of which I speak was one of the cast of the super-film, "Black Africa", a celluloid epic of the clashing of elemental passions in a land where might is right and the strong man comes into his own. Its capture in its native jungle was said to have cost the lives of some half-dozen members of the expedi-tion, and at the time when this story begins it was lodged in a stout cage on the Perfecto-Zizzbaum lot at a salary of seven hundred and fifty dollars a week, with billing guaranteed in letters not smaller than those of Edmund Wigham and Luella Benstead, the stars.'

In ordinary circumstances (said Mr Mulliner) this gorilla would have been to my distant cousin Montrose merely one of a thousand fellow-workers on the lot. If you had asked him, he would have said that he wished the animal every kind of success in its chosen profession but that, for all the chance there was of them ever, as it were, getting together, they were just ships that pass in the night. It is doubtful, indeed, if he would even have bothered to go down to its cage and look at it had not Rosalie Beamish asked him to do so. As he put it to himself, if a man's duties brought him into constant personal contact with Mr Schnellenhamer, the President of the Corporation, where was the sense of wasting time looking at gorillas? *Blasé* about sums up his attitude.

But Rosalie was one of the extra girls in 'Black Africa' and so had a natural interest in a brother-artist. And as she and Montrose were engaged to be married her word, of course, was law. Montrose had been planning to play draughts that afternoon with his friend, George Pybus, of the Press department, but he good-naturedly cancelled the fixture and accompanied Rosalie to the animal's head-quarters.

He was more than ordinarily anxious to oblige her to-day, because they had recently been having a little tiff. Rosalie had been urging him to go to Mr Schnellenhamer and ask for a rise of salary: and this Montrose, who was excessively timid by nature, was reluctant to do. There was something about being asked to pay out money that always aroused the head of the firm's worst passions.

When he met his betrothed outside the commissary, he was relieved to find her in a more amiable mood than she had been of late. She prattled merrily of this and that as they walked along, and Montrose was congratulating himself that there was not a cloud on the sky when, arriving at the cage, he found Captain Jack Fosdyke there, prodding at the gorilla with a natty cane.

This Captain Jack Fosdyke was a famous explorer who had been engaged to superintend the production of 'Black Africa'. And the fact that Rosalie's professional duties necessitated a rather close association with him had caused Montrose a good deal of uneasiness. It was not that he did not trust her, but love makes a man jealous and he knew the fascination of these lean, brown, hard-bitten adventurers of the wilds.

As they came up, the explorer turned, and Montrose did not like the chummy look in the eye which he cocked at the girl. Nor, for the matter of that, did he like the other's bold smile. And he wished that in addressing Rosalie, Captain Fosdyke would not preface his remarks with the words 'Ah, there, girlie.'

'Ah, there, girlie,' said the Captain. 'Come to see the monk?'

Rosalie was staring open-mouthed through the bars. 'Doesn't he look fierce!' she cried.

Captain Jack Fosdyke laughed carelessly.

'Tchah!' he said, once more directing the ferrule of his cane at the animal's ribs. 'If you had led the rough, tough, slam-bang, every-man-for-himself life I have, you wouldn't be frightened of gorillas. Bless my soul, I remember once in Equatorial Africa I was strolling along with my elephant gun and my trusty native bearer, 'Mlongi, and a couple of the brutes dropped out of a tree and started throwing their weight about and behaving as if the place belonged to them. I soon put a stop to that, I can tell you. Bang, bang, left and right, and two more skins for my collection. You have to be firm with gorillas. Dining anywhere to-night, girlie?'

'I am dining with Mr Mulliner at the Brown Derby.'

'Mr who?'

'This is Mr Mulliner.'

'Oh, that?' said Captain Fosdyke, scrutinizing Montrose in a supercilious sort of way as if he had just dropped out of a tree before him. 'Well, some other time, eh?'

And, giving the gorilla a final prod, he sauntered away.

Rosalie was silent for a considerable part of the return journey. When at length she spoke it was in a vein that occasioned Montrose the gravest concern.

'Isn't he wonderful!' she breathed. 'Captain Fosdyke, I mean.'

'Yes,' said Montrose coldly.

'I think he's splendid. So strong, so intrepid. Have you asked Mr Schnellenhamer for that raise yet?'

'Er – no,' said Montrose. 'I am – how shall I put it? – biding my time.'

There was another silence.

'Captain Fosdyke isn't afraid of Mr Schnellenhamer,' said Rosalie pensively. 'He slaps him on the back.'

'Nor am I afraid of Mr Schnellenhamer,' replied Montrose, stung. 'I would slap him on the back myself if I considered that it would serve any useful end. My delay in asking for that raise is simply due to the fact that in these matters of finance a certain tact and delicacy have to be observed. Mr Schnellenhamer is a busy man, and I have enough consideration not to intrude my personal affairs on him at a time when he is occupied with other matters.'

'I see,' said Rosalie, and there the matter rested. But Montrose remained uneasy. There had been a gleam in her eyes and a rapt expression on her face as she spoke of Captain Fosdyke which he had viewed with concern. Could it be, he asked himself, that she was falling a victim to the man's undeniable magnetism? He decided to consult his friend, George Pybus, of the Press department, on the matter. George was a knowledgeable young fellow and would doubtless have something constructive to suggest.

George Pybus listened to his tale with interest and said it reminded him of a girl he had loved and lost in Des Moines, Iowa.

'She ditched me for a prizefighter,' said George. 'There's no getting away from it, girls do get fascinated by the strong, tough male.'

Montrose's heart sank.

'You don't really think —?'

'It is difficult to say. One does not know how far this thing has gone. But I certainly feel that we must lose no time in drafting out some scheme whereby you shall acquire a glamour which will counteract the spell of this Fosdyke. I will devote a good deal of thought to the matter.'

And it was on the very next afternoon, as he sat with Rosalie in the commissary sharing with her a Steak Pudding Marlene Dietrich, that Montrose noticed that the girl was in the grip of some strong excitement.

'Monty,' she exclaimed, almost before she had dug out the first kidney, 'do you know what Captain Fosdyke said this morning?'

Montrose choked.

'If that fellow has been insulting you,' he cried, 'I'll ... Well, I shall be extremely annoyed,' he concluded with a good deal of heat.

'Don't be silly. He wasn't talking to me. He was speaking to Luella Benstead. You know she's getting married again soon ...'

'Odd how these habits persist.'

'... and Captain Fosdyke said why didn't she get married in the gorilla's cage. For the publicity.'

'He did?'

Montrose laughed heartily. A quaint idea, he felt. Bizarre, even.

'She said she wouldn't dream of it. And then Mr Pybus, who happened to be standing by, suddenly got the most wonderful idea. He came up to me and said why shouldn't you and I get married in the gorilla's cage.'

Montrose's laughter died away.

'You and I?'

'Yes.'

'George Pybus suggested that?'

'Yes.'

Montrose groaned in spirit. He was telling himself that he might have known that something like this would have been the result of urging a member of the Press department to exercise his intellect. The brains of members of the Press departments of motion-picture studios resemble soup at a cheap restaurant. It is wiser not to stir them.

'Think what a sensation it would make! No more extra work for me after that. I'd get parts, and good ones. A girl can't get anywhere in this business without publicity.'

Montrose licked his lips. They had become very dry. He was thinking harshly of George Pybus. It was just loose talking like George Pybus's, he felt, that made half the trouble in this world.

'But don't you feel,' he said, 'that there is something a little undignified about publicity? In my opinion, a true artist ought to be above it. And I think you should not overlook another, extremely vital aspect of the matter. I refer to the deleterious effect which such an exhibition as Pybus suggests would have upon those who read about it in the papers. Speaking for myself,' said Montrose, 'there is nothing I should enjoy more than a quiet wedding in a gorilla's cage. But has one the right to pander to the morbid tastes of a sensation-avid public? I am not a man who often speaks of these deeper things – on the surface, no doubt, I seem careless and happy-go-lucky – but I do hold very serious views on a citizen's duties in this fevered modern age. I consider that each one of us should do all that lies in his power to fight the ever-growing trend of the public mind towards the morbid and the hectic. I have a very real feeling that the body politic can never become healthy while this appetite for sensation persists. If America is not to go the way of Babylon and Rome, we must come back to normalcy and the sane outlook. It is not much that a man in my humble position can do to stem the tide, but at least I can refrain from adding fuel to its flames by getting married in gorillas' cages.'

Rosalie was gazing at him incredulously.

'You don't mean you won't do it?'

'It would not be right.'

'I believe you're scared.'

'Nothing of the kind. It is purely a question of civic conscience.'

'You *are* scared. To think,' said Rosalie vehemently, 'that I should have linked my lot with a man who's afraid of a teentsy-weentsy gorilla.'

Montrose could not let this pass.

'It is not a teentsy-weentsy gorilla. I should describe the animal's muscular development as well above the average.'

'And the keeper would be outside the cage with a spiked stick.'

'*Outside* the cage!' said Montrose thoughtfully.

Rosalie sprang to her feet in sudden passion.

'Good-bye!'

'But you haven't finished your steak-pudding.'

'Good-bye,' she repeated. 'I see now what your so-called love is worth. If you are going to start denying me every little thing before we're married, what would you be like after? I'm glad I have discovered your true character in time. Our engagement is at an end.'

Montrose was pale to the lips, but he tried to reason with her.

'But, Rosalie,' he urged, 'surely a girl's wedding-day ought to be something for her to think of all her life – to recall with dreamily smiling lips as she knits the tiny garments or cooks the evening meal for the husband she adores. She ought to be able to look back and live again through the solemn hush in the church, savour once more the sweet scent of the lilies-of-the-valley, hear the rolling swell of the organ and the grave voice of the clergyman reading the service. What memories would you have if you carried out this plan that you suggest? One only – that of a smelly monkey. Have you reflected upon this, Rosalie?'

But she was obdurate.

'Either you marry me in the gorilla's cage, or you don't marry me at all. Mr Pybus says it is certain to make the front page, with photographs and possibly even a short editorial on the right stuff being in the modern girl despite her surface irresponsibility.'

'You will feel differently to-night, dear, when we meet for dinner.'

'We shall not meet for dinner. If you are interested, I may inform you that Captain Fosdyke invited me to dine with him and I intend to do so.'

'Rosalie!'

'There is a man who really is a man. When he meets a gorilla, he laughs in its face.'

'Very rude.'

'A million gorillas couldn't frighten him. Good-bye, Mr Mulliner. I must go and tell him that when I said this morning that I had a previous engagement I was mistaken.'

She swept out, and Montrose went on with his steak-pudding like one in a dream.

It is possible (said Mr Mulliner, taking a grave sip of his hot Scotch and lemon and surveying the company with a thoughtful eye) that what I have told you may have caused you to form a dubious opinion of my distant cousin Montrose. If so, I am not surprised. In the scene which I have just related, no one is better aware than myself that he has not shown up well. Reviewing his shallow arguments, we see through them, as Rosalie did: and, like Rosalie, we realize that he had feet of clay – and cold ones, to boot.

But I would urge in extenuation of his attitude that Montrose Mulliner, possibly through some constitutional defect such as an insufficiency of hormones, had been from childhood timorous in the extreme. And his work as an assistant director had served very noticeably to increase this innate pusillanimity.

It is one of the drawbacks to being an assistant director that virtually everything that happens to him is of a nature to create an inferiority-complex – or, if one already exists, to deepen it. He is habitually addressed as 'Hey, you' and alluded to in the third person as 'that fathead'. If anything goes wrong on the set, he gets the blame and is ticked off not only by the producer but also by the director and all the principals involved. Finally, he has to be obsequious to so many people that it is little wonder that he comes in time to resemble one of the more shrinking and respectful breeds of rabbit. Five years of assistant-directing had so sapped Montrose's *morale* that nowadays he frequently found himself starting up and apologizing in his sleep.

It is proof, then, of the great love which he had for Rosalie Beamish that, encountering Captain Jack Fosdyke a few days later, he should have assailed him with bitter reproaches. Only love could have impelled him to act in a manner so foreign to his temperament.

The fact was, he blamed the Captain for all that had occurred. He considered that he had deliberately unsettled Rosalie and influenced her mind with the set purpose of making her dissatisfied with the man to whom she had plighted her troth.

'If it wasn't for you,' he concluded warmly, 'I feel sure I could have reasoned her out of what is nothing but a passing girlish whim. But you have infatuated her, and now where do I get off?'

The Captain twirled his moustache airily.

'Don't blame me, my boy. All my life I have been cursed by this fatal attraction of mine for the sex. Poor little moths, they will beat their wings against the bright light of my personality. Remind me to tell you some time of an interesting episode which occurred in the harem of the King of the 'Mbongos. There is something about me which is – what shall I say? – hypnotic. It is not my fault that this girl has compared us. It was inevitable that she should compare us. And having compared us, what does she see? On the one hand, a man with a soul of chilled steel who can look his gorilla in the eye and make it play ball. On the other – I use the term in the kindliest possible sense – a crawling worm. Well, good-bye, my boy, glad to have seen you and had this little chat,' said Captain Fosdyke. 'I like you young fellows to bring your troubles to me.'

For some moments after he had gone, Montrose remained standing motionless, while all the repartees which he might have made surged through his mind in a glittering procession. Then his thoughts turned once more to the topic of gorillas.

It is possible that it was the innuendoes uttered by Captain Fosdyke that now awoke in Montrose something which bore a shadowy resemblance to fortitude. Certainly, until this conversation, he had not intended to revisit the gorilla's cage, one sight of its occupant having been ample for him. Now, stung by the other's slurs, he decided to go and have another look at the brute. It might be that further inspection would make it seem less formidable. He had known this to happen before. The first time he had seen Mr Schnellenhamer, for example, he had had something not unlike a fit of what our grandparents used to call the 'vapours'. Now, he could bear him with at least an assumption of nonchalance.

He made his way to the cage, and was presently exchanging glances with the creature through the bars.

Alas, any hope he may have had that familiarity would breed contempt died as their eyes met. Those well-gnashed teeth, that hideous shagginess (a little reminiscent of a stockbroker motoring to Brighton in a fur coat) filled him with all the old familiar qualms. He tottered back and, with some dim idea of pulling himself together, took a banana from the bag which he had bought at the commissary to see him through the long afternoon. And, as he did so, there suddenly flashed upon him the recollection of an old saw which he had heard in his infancy – The Gorilla Never Forgets. In other words, do the square thing by gorillas, and they will do the square thing by you.

His heart leaped within him. He pushed the banana through the bars with a cordial smile, and was rejoiced to find it readily accepted. In rapid succession he passed over the others. A banana a day keeps the gorilla away, he felt jubilantly. By standing treat to this animal regardless of cost, he reasoned, he would so ingratiate himself with it as to render the process of getting married in its cage both harmless and agreeable. And it was only when his guest had finished the last of the fruit that he realized with a sickening sense of despair that he had got his facts wrong and that his whole argument, based on a false premiss, fell to the ground and became null and void.

It was the elephant who never forgot – not the gorilla. It all came back to him now. He was practically sure that gorillas had never been mentioned in connexion with the subject of mnemonics. Indeed, for all he knew, these creatures might be famous for the shortness of their memory – with the result that if later on he were to put on pin-striped trousers and a top hat and enter this animal's cage with Rosalie on his arm and the studio band playing the Wedding March, all recollection of those bananas would probably have passed completely from its fat head, and it would totally fail to recognize its benefactor.

Moodily crumpling the bag, Montrose turned away. This, he felt, was the end.

I have a tender heart (said Mr Mulliner), and I dislike to dwell on the spectacle of a human being groaning under the iron heel of Fate. Such morbid gloating, I consider, is better left to the Russians. I will spare you, therefore, a detailed analysis of my distant cousin Montrose's emotion as the long day wore on. Suffice it to say that by a few minutes to five o'clock he had become a mere toad beneath the harrow. He wandered aimlessly to and fro about the lot in the growing dusk, and it seemed to him that the falling shades of evening resembled the cloud that had settled upon his life.

He was roused from these meditations by a collision with some solid body and, coming to himself, discovered that he had been trying to walk through his old friend, George Pybus of the Press department. George was standing beside his car, apparently on the point of leaving for the day.

It is one more proof of Montrose Mulliner's gentle nature that he did not reproach George Pybus for the part he had taken in darkening his outlook. All he did was to gape and say:

'Hullo! You off?'

George Pybus climbed into the car and started the engine.

'Yes,' he said, 'and I'll tell you why. You know that gorilla?'

With a shudder which he could not repress Montrose said he knew the gorilla.

'Well, I'll tell you something,' said George Pybus. 'Its agent has been complaining that we've been throwing all the publicity to Luella Benstead and Edmund Wigham. So the boss sent out a hurry call for quick thinking. I told him that you and Rosalie Beamish were planning to get married in its cage, but I've seen Rosalie and she tells me you've backed out. Scarcely the spirit I should have expected in you, Montrose.'

Montrose did his best to assume a dignity which he was far from feeling.

'One has one's code,' he said. 'One dislikes to pander to the morbidity of a sensation-avid ...'

'Well, it doesn't matter, anyway,' said George Pybus, 'because I got another idea, and a better one. This one is a pippin. At five sharp this evening, Standard Pacific time, that gorilla's going to be let out of its cage and will menace hundreds. If that doesn't land him on the front page …'

Montrose was appalled.

'But you can't do that!' he gasped. 'Once let that awful brute out of its cage and it may tear people to shreds.'

George Pybus reassured him.

'Nobody of any consequence. The stars have all been notified and are off the lot. So are the directors. Also the executives, all except Mr Schnellenhamer, who is cleaning up some work in his office. He will be quite safe there, of course. Nobody ever got into Mr Schnellenhamer's office without waiting four hours in the ante-room. Well, I must be off,' said George Pybus. 'I've got to dress and get out to Malibu for dinner.'

And, so speaking, he trod on the accelerator and was speedily lost to view in the gathering darkness.

It was a few moments later that Montrose, standing rooted to the spot, became aware of a sudden distant uproar: and, looking at his watch, he found that it was precisely five o'clock.

The spot to which Montrose had been standing rooted was in that distant part of the lot where the outdoor sets are kept permanently erected, so that a director with – let us suppose – a London street scene to shoot is able instantly to lay his hands on a back-alley in Algiers, a medieval castle, or a Parisian boulevard – none of which is any good to him but which make him feel that the studio is trying to be helpful.

As far as Montrose's eye could reach, Spanish patios, thatched cottages, tenement buildings, estaminets, Oriental bazaars, Kaffir kraals and the residences of licentious New York clubmen stood out against the evening sky: and the fact that he selected as his haven of refuge one of the tenement buildings was due to its being both tallest and nearest.

Like all outdoor sets, it consisted of a front just like the real thing and a back composed of steps and platforms. Up these steps he raced, and on the topmost of the platforms he halted and sat down. He was still unable to think very coherently, but in a dim sort of way he was rather proud of his agility and resource. He felt that he had met a grave crisis well. He did not know what the record was for climbing a flight of steps with a gorilla loose in the neighbourhood, but he would have felt surprise if informed that he had not lowered it.

The uproar which had had such a stimulating effect upon him was now increasing in volume: and, oddly, it appeared to have become stationary. He glanced down through the window of his tenement building, and was astonished to observe below him a dense crowd. And what perplexed him most about this crowd was that it was standing still and looking up.

Scarcely, felt Montrose, intelligent behaviour on the part of a crowd with a savage gorilla after it.

There was a good deal of shouting going on, but he found himself unable to distinguish any words. A woman who stood in the forefront of the throng appeared particularly animated. She was waving an umbrella in a rather neurotic manner.

The whole thing, as I say, perplexed Montrose. What these people thought they were doing, he was unable to say. He was still speculating on the matter when a noise came to his ears.

It was the crying of a baby.

Now, with all these mother-love pictures so popular, the presence of a baby on the lot was not in itself a thing to occasion surprise. It is a very unambitious mother in Hollywood who, the moment she finds herself and child doing well, does not dump the little stranger into a perambulator and wheel it round to the casting-office in the hope of cashing in. Ever since he had been with the Perfecto-Zizzbaum, Montrose had seen a constant stream of offspring riding up and trying to break into the game. It was not, accordingly, the fact of a baby being among those present that surprised him. What puzzled him about this particular baby was that it seemed to be so close at hand. Unless the acoustics were playing odd tricks, the infant, he was convinced, was sharing this eyrie of his. And how a mere baby, handicapped probably by swaddling-clothes and a bottle, could have shinned up all those steps bewildered him to such an extent that he moved along the planks to investigate.

And he had not gone three paces when he paused, aghast. With its hairy back towards him, the gorilla was crouching over something that lay on the ground. And another bellow told him that this was the baby in person: and instantly Montrose saw what must have occurred. His reading of magazine stories had taught him that, once a gorilla gets loose, the first thing it does is to snatch a baby from a perambulator and climb to the nearest high place. It is pure routine.

This, then, was the position in which my distant cousin Montrose found himself at eight minutes past five on this misty evening. A position calculated to test the fortitude of the sternest.

Now, it has been well said that with nervous, highly-strung men like Montrose Mulliner, a sudden call upon their manhood is often enough to revolutionize their whole character. Psychologists have frequently commented on this. We are too ready, they say, to dismiss as cowards those who merely require the stimulus of the desperate emergency to bring out all their latent heroism. The crisis comes, and the cravens turns magically into the paladin.

With Montrose, however, this was not the case. Ninety-nine out of a hundred of those who knew him would have scoffed at the idea of him interfering with an escaped gorilla to save the life of a child, and they would have been right. To tiptoe backwards, holding his breath, was with Montrose Mulliner the work of a moment. And it was the fact that he did it so quickly that wrecked his plans. Stubbing a heel on a loose board in his haste, he fell backwards with a crash. And when the stars had ceased to obscure his vision, he found himself gazing up into the hideous face of the gorilla.

On the last occasion when the two had met, there had been iron bars between them: and even with this safeguard Montrose, as I have said, had shrunk from the creature's evil stare. Now, meeting the brute as it were socially, he experienced a thrill of horror such as had never come to him even in nightmares. Closing his eyes, he began to speculate as to which limb, when it started to tear him limb from limb, the animal would start with.

The one thing of which he was sure was that it would begin operations by uttering a fearful snarl: and when the next sound that came to his ears was a deprecating cough he was so astonished that he could keep his eyes closed no longer. Opening them, he found the gorilla looking at him with an odd, apologetic expression on its face.

'Excuse me, sir,' said the gorilla, 'but are you by any chance a family man?'

For an instant, on hearing the question, Montrose's astonishment deepened. Then he realized what must have happened. He must have been torn limb from limb without knowing it, and now he was in heaven. Though even this did not altogether satisfy him as an explanation, for he had never expected to find gorillas in heaven.

The animal now gave a sudden start.

'Why, it's you! I didn't recognize you at first. Before going any further, I should like to thank you for those bananas. They were delicious. A little something round about the middle of the afternoon picks one up quite a bit, doesn't it?'

Montrose blinked. He could still hear the noise of the crowd below. His bewilderment increased.

'You speak very good English for a gorilla,' was all he could find to say. And, indeed, the animal's diction had been remarkable for its purity.

The gorilla waved the compliment aside modestly.

'Oh, well, Balliol, you know. Dear old Balliol. One never quite forgets the lessons one learned at Alma Mater, don't you think? You are not an Oxford man, by any chance?'

'No.'

'I came down in '26. Since then I have been knocking around a good deal, and a friend of mine in the circus business suggested to me that the gorilla field was not overcrowded. Plenty of room at the top, was his expression. And I must say,' said the gorilla, 'I've done pretty well at it. The initial expenditure comes high, of course ... you don't get a skin like this for nothing ... but there's virtually no overhead. Of course, to become a co-star in a big feature film, as I have done, you need a good agent. Mine, I am glad to say, is a capital man of business. Stands no nonsense from these motion-picture magnates.'

Montrose was not a quick thinker, but he was gradually adjusting his mind to the facts.

'Then you're not a real gorilla?'

'No, no. Synthetic, merely.'

'You wouldn't tear anyone limb from limb?'

'My dear chap! My idea of a nice time is to curl up with a good book. I am happiest among my books.'

Montrose's last doubts were resolved. He extended his hand cordially.

'Pleased to meet you, Mr ...'

'Waddesley-Davenport. Cyril Waddesley-Davenport. And I am extremely happy to meet you, Mr ...'

'Mulliner. Montrose Mulliner.'

They shook hands warmly. From down below came the hoarse uproar of the crowd. The gorilla started.

'The reason I asked you if you were a family man,' it said, 'was that I hoped you might be able to tell me what is the best method of procedure to adopt with a crying baby. I don't seem able to stop the child. And all my own silly fault, too. I see now I should never have snatched it from its perambulator. If you want to know what is the matter with me, I am too much the artist. I simply had to snatch that baby. It was how I saw the scene. I *felt* it ... felt it *here*,' said the gorilla, thumping the left side of its chest. 'And now what?'

Montrose reflected.

'Why don't you take it back?'

'To its mother?'

'Certainly.'

'But ...' The gorilla pulled doubtfully at its lower lip. 'You have seen that crowd. Did you happen to observe a woman standing in the front row waving an umbrella?'

'The mother?'

'Precisely. Well, you know as well as I do, Mulliner, what an angry woman can do with an umbrella.'

Montrose thought again.

'It's all right,' he said. 'I have it. Why don't you sneak down the back steps? Nobody will see you. The crowd's in front, and it's almost dark.'

The gorilla's eyes lit up. It slapped Montrose gratefully on the shoulder.

'My dear chap! The very thing. But as regards the baby ...'

'I will restore it.'

'Capital! I don't know how to thank you, dear fellow,' said the gorilla. 'By Jove, this is going to be a lesson to me in future not to give way to the artist in me. You don't know how I've been feeling about that umbrella. Well, then, in case we don't meet again, always remember that the Lotos Club finds me when I am in New York. Drop in any time you happen to be in that neighbourhood and we'll have a bite to eat and a good talk.'

And what of Rosalie, meanwhile? Rosalie was standing between the bereaved mother, using all her powers of cajolery to try to persuade Captain Jack Fosdyke to go to the rescue: and the Captain was pleading technical difficulties that stood in the way.

'Dash my buttons,' he said, 'if only I had my elephant gun and my trusty native bearer, 'Mlongi, here, I'd pretty soon know what to do about it. As it is, I'm handicapped.'

'But you told me yesterday that you had often strangled gorillas with your bare hands.'

'Not *gor*-illas, dear lady – *por*-illas. A species of South American wombat, and very good eating they make, too.'

'You're afraid!'

'Afraid? Jack Fosdyke afraid? How they would laugh on the Lower Zambesi if they could hear you say that.'

'You are! You, who advised me to have nothing to do with the man I love because he was of a mild and diffident nature.'

Captain Jack Fosdyke twirled his moustache.

'Well, I don't notice,' he sneered, 'that he ...' He broke off, and his jaw slowly fell. Round the corner of the building was walking Montrose Mulliner. His bearing was erect, even jaunty, and he carried the baby in his arms. Pausing for an instant to allow the busily-clicking cameras to focus him, he advanced towards the stupefied mother and thrust the child into her arms.

'That's that,' he said carelessly, dusting his fingers. 'No, no, please,' he went on. 'A mere nothing.'

For the mother was kneeling before him, endeavouring to kiss his hand. It was not only maternal love that prompted the action. That morning she had signed up her child at seventy-five dollars a week for the forthcoming picture, 'Tiny Fingers' and all through these long, anxious minutes it had seemed as though the contract must be a total loss.

Rosalie was in Montrose's arms, sobbing.

'Oh, Monty!'

'There, there!'

'How I misjudged you!'

'We all make mistakes.'

'I made a bad one when I listened to that man there,' said Rosalie, darting a scornful look at Captain Jack Fosdyke. 'Do you realize that, for all his boasting, he would not move a step to save that poor child?'

'Not a step?'

'Not a single step.'

'Bad, Fosdyke,' said Montrose. 'Rather bad. Not quite the straight bat, eh?'

'Tchah!' said the baffled man, and he turned on his heel and strode away. He was still twirling his moustache, but a lot that got him.

Rosalie was clinging to Montrose.

'You aren't hurt? Was it a fearful struggle?'

'Struggle?' Montrose laughed. 'Oh, dear no. There was no struggle. I very soon showed the animal that I was going to stand no nonsense. I generally find with gorillas that all one needs is the power of the human eye. By the way, I've been thinking it over and I realize that I may have been a little unreasonable about that idea of yours. I still would prefer to get married in some nice, quiet church, but if you feel you want the ceremony to take place in that animal's cage, I shall be delighted.'

She shivered.

'I couldn't do it. I'd be scared.'

Montrose smiled understandingly.

'Ah, well,' he said, 'it is perhaps not unnatural that a delicately nurtured woman should be of less tough stuff than the more rugged male. Shall we be strolling along? I want to look in on Mr Schnellenhamer, and arrange about that raise of mine. You won't mind waiting while I pop in at his office?'

'My hero!' whispered Rosalie.

CHAPTER 9

The Nodder

THE presentation of the super film 'Baby Boy' at the Bijou Dream in the High Street had led to an animated discussion in the bar-parlour of the Angler's Rest. Several of our prominent first-nighters had dropped in there for a much-needed restorative after the performance, and the conversation had turned to the subject of child stars in the motion-pictures.

'I understand they're all midgets, really,' said a Rum and Milk.

'That's what I heard, too,' said a Whisky and Splash. 'Somebody told me that at every studio in Hollywood they have a special man who does nothing but go round the country, combing the circuses, and when he finds a good midget he signs him up.'

Almost automatically we looked at Mr Mulliner, as if seeking from that unfailing fount of wisdom an authoritative pronouncement on this difficult point. The Sage of the bar-parlour sipped his hot Scotch and lemon for a moment in thoughtful silence.

'The question you have raised,' he said at length, 'is one that has occupied the minds of thinking men ever since these little excrescences first became popular on the screen. Some argue that mere children could scarcely be so loathsome. Others maintain that a right-minded midget would hardly stoop to some of the things these child stars do. But, then, arising from that, we have to ask ourselves: Are midgets right-minded? The whole thing is very moot.'

'Well, this kid we saw to-night,' said the Rum and Milk. 'This Johnny Bingley. Nobody's going to tell me he's only eight years old.'

'In the case of Johnny Bingley,' assented Mr Mulliner, 'your intuition has not led you astray. I believe he is in the early forties. I happen to know all about him because it was he who played so important a part in the affairs of my distant connexion, Wilmot.'

'Was your distant connexion Wilmot a midget?'

'No. He was a Nodder.'

'A what?'

Mr Mulliner smiled.

'It is not easy to explain to the lay mind the extremely intricate ramifications of the personnel of a Hollywood motion-picture organization. Putting it as briefly as possible, a Nodder is something like a Yes-Man, only lower

in the social scale. A Yes-Man's duty is to attend con-
ferences and say "Yes". A Nodder's, as the name implies,
is to nod. The chief executive throws out some statement
of opinion, and looks about him expectantly. This is the
cue for the senior Yes-Man to say yes. He is followed, in
order of precedence, by the second Yes-Man – or Vice-
Yesser, as he is sometimes called – and the junior Yes-
Man. Only when all the Yes-Men have yessed, do the
Nodders begin to function. They nod.'

A Pint of Half-and-Half said it didn't sound much of a
job.

'Not very exalted,' agreed Mr Mulliner. 'It is a position
which you might say, roughly, lies socially somewhere in
between that of the man who works the wind-machine and
that of a writer of additional dialogue There is also a class
of Untouchables who are known as Nodders' assistants,
but this is a technicality with which I need not trouble you.
At the time when my story begins, my distant connexion
Wilmot was a full Nodder. Yet, even so, there is no doubt
that he was aiming a little high when he ventured to aspire
to the hand of Mabel Potter, the private secretary of Mr
Schnellenhamer, the head of the Perfecto-Zizzbaum Corporation.

'Indeed, between a girl so placed and a man in my distant connexion's position there could, in ordinary circumstances, scarcely have been anything in the nature of
friendly intercourse. Wilmot owed his entry to her good
graces to a combination of two facts – the first, that in his
youth he had been brought up on a farm and so was familiar
with the customs and habits of birds; the second, that before coming to Hollywood, Miss Potter had been a bird-
imitator in vaudeville.'

Too little has been written of vaudeville bird-imitators
and their passionate devotion to their art: but everybody
knows the saying, Once a Bird-Imitator, Always a Bird-
Imitator. The Mabel Potter of to-day might be a mere
lovely machine for taking notes and tapping out her employer's correspondence, but within her there still burned

the steady flame of those high ideals which always animate a girl who has once been accustomed to render to packed houses the liquid notes of the cuckoo, the whip-poor-will, and other songsters who are familiar to you all.

That this was so was revealed to Wilmot one morning when, wandering past an outlying set, he heard raised voices within and, recognizing the silver tones of his adored one, paused to listen. Mabel Potter seemed to be having some kind of an argument with a director.

'Considering,' she was saying, 'that I only did it to oblige and that it is in no sense a part of my regular duties for which I draw my salary, I must say ...'

'All right, all right,' said the director.

'... that you have a nerve calling me down on the subject of cuckoos. Let me tell you, Mr Murgatroyd, that I have made a lifelong study of cuckoos and know them from soup to nuts. I have imitated cuckoos in every theatre on every circuit in the land. Not to mention urgent offers from England, Australia and ...'

'I know, I know,' said the director.

'... South Africa, which I was compelled to turn down because my dear mother, then living, disliked ocean travel. My cuckoo is world-famous. Give me time to go home and fetch it and I'll show you the clipping from the *St Louis Post-Democrat* where it says ...'

'I know, I know, I know,' said the director, 'but, all the same, I think I'll have somebody do it who'll do it my way.'

The next moment Mabel Potter had swept out, and Wilmot addressed her with respectful tenderness.

'Is something the matter, Miss Potter? Is there anything I can do?'

Mabel Potter was shaking with dry sobs. Her self-esteem had been rudely bruised.

'Well, look,' she said. 'They ask me as a special favour to come and imitate the call of the cuckoo for this new picture, and when I do it Mr Murgatroyd says I've done it wrong.'

'The hound,' breathed Wilmot.

'He says a cuckoo goes Cuckoo, Cuckoo, when everybody who has studied the question knows that what it really goes is Wuckoo, Wuckoo.'

'Of course. Not a doubt about it. A distinct "W" sound.'

'As if it had got something wrong with the roof of its mouth.'

'Or had omitted to have its adenoids treated.'

'Wuckoo, Wuckoo ... Like that.'

'Exactly like that,' said Wilmot.

The girl gazed at him with a new friendliness.

'I'll bet you've heard rafts of cuckoos.'

'Millions. I was brought up on a farm.'

'These know-it-all directors make me tired.'

'Me, too,' said Wilmot. Then, putting his fate to the touch, to win or lose it all, 'I wonder, Miss Potter, if you would care to step round to the commissary and join me in a small coffee?'

She accepted gratefully, and from that moment their intimacy may be said to have begun. Day after day, in the weeks that followed, at such times as their duties would permit, you would see them sitting together either in the commissary or on the steps of some Oriental palace on the outskirts of the lot; he gazing silently up into her face; she, an artist's enthusiasm in her beautiful eyes, filling the air with the liquid note of the Baltimore oriole or possibly the more strident cry of the African buzzard. While ever and anon, by special request, she would hitch up the muscles of the larynx and go 'Wuckoo, Wuckoo.'

But when at length Wilmot, emboldened, asked her to be his wife, she shook her head.

'No,' she said, 'I like you, Wilmot. Sometimes I even think that I love you. But I can never marry a mere serf.'

'A what was that?'

'A serf. A peon. A man who earns his living by nodding his head at Mr Schnellenhamer. A Yes-man would be bad enough, but a Nodder!'

She paused, and Wilmot, from sheer force of habit, nodded.

'I am ambitious,' proceeded Mabel. 'The man I marry must be a king among men ... well, what I mean, at least a supervisor. Rather than wed a Nodder, I would starve in the gutter.'

The objection to this as a practical policy was, of course, that, owing to the weather being so uniformly fine all the year round, there are no gutters in Hollywood. But Wilmot was too distressed to point this out. He uttered a heart-stricken cry not unlike the mating-call of the Alaskan wild duck and began to plead with her. But she was not to be moved.

'We will always be friends,' she said, 'but marry a Nodder, no.'

And with a brief 'Wuckoo' she turned away.

There is not much scope or variety of action open to a man whose heart has been shattered and whose romance has proved an empty dream. Practically speaking, only two courses lie before him. He can go out West and begin a new life, or he can drown his sorrow in drink. In Wilmot's case, the former of these alternatives was rendered impossible by the fact that he was out West already. Little wonder, then, that as he sat in his lonely lodging that night his thoughts turned ever more and more insistently to the second.

Like all the Mulliners, my distant connexion Wilmot had always been a scrupulously temperate man. Had his love-life but run smoothly, he would have been amply contented with a nut sundae or a malted milk after the day's work. But now, with desolation staring him in the face, he felt a fierce urge towards something with a bit more kick in it.

About half-way down Hollywood Boulevard, he knew, there was a place where, if you knocked twice and whistled 'My Country, 'tis of Thee', a grille opened and a whiskered face appeared. The Face said 'Well?' and you said 'Service and Co-operation', and then the door was unbarred and you saw before you the primrose path that led to perdition. And as this was precisely what, in his present mood, Wilmot most desired to locate, you will readily understand how it came about that, some hour and a half later, he was seated at a table in this establishment, feeling a good deal better.

How long it was before he realized that his table had another occupant he could not have said. But came a moment when, raising his glass, he found himself looking into the eyes of a small child in a Lord Fauntleroy costume, in whom he recognized none other than Little Johnny Bingley, the Idol of American Motherhood – the star of this picture, 'Baby Boy', which you, gentlemen, have just been witnessing at the Bijou Dream in the High Street.

To say that Wilmot was astonished at seeing this infant in such surroundings would be to overstate the case. After half an hour at this home-from-home the customer is seldom in a condition to be astonished at anything – not even a gamboge elephant in golfing costume. He was, however, sufficiently interested to say 'Hullo'.

'Hullo,' replied the child. 'Listen,' he went on, placing a cube of ice in his tumbler, 'don't tell old Schnellenhamer you saw me here. There's a morality clause in my contract.'

'Tell who?' said Wilmot.

'Schnellenhamer.'

'How do you spell it?'

'I don't know.'

'Nor do I,' said Wilmot. 'Nevertheless, be that as it may,' he continued, holding out his hand impulsively, 'he shall never learn from me.'

'Who won't?' said the child.

'He won't,' said Wilmot.

'Won't what?' asked the child.

'Learn from me,' said Wilmot.

'Learn what?' inquired the child.

'I've forgotten,' said Wilmot.

They sat for a space in silence, each busy with his own thoughts.

'You're Johnny Bingley, aren't you?' said Wilmot.

'Who is?' said the child.

'You are.'

'I'm what?'

'Listen,' said Wilmot. 'My name's Mulliner. That's what it is. Mulliner. And let them make the most of it.'

'Who?'

'I don't know,' said Wilmot.

He gazed at his companion affectionately. It was a little difficult to focus him, because he kept flickering, but Wilmot could take the big, broad view about that. If the heart is in the right place, he reasoned, what does it matter if the body flickers?

'You're a good chap, Bingley.'

'So are you, Mulliner.'

'Both good chaps?'

'Both good chaps.'

'Making two in all?' asked Wilmot, anxious to get this straight.

'That's how I work it out.'

'Yes, two,' agreed Wilmot, ceasing to twiddle his fingers. 'In fact, you might say both gentlemen.'

'Both gentlemen is correct.'

'Then let us see what we have got. Yes,' said Wilmot, as he laid down the pencil with which he had been writing figures on the table-cloth. 'Here are the final returns, as I get them. Two good chaps, two gentlemen. And yet,' he said, frowning in a puzzled way, 'that seems to make four, and there are only two of us. However,' he went on, 'let that go. Immaterial. Not germane to the issue. The fact we have to face, Bingley, is that my heart is heavy.'

'You don't say!'

'I do say. Heavy, Hearty. My bing is heavy.'

'What's the trouble?'

Wilmot decided to confide in this singularly sympathetic infant. He felt he had never met a child he liked better.

'Well, it's like this.'

'What is?'

'This is.'

'Like what?'

'I'm telling you. The girl I love won't marry me.'

'She won't?'

'So she says.'

'Well, well,' said the child star commiseratingly. 'That's too bad. Spurned your love, did she?'

'You're dern tooting she spurned my love,' said Wilmot. 'Spurned it good and hard. Some spurning!'

'Well, that's how it goes,' said the child star. 'What a world!'

'You're right, what a world.'

'I shouldn't wonder if it didn't make your heart heavy.'

'You bet it makes my heart heavy,' said Wilmot, crying softly. He dried his eyes on the edge of the table-cloth. 'How can I shake off this awful depression?' he asked.

The child star reflected.

'Well, I'll tell you,' he said. 'I know a better place than this one. It's out Venice way. We might give it a try.'

'We certainly might,' said Wilmot.

'And then there's another one down at Santa Monica.'

'We'll go there, too,' said Wilmot. 'The great thing is to keep moving about and seeing new scenes and fresh faces.'

'The faces are always nice and fresh down at Venice.'

'Then let's go,' said Wilmot.

It was at eleven o'clock on the following morning that Mr Schnellenhamer burst in upon his fellow-executive, Mr Levitsky, with agitation written on every feature of his expressive face. The cigar trembled between his lips.

'Listen!' he said. 'Do you know what?'

'Listen!' said Mr Levitsky. 'What?'

'Johnny Bingley has just been in to see me.'

'If he wants a raise of salary, talk about the Depression.'

'Raise of salary? What's worrying me is how long is he going to be worth he salary he's getting.'

'Worth it?' Mr Levitsky stared. 'Johnny Bingley? The

Child With The Tear Behind The Smile? The Idol Of American Motherhood?'

'Yes, and how long is he going to be the idol of American Motherhood after American Motherhood finds out he's a midget from Connolly's Circus, and an elderly, hard-boiled midget, at that?'

'Well, nobody knows that but you and me.'

'Is that so?' said Mr Schnellenhamer. 'Well, let me tell you, he was out on a toot last night with one of my Nodders and he comes to me this morning and says he couldn't actually swear he told this guy he was a midget, but, on the other hand, he rather thinks he must have done. He says that between the time they were thrown out of Mike's Place and the time he stabbed the waiter with the pickle-fork there's a sort of gap in his memory, a kind of blur, and he thinks it may have been then, because by that time they had got pretty confidential and he doesn't think he would have had any secrets from him.'

All Mr Levitsky's nonchalance had vanished.

'But if this fellow – what's his name?'

'Mulliner.'

'If this fellow Mulliner sells this story to the Press Johnny Bingley won't be worth a nickel to us. And his contract calls for two more pictures at two hundred and fifty thousand each.'

'That's right.'

'But what are we to do?'

'You tell me.'

Mr Levitsky pondered.

'Well, first of all,' he said, 'we'll have to find out if this Mulliner really knows.'

'We can't ask him.'

'No, but we'll be able to tell by his manner. A fellow with a stranglehold on the Corporation like that isn't going to be able to go on acting same as he's always done. What sort of a fellow is he?'

'The ideal Nodder,' said Mr Schnellenhamer regretfully. 'I don't know when I've had a better. Always on his cues.

Never tries to alibi himself by saying he had a stiff neck. Quiet ... Respectful ... What's that word that begins with a "d"?'

'Damn?'

'Deferential. And what's the word beginning with an "o"?'

'Oyster?'

'Obsequious. That's what he is. Quiet, respectful, deferential, and obsequious – that's Mulliner.'

'Well, then, it'll be easy to see. If we find him suddenly not being all what you said ... if he suddenly ups and starts to throw his weight about, understand what I mean ... why, then we'll know that he knows that Little Johnny Bingley is a midget.'

'And then?'

'Why, then we'll have to square him. And do it right, too. No half-measures.'

Mr Schnellenhamer tore at his hair. He seemed disappointed that he had no straws to stick in it.

'Yes,' he agreed, the brief spasm over, 'I suppose it's the only way. Well, it won't be long before we know. There's a story-conference in my office at noon, and he'll be there to nod.'

'We must watch him like a lynx.'

'Like a what?'

'Lynx. Sort of wild-cat. It watches things.'

'Ah,' said Mr Schnellenhamer, 'I get you now. What confused me at first was that I thought you meant golf-links.'

The fears of the two magnates, had they but known it, were quite without foundation. If Wilmot Mulliner had ever learned the fatal secret, he had certainly not remembered it next morning. He had woken that day with a confused sense of having passed through some soul-testing experience, but as regarded details his mind was a blank. His only thought as he entered Mr Schnellenhamer's office for the conference was a rooted conviction that, unless he kept very still, his head would come apart in the middle.

Nevertheless, Mr Schnellenhamer, alert for significant and sinister signs, plucked anxiously at Mr Levitsky's sleeve.

'Look!'

'Eh?'

'Did you see that?'

'See what?'

'That fellow Mulliner. He sort of quivered when he caught my eye, as if in unholy glee.'

'He did?'

'It seemed to me he did.'

As a matter of fact, what had happened was that Wilmot, suddenly sighting his employer, had been unable to restrain a quick shudder of agony. It seemed to him that somebody had been painting Mr Schnellenhamer yellow. Even at the best of times, the President of the Perfecto-Zizzbaum, considered as an object for the eye, was not everybody's money. Flickering at the rims and a dull orange in colour, as he appeared to be now, he had smitten Wilmot like a blow, causing him to wince like a salted snail.

Mr Levitsky was regarding the young man thoughtfully.

'I don't like his looks,' he said.

'Nor do I,' said Mr Schnellenhamer.

'There's a kind of horrid gloating in his manner.'

'I noticed it, too.'

'See how he's just buried his head in his hands, as if he were thinking out dreadful plots?'

'I believe he knows everything.'

'I shouldn't wonder if you weren't right. Well, let's start the conference and see what he does when the time comes for him to nod. That's when he'll break out if he's going to.'

As a rule, these story-conferences were the part of his work which Wilmot most enjoyed. His own share in them was not exacting, and, as he often said, you met such interesting people.

To-day, however, though there were eleven of the

studio's weirdest authors present, each well worth more than
a cursory inspection, he found himself unable to overcome
the dull listlessness which had been gripping him since he
had first gone to the refrigerator that morning to put ice
on his temples. As the poet Keats puts it in his 'Ode to a
Nightingale', his head ached and a drowsy numbness
pained his sense. And the sight of Mabel Potter, recalling
to him those dreams of happiness which he had once dared
to dream and which now could never come to fulfilment,
plunged him still deeper into the despondency. If he had
been a character in a Russian novel, he would have gone
and hanged himself in the barn. As it was, he merely sat
staring before him and keeping perfectly rigid.

Most people, eyeing him, would have been reminded
of a corpse which had been several days in the water: but
Mr Schnellenhamer thought he looked like a leopard about
to spring, and he mentioned this to Mr Levitsky in an
undertone.

'Bend down. I want to whisper.'

'What's the matter?'

'He looks to me just like a crouching leopard.'

'I beg your purdon,' said Mabel Potter, who, her duty
being to take notes of the proceedings, was seated at her
employer's side. 'Did you say "crouching leopard" or
"grouchy shepherd"?'

Mr Schnellenhamer started. He had forgotten the risk of
being overheard. He felt that he had been incautious.

'Don't put that down,' he said. 'It wasn't part of the conference. Well, now, come on, come on,' he proceeded, with
a pitiful attempt at the bluffness which he used at con-
ferences, 'let's get at it. Where did we leave off yesterday,
Miss Potter?'

Mabel consulted her notes.

'Cabot Delancy, a scion of an old Boston family, has
gone to try to reach the North Pole in a submarine, and
he's on an iceberg, and the scenes of his youth are passing
before his eyes.'

'What scenes?'

'You didn't get to what scenes.'

'Then that's where we begin,' said Mr Schnellenhamer. 'What scenes pass before this fellow's eyes?'

One of the authors, a weedy young man in spectacles, who had come to Hollywood to start a Gyffte Shoppe and had been scooped up in the studio's drag-net and forced into the writing-staff much against his will, said why not a scene where Cabot Delancy sees himself dressing his window with kewpie-dolls and fancy note-paper.

'Why kewpie-dolls?' asked Mr Schnellenhamer testily.

The author said they were a good selling line.

'Listen!' said Mr Schnellenhamer brusquely. 'This Delancy never sold anything in his life. He's a millionaire. What we want is something romantic.'

A diffident old gentleman suggested a polo-game.

'No good,' said Mr Schnellenhamer. 'Who cares anything about polo? When you're working on a picture you've got to bear in mind the small-town population of the Middle West. Aren't I right?'

'Yes,' said the senior Yes-man.

'Yes,' said the Vice-Yesser.

'Yes,' said the junior Yes-man.

And all the Nodders nodded. Wilmot, waking with a start to the realization that duty called, hurriedly inclined his throbbing head. The movement made him feel as if a red-hot spike had been thrust through it, and he winced. Mr Levitsky plucked at Mr Schnellenhamer's sleeve.

'He scowled!'

'I thought he scowled, too.'

'As it might be with sullen hate.'

'That's the way it struck me. Keep watching him.'

The conference proceeded. Each of the authors put forward a suggestion, but it was left for Mr Schnellenhamer to solve what had begun to seem an insoluble problem.

'I've got it,' said Mr Schnellenhamer. 'He sits on this iceberg and he seems to see himself – he's always been an athlete, you understand – he seems to see himself scoring the winning goal in one of these polo-games. Everybody's interested in polo nowadays. Aren't I right?'

'Yes,' said the senior Yes-man.

'Yes,' said the Vice-Yesser.

'Yes,' said the junior Yes-man.

Wilmot was quicker off the mark this time. A conscientious employee, he did not intend mere physical pain to cause him to fall short in his duty. He nodded quickly, and returned to the 'ready' a little surprised that his head was still attached to its moorings. He had felt so certain it was going to come off that time.

The effect of this quiet, respectful, deferential and obsequious nod on Mr. Schnellenhamer was stupendous. The anxious look had passed from his eyes. He was convinced now that Wilmot knew nothing. The magnate's confidence mounted high. He proceeded briskly. There was a new strength in his voice.

'Well,' he said, 'that's set for one of the visions. We want two, and the other's got to be something that'll pull in the women. Something touching and sweet and tender.'

The young author in spectacles thought it would be kind of touching and sweet and tender if Cabot Delancy remembered the time he was in his Gyffte Shoppe and a beautiful girl came in and their eyes met as he wrapped up her order of Indian bead-work.

Mr Schnellenhamer banged the desk.

'What is all this about Gyffte Shoppes and Indian bead-work? Don't I tell you this guy is a prominent clubman? Where would he get a Gyffte Shoppe? Bring a girl into it, yes – so far you're talking sense. And let him gaze into her eyes – certainly he can gaze into her eyes. But not in any Gyffte Shoppe. It's got to be a lovely, peaceful, old-world exterior set, with bees humming and doves cooing and trees waving in the breeze. Listen!' said Mr Schnellenhamer. 'It's spring, see, and all around is the beauty of Nature in the first shy sun-glow. The grass that waves. The buds that ... what's the word?'

'Bud?' suggested Mr Levitsky.

'No, it's two syllables,' said Mr Schnellenhamer, speaking a little self-consciously, for he was modestly proud of knowing words of two syllables.

'Burgeon?' hazarded an author who looked liked a trained seal.

'I beg your pardon,' said Mabel Potter. 'A burgeon's a sort of fish.'

'You're thinking of sturgeon,' said the author.

'Excuse it, please,' murmured Mabel. 'I'm not strong on fishes. Birds are what I'm best at.'

'We'll have birds, too,' said Mr Schnellenhamer jovially. 'All the birds you want. Especially the cuckoo. And I'll tell you why. It gives us a nice little comedy touch. This fellow's with this girl in this old-world garden where everything's burgeoning ... and when I say burgeoning I mean burgeoning. That burgeoning's got to be done *right*, or somebody'll get fired ... and they're locked in a close embrace. Hold as long as the Philadelphia censors'll let you, and then comes your nice little comedy touch. Just as these two young folks are kissing each other without a thought of anything else in the world, suddenly a cuckoo close by goes "Cuckoo! Cuckoo!" Meaning how goofy they are. That's good for a laugh, isn't it?'

'Yes,' said the senior Yes-man.

'Yes,' said the Vice-Yesser.

'Yes,' said the junior Yes-man.

And then, while the Nodders' heads – Wilmot's among them – were trembling on their stalks preparatory to the downward swoop, there spoke abruptly a clear female voice. It was the voice of Mabel Potter, and those nearest her were able to see that her face was flushed and her eyes gleaming with an almost fanatic light. All the bird-imitator in her had sprung to sudden life.

'I beg your purdon, Mr Schnellenhamer, that's wrong.'

A deadly stillness had fallen on the room. Eleven authors sat transfixed in their chairs, as if wondering if they could believe their twenty-two ears. Mr Schnellenhamer uttered a little gasp. Nothing like this had ever happened to him before in his long experience.

'What did you say?' he asked incredulously. 'Did you say that I ... *I* ... was wrong?'

Mabel met his gaze steadily. So might Joan of Arc have faced her inquisitors.

' 'The cuckoo,' she said, 'does not go "Cuckoo, cuckoo" ... it goes "Wuckoo, wuckoo". A distinct "*W*" sound.'

A gasp at the girl's temerity ran through the room. In the eyes of several of those present there was something that was not far from a tear. She seemed so young, so fragile.

Mr Schnellenhamer's joviality had vanished. He breathed loudly through his nose. He was plainly mastering himself with a strong effort.

'So I don't know the low-down on cuckoos?'

'Wuckoos,' corrected Mabel.

'Cuckoos!'

'Wuckoos!'

'You're fired,' said Mr Schnellenhamer.

Mabel flushed to the roots of her hair.

'It's unfair and unjust,' she cried. 'I'm right, and anybody who's studied cuckoos will tell you I'm right. When it was a matter of burgeons, I was mistaken, and I admitted that I was mistaken, and apologized. But when it comes to cuckoos, let me tell you you're talking to somebody who has imitated the call of the cuckoo from the Palace, Portland, Oregon, to the Hippodrome, Sumquamset, Maine, and taken three bows after every performance. Yes, sir, I know my cuckoos! And if you don't believe me I'll put it up to Mr Mulliner there, who was born and bred on a farm and has heard more cuckoos in his time than a month of Sundays. Mr Mulliner, how about it? Does the cuckoo go "Cuckoo"?'

Wilmot Mulliner was on his feet, and his eyes met hers with the love-light in them. The spectacle of the girl he loved in distress and appealing to him for aid had brought my distant connexion's better self to the surface as if it had been jerked up on the end of a pin. For one brief instant he had been about to seek safety in a cowardly cringing to the side of those in power. He loved Mabel Potter madly, desperately, he had told himself in that short, sickening moment of poltroonery, but Mr Schnellenhamer was the man who signed the cheques: and the thought of risking his displeasure and being summarily dismissed had appalled him. For there is no spiritual anguish like that of the man who, grown accustomed to opening the crackling envelope each Saturday morning, reaches out for it one day and finds that it is not there. The thought of the Perfecto-Zizzbaum cashier ceasing to be a fount of gold and becoming just a man with a walrus moustache had turned Wilmot's spine to Jell-o. And for an instant, as I say, he had been on the point of betraying this sweet girl's trust.

But now, gazing into her eyes, he was strong again. Come what might, he would stand by her to the end.

'No!' he thundered, and his voice rang through the room like a trumpet-blast. 'No, it does not go "Cuckoo". You have fallen into a popular error, Mr Schnellenhamer. The bird wooks, and, by heaven, I shall never cease to maintain that it wooks, no matter what offence I give to powerful vested interests. I endorse Miss Potter's view wholeheartedly and without compromise. I say the cuckoo does not cook. It wooks, so make the most of it!'

There was a sudden whirring noise. It was Mabel Potter shooting through the air into his arms.

'Oh, Wilmot!' she cried.

He glared over her back-hair at the magnate.

' "Wuckoo, wuckoo!" ' he shouted, almost savagely.

He was surprised to observe that Mr Schnellenhamer and Mr Levitsky were hurriedly clearing the room. Authors had begun to stream through the door in a foaming torrent. Presently, he and Mabel were alone with the two directors of the destinies of the Perfecto-Zizzbaum Corporation, and Mr Levitsky was carefully closing the door, while Mr Schnellenhamer came towards him, a winning, if nervous, smile upon his face.

'There, there, Mulliner,' he said.

And Mr Levitsky said 'There, there,' too.

'I can understand your warmth, Mulliner,' said Mr Schnellenhamer. 'Nothing is more annoying to the man who knows than to have people making these silly mistakes. I consider the firm stand you have taken as striking evidence of your loyalty to the Corporation.'

'Me, too,' said Mr Levitsky. 'I was admiring it myself.'

'For you are loyal to the Corporation, Mulliner, I know. You would never do anything to prejudice its interests, would you?'

'Sure he wouldn't,' said Mr Levitsky.

'You would not reveal the Corporation's little secrets, thereby causing it alarm and despondency, would you, Mulliner?'

'Certainly he wouldn't,' said Mr Levitsky. 'Especially now that we're going to make him an executive.'

'An executive?' said Mr Schnellenhamer, starting.

'An executive,' repeated Mr Levitsky firmly. 'With brevet rank as a brother-in-law.'

Mr Schnellenhamer was silent for a moment. He seemed to be having a little trouble in adjusting his mind to this extremely drastic step. But he was a man of sterling sense who realized that there are times when only the big gesture will suffice.

'That's right,' he said. 'I'll notify the legal department and have the contract drawn up right away.'

'That will be agreeable to you, Mulliner?' inquired Mr Levitsky anxiously. 'You will consent to become an executive?'

Wilmot Mulliner drew himself up. It was his moment. His head was still aching, and he would have been the last person to claim that he knew what all this was about: but this he did know – that Mabel was nestling in his arms and that his future was secure.

'I …'

Then words failed him, and he nodded.

CHAPTER 10

The Juice of an Orange

A SUDDEN cat shot in through the door of the bar-parlour of the Angler's Rest, wearing the unmistakable air of a cat which has just been kicked by a powerful foot. At the same moment there came from without sounds indicative of a strong man's wrath: and recognizing the voice of Ernest Biggs, the inn's popular landlord, we stared at one another in amazement. For Ernest had always been celebrated for the kindliness of his disposition. The last man, one would have thought, to raise a number eleven shoe against a faithful friend and good mouser.

It was a well-informed Rum and Milk who threw light on the mystery.

'He's on a diet,' said the Rum and Milk. 'On account of gout.'

Mr Mulliner sighed.

'A pity,' he said, 'that dieting, so excellent from a purely physical standpoint, should have this unfortunate effect on the temper. It seems to sap the self-control of the stoutest.'

'Quite,' said the Rum and Milk. 'My stout Uncle Henry ...'

'And yet,' proceeded Mr Mulliner, 'I have known great happiness result from dieting. Take, for example, the case of my distant connexion, Wilmot.'

'Is that the Wilmot you were telling us about the other night?'

'Was I telling you about my distant connexion Wilmot the other night?'

'The fellow I mean was a Nodder at Hollywood, and he found out that the company's child star, Little Johnny Bingley, was a midget, so to keep his mouth shut they made him an executive, and he married a girl named Mabel Potter.'

'Yes, that was Wilmot. You are mistaken, however, in supposing that he married Mabel Potter at the conclusion of that story.'

'But you distinctly said she fell into his arms.'

'Many a girl has fallen into a man's arms,' said Mr Mulliner gravely, 'only to wriggle out of them at a later date.'

We left Wilmot, as you very rightly say (said Mr Mulliner) in an extremely satisfactory position, both amatory and financial. The only cloud there had ever been between himself and Mabel Potter had been due, if you recollect, to the fact that she considered his attitude towards Mr Schnellenhamer, the head of the Corporation, too obsequious and deferential. She resented his being a Nodder. Then he was promoted to the rank of executive, so there he was, reconciled to the girl he loved and in receipt of a most satisfactory salary. Little wonder that he felt that the happy ending had arrived.

One effect of his new-found happiness on my distant connexion Wilmot was to fill him with the utmost benevolence and goodwill towards all humanity. His sunny smile was the talk of the studio, and even got a couple of lines in Louella Parsons's column in the *Los Angeles Examiner*. Love, I believe, often has this effect on a young man. He went about the place positively seeking for ways of doing his fellow human beings good turns. And when one morning Mr Schnellenhamer summoned him to his office Wilmot's chief thought was that he hoped that the magnate was going to ask some little favour of him, because it would be a real pleasure to him to oblige.

He found the head of the Perfecto-Zizzbaum Corporation looking grave.

'Times are hard, Mulliner,' said Mr Schnellenhamer.

'And yet,' replied Wilmot cheerily, 'there is still joy in the world; still the happy laughter of children and the singing of blue-birds.'

'That's all right about blue-birds,' said Mr Schnellenhamer, 'but we've got to cut down expenses. We'll have to do some salary-slicing.'

Wilmot was concerned. This seemed to him morbid.

'Don't dream of cutting your salary, Chief,' he urged. 'You're worth every cent of it. Besides, reflect. It you reduce your salary, it will cause alarm. People will go about saying that things must be in a bad way. It is your duty to the community to be a man and bite the bullet and, no matter how much it may irk you, to stick to your eight hundred thousand dollars a year like glue.'

'I wasn't thinking of cutting my salary so much,' said Mr Schnellenhamer. 'Yours, more, if you see what I mean.'

'Oh, mine?' cried Wilmot buoyantly. 'Ah, that's different. That's another thing altogether. Yes, that's certainly an idea. If you think it will be of assistance and help to ease matters for all these dear chaps on the P-F lot, by all means cut my salary. About how much were you thinking of?'

'Well, you're getting fifteen hundred a week.'

'I know, I know,' said Wilmot. 'It's a lot of money.'

'I thought if we said seven hundred and fifty from now on …'

'It's an awkward sort of sum,' said Wilmot dubiously. 'Not round, if you follow me. I would suggest five hundred.'

'Or four?'

'Four, if you prefer it.'

'Very well,' said Mr Schnellenhamer. 'Then from now on we'll put you on the books as three. It's a more convenient sum than four,' he explained. 'Makes less bookkeeping.'

'Of course,' said Wilmot. 'Of course. What a perfectly lovely day it is, is it not? I was thinking as I came along here that I had never seen the sun shining more brightly. One just wanted to be out and about, doing lots of good on every side. Well, I'm delighted if I have been able to do anything in my humble way to make things easier for you, Chief. It has been a real pleasure.'

And with a merry 'Tra-la' he left the room and made his way to the commissary, where he had arranged to give Mabel Potter lunch.

She was a few minutes late in arriving, and he presumed that she had been detained on some matter by Mr Schnellenhamer, whose private secretary, if you remember, she was. When she arrived, he was distressed to see that her lovely face was overcast, and he was just about to say something about blue-birds when she spoke abruptly.

'What is all this I hear from Mr Schnellenhamer?'

'I don't quite understand,' said Wilmot.

'About your taking a salary cut.'

'Oh, that. I see. I suppose he drafted out a new agreement for you to take to the legal department. Yes,' said Wilmot, 'Mr Schnellenhamer sent for me this morning, and I found him very worried, poor chap. There is a worldwide money shortage at the moment, you see, and industry is in a throttled state and so on. He was very upset about it. However, we talked things over, and fortunately we found a way out. I've reduced my salary. It has eased things all round.'

Mabel's face was stony.

'Has it?' she said bitterly. 'Well, let me tell you that, as far as I'm concerned, it has done nothing of the sort. You have failed me, Wilmot. You have forfeited my respect. You have proved to me that you are still the same cold asparagus-backboned worm who used to cringe to Mr Schnellenhamer. I thought, when you became an executive, that you would have the soul of an executive. I find that at heart you are still a Nodder. The man I used to think you – the strong, dominant man of my dreams – would have told Mr Schnellenhamer to take a running jump up an alley at the mere hint of a cut in the weekly envelope. Ah, yes, how woefully I have been deceived in you. I think that we had better consider our engagement at an end.'

Wilmot tottered.

'You are not taking up my option?' he gasped.

'No. You are at liberty to make arrangements elsewhere. I can never marry a poltroon.'

'But, Mabel ...'

'No. I mean it. Of course,' she went on more gently, 'if one day you should prove yourself worthy of my love, that is another matter. Give me evidence that you are a man among men, and then I'm not saying. But, meanwhile, the scenario reads as I have outlined.'

And with a cold, averted face she passed on into the commissary alone.

The effect of this thunderbolt on Wilmot Mulliner may readily be imagined. It had never occurred to him that Mabel might take this attitude towards what seemed to him an action of the purest altruism. Had he done wrong? he asked himself. Surely, to bring the light of happiness into the eyes of a motion-picture magnate was not a culpable thing. And yet Mabel thought otherwise, and, so thinking, had given him the air. Life, felt Wilmot, was very difficult.

For some moments he debated within himself the possibility of going back to his employer and telling him he had changed his mind. But no, he couldn't do that. It would be like taking chocolate from an already chocolated child. There seemed to Wilmot Mulliner nothing that he could do. It was just one of those things. He went into the commissary, and, taking a solitary table at some distance from the one where the haughty girl sat, ordered Hungarian goulash, salad, two kinds of pie, ice-cream, cheese and coffee. For he had always been a good trencherman and sorrow seemed to sharpen his appetite.

And this was so during the days that followed. He found himself eating a good deal more than usual, because food seemed to dull the pain at his heart. Unfortunately, in doing so, it substituted another in his stomach.

The advice all good doctors give to those who have been disappointed in love is to eat lightly. Fail to do this, and the result is as inevitable as the climax of a Greek tragedy. No man, however gifted his gastric juices, can go on indefinitely brooding over a lost love and sailing into the starchy foods simultaneously. It was not long before indigestion gripped Wilmot, and for almost the first time in his life he was compelled to consult a physician. And the one he selected was a man of drastic views.

'On rising,' he told Wilmot, 'take the juice of an orange. For luncheon, the juice of an orange. And for dinner the juice' – he paused a moment before springing the big surprise –'of an orange. For the rest, I am not an advocate of nourishment between meals, but I am inclined to think that, should you become faint during the day – or possibly the night – there will be no harm in your taking ... well, yes, I really see no reason why you should not take the juice of – let us say – an orange.'

Wilmot stared. His manner resembled that of a wolf on the steppes of Russia who, expecting a peasant, is fobbed off with wafer biscuit.

'But aren't you leaving out something? '

'I beg your pardon?'

'How about steaks?'

'Most decidedly no steaks.'

'Chops, then?'

'Absolutely no chops.'

'But the way I figure it out – check my figures in case I'm wrong – you're suggesting that I live solely on orange-juice.'

'On the juice of an orange,' corrected the doctor. 'Precisely. Take your orange. Divide it into two equal parts. Squeeze on a squeezer. Pour into a glass ... or cup,' he added, for he was not the man to be finicky about small details, 'and drink.'

Put like that, it sounded a good and even amusing trick, but Wilmot left the consulting-room with his heart bowed down. He was a young man who all his life had been accustomed to take his meals in a proper spirit of seriousness, grabbing everything there was and, if there was no more, filling up with biscuits and butter. The vista which this doctor had opened up struck him as bleak to a degree and I think that, had not a couple of wild cats at this moment suddenly started a rather ugly fight inside him, he would have abandoned the whole project.

The cats, however, decided him. He stopped at the nearest market and ordered a crate of oranges to be dispatched to his address. Then, having purchased a squeezer, he was ready to begin the new life.

It was some four days later that Mr Schnellenhamer, as he sat in conference with his fellow-magnate, Mr Levitsky – for these zealous men, when they had no one else to confer with, would confer with one another – was informed that Mr Eustiss Vanderleigh desired to see him. A playwright, this Vanderleigh, of the Little Theatre school, recently shipped to Hollywood in a crate of twelve.

'What does he want?' asked Mr Schnellenhamer.

'Probably got some grievance of some kind,' said Mr Levitsky. 'These playwrights make me tired. One sometimes wishes the old silent days were back again.'

'Ah,' said Mr Schnellenhamer wistfully. 'Well, send him in.'

Eustiss Vanderleigh was a dignified young man with tortoiseshell-rimmed spectacles and flowing front hair. His voice was high and plaintive.

'Mr Schnellenhamer,' he said, 'I wish to know what rights I have in this studio.'

'Listen . . .' began the magnate truculently.

Eustiss Vanderleigh held up a slender hand.

'I do not allude to my treatment as an artist and a craftsman. With regard to that I have already said my say. Though I have some slight reputation as a maker of plays, I have ceased to complain that my rarest scenes are found unsuitable for the medium of the screen. Nor do I dispute the right, however mistaken, of a director to assert that my subtlest lines are – to adopt his argot – "cheesy." All this I accept as part of the give and take of Hollywood life. But there is a limit, and what I wish to ask you, Mr Schnellenhamer, is this: Am I to be hit over the head with crusty rolls?'

'Who's been hitting you over the head with crusty rolls?'

'One of your executives. A man named Mulliner. The incident to which I allude occurred to-day at the luncheon hour in the commissary. I was entertaining a friend at the meal, and, as he seemed unable to make up his mind as to the precise nature of the refreshment which he desired, I began to read aloud to him the various items on the bill of fare. I had just mentioned roast pork with boiled potatoes and cabbage and was about to go on to Mutton Stew Joan Clarkson, when I was conscious of a violent blow or buffet on the top of the head. And turning, I perceived this man Mulliner with a shattered roll in his hand and on his face the look of a soul in torment. Upon my inquiring into his motives for the assault, he merely muttered something which I understood to be "You and your roast pork", and went on sipping his orange-juice – a beverage of which he appears to be inordinately fond, for I have seen him before in the commissary and he seems to take nothing else. However, that is neither here nor there. The question to which I desire an answer is this: How long is this going on? Must I expect, whenever I enter the studio's place of refreshment, to undergo furious assaults with crusty rolls, or are you prepared to exert your authority and prevent a repetition of the episode?'

Mr Schnellenhamer stirred uneasily.

'I'll look into it.'

'If you would care to feel the bump or contusion …?'

'No, you run along. I'm busy now with Mr Levitsky.'

The playwright withdrew, and Mr Schnellenhamer frowned thoughtfully.

'Something'll have to be done about this Mulliner,' he said. 'I don't like the way he's acting. Did you notice him at the conference yesterday?'

'Not specially. What did he do?'

'Well, listen,' said Mr Schnellenhamer, 'he didn't give

me the idea of willing service and selfless co-operation.
Every time I said anything, it seemed to me he did something funny with the corner of his mouth. Drew it up in a
twisted way that looked kind of ... what's that word beginning with an "s"?'

'Cynical?'

'No, a snickle is a thing you cut corn with. Ah, I've got
it. Sardinic. Every time I spoke he looked sardinic.'

Mr Levitsky was out of his depth.

'Like a sardine, do you mean?'

'No, not like a sardine. Sort of cold and sneering, like
Glutz of the Medulla-Oblongata the other day on the golf-
links when he asked me how many I'd taken in the rough
and I said one.'

'Maybe his nose was tickling.'

'Well, I don't pay my staff to have tickling noses in the
company's time. If they want tickling noses, they must
have them after hours. Besides, it couldn't have been that,
or he'd have scratched it. No, the way it looks to me, this
Mulliner has got too big for his boots and is seething with
rebellion. We've another story-conference this afternoon.
You watch him and you'll see what I mean. Kind of tough
and ugly he looks, like something out of a gangster film.'

'I get you. Sardinic.'

'That's the very word,' said Mr Schnellenhamer. 'And
if it goes on I'll know what to do about it. There's no room
in this corporation for fellows who sit around drawing up
the corners of their mouths and looking sardinical.'

'Or hitting playwrights with crusty rolls.'

'No, there you go too far,' said Mr Schnellenhamer.
'Playwrights ought to be hit with crusty rolls.'

Meanwhile, unaware that his bread-and-butter – or, as it
would be more correct to say, his orange-juice – was in
danger, Wilmot Mulliner was sitting in a corner of the
commissary, glowering sullenly at the glass which had
contained his midday meal. He had fallen into a reverie,
and was musing on some of the characters in History whom

he most admired ... Genghis Khan ... Jack the Ripper ...
Attila the Hun ...

There was a chap, he was thinking. That Attila. Used to
go about taking out people's eyeballs and piling them in
neat heaps. The ideal way, felt Wilmot, of getting through
the long afternoon. He was sorry Attila was no longer
with us. He thought the man would have made a nice
friend.

For the significance of the scene which I have just described will not have been lost on you. In the short space of
four days, dieting had turned my distant connexion Wilmot
from a thing of almost excessive sweetness and light to a
soured misanthrope.

It has sometimes seemed to me (said Mr Mulliner, thoughtfully sipping his hot Scotch and lemon) that to the modern
craze for dieting may be attributed all the unhappiness
which is afflicting the world to-day. Women, of course,
are chiefly responsible. They go in for these slimming systems, their sunny natures become warped, and they work
off the resultant venom on their men-folk. These, looking
about them for someone they can take it out of, pick on the
males of the neighbouring country, who themselves are
spoiling for a fight because their own wives are on a diet,
and before you know where you are war has broken out
with all its attendant horrors.

This is what happened in the case of China and Japan. It
is this that lies at the root of all the unpleasantness in the
Polish Corridor. And look at India. Why is there unrest in
India? Because its inhabitants eat only an occasional handful of rice. The day when Mahatma Gandhi sits down to a
good juicy steak and follows it up with roly-poly pudding
and a spot of Stilton, you will see the end of all this nonsense of Civil Disobedience.

Till then we must expect Trouble, Disorder ... in a word
Chaos.

However, these are deep waters. Let us return to my distant connexion, Wilmot.

In the brief address which he had made when prescribing, the doctor, as was his habit, had enlarged upon the spiritual uplift which might be expected to result from an orange-juice diet. The juice of an orange, according to him, was not only rich in the essential vitamins but contained also mysterious properties which strengthened and enlarged the soul. Indeed, the picture he had drawn of the soul squaring its elbows and throwing out its chest had done quite a good deal at the time to soothe the anguish that had afflicted Wilmot when receiving his sentence.

After all, the young man had felt, unpleasant though it might be to suffer the physical torments of a starving python, it was jolly to think that one was going to become a sort of modern St Francis of Assisi.

And now, as we have seen, the exact opposite had proved to be the case. Now that he had been called upon to convert himself into a mere vat or container for orange-juice, Wilmot Mulliner had begun to look on his fellow-man with a sullen loathing. His ready smile had become a tight-lipped sneer. And as for his eye, once so kindly, it could have been grafted on to the head of a man-eating shark and no questions asked.

The advent of a waitress, who came to clear away his glass, and the discovery that he was alone in the deserted commissary, awoke Wilmot to a sense of the passage of time. At two o'clock he was due in Mr Schnellenhamer's office, to assist at the story-conference to which the latter had alluded in his talk with Mr Levitsky. He glanced at his watch and saw that it was time to be moving.

His mood was one of sullen rebellion. He thought of Mr Schnellenhamer with distaste. He was feeling that, if Mr Schnellenhamer started to throw his weight about, he, Wilmot Mulliner, would know what to do about it.

In these circumstances, the fact that Mr Schnellenhamer, having missed his lunch that day owing to the numerous calls upon him, had ordered a plateful of sandwiches to be placed upon his desk takes upon itself no little of the dramatic. A scenario-writer, informed of the facts of the case, would undoubtedly have thought of those sandwiches as Sandwiches of Fate.

It was not at once that Wilmot perceived the loathsome objects. For some minutes only the familiar features of a story-conference penetrated to his consciousness. Mr Schnellenhamer was criticizing a point that had arisen in connexion with the scenario under advisement.

'This guy, as I see it,' he was saying, alluding to the hero of the story, 'is in a spot. He's seen his wife kissing a fellow and, not knowing it was really her brother, he's gone off to Africa, shooting big game, and here's this lion has got him down and is starting to chew the face off him. He gazes into its hideous eyes, he hears its fearful snarls, and he knows the end is near. And where I think you're wrong, Levitsky, is in saying that that's the spot for our big cabaret sequence.'

'A vision,' explained Mr Levitsky.

'That's all right about visions. I don't suppose there's a man in the business stronger for visions than I am. But only in their proper place. What I say is what we need here is for the United States Marines to arrive. Aren't I right?'

He paused and looked about him like a hostess collecting eyes at a dinner-party. The Yessers yessed. The Nodders' heads bent like poplars in a breeze.

'Sure I am,' said Mr Schnellenhamer. 'Make a note, Miss Potter.'

And with a satisfied air he reached out and started eating a sandwich.

Now, the head of the Perfecto-Zizzbaum Motion Picture Corporation was not one of those men who can eat sandwiches aloofly and, as it were, surreptitiously. When he ate a sandwich there was no concealment or evasion. He was patently, for all eyes to see, all ears to hear, a man eating a sandwich. There was a brio, a gusto, about the performance which stripped it of all disguise. His sandwich flew before him like a banner.

The effect on Wilmot Mulliner was stupendous. As I say, he had not been aware that there were sandwiches among those present and the sudden and unexpected crunching went through him like a knife.

Poets have written feelingly of many a significant and compelling sound . . . the breeze in the trees; the roar of waves breaking on a stern and rockbound coast; the coo of doves in immemorial elms; and the song of the nightingale. But none of these can speak to the very depths of the soul like the steady champing of beef sandwiches when the listener is a man who for four days has been subsisting on the juice of an orange.

In the case of Wilmot Mulliner, it was as if the sound of those sandwiches had touched a spring, releasing all the dark forces within him. A tigerish light had come into his eyes, and he sat up in his chair, bristling.

The next moment those present were startled to observe him leap to his feet, his face working violently.

'Stop that!'

Mr Schnellenhamer quivered. His jaw and sandwich fell. He caught Mr Levitsky's eye. Mr Levitsky's jaw had fallen, too.

'Stop it, I say!' thundered Wilmot. 'Stop eating those sandwiches immediately!'

He paused, panting with emotion. Mr Schnellenhamer had risen and was pointing a menacing finger. A deathly silence held the room.

And then, abruptly, into this silence there cut the shrill, sharp, wailing note of a siren. And the magnate stood spellbound, the words 'You're fired!' frozen on his lips. He knew what that sound meant.

One of the things which have caused the making of motion pictures to be listed among the Dangerous Trades is the fact that it has been found impossible to dispense with the temperamental female star. There is a public demand for her, and the Public's word is law. The consequence is that in every studio you will find at least one gifted artiste, the mere mention of whose name causes the strongest to tremble like aspens. At the Perfecto-Zizzbaum this position was held by Hortensia Burwash, the Empress of Molten Passion.

Temperament is a thing that cuts both ways. It brings in the money, but it also leads to violent outbursts on the part of its possessor similar to those so common among the natives of the Malay States. Every Hortensia Burwash picture grossed five million, but in the making of them she was extremely apt, if thwarted in some whim, to run *amok*, sparing neither age nor sex.

A procedure, accordingly, had been adopted not unlike that in use during air raids in the war. At the first sign that the strain had become too much for Miss Burwash, a siren sounded, warning all workers on the lot to take cover. Later, a bugler, blowing the 'All Clear', would inform those in the danger zone that the star had now kissed the director and resumed work on the set.

It was this siren that had interrupted the tense scene which I have been describing.

For some moments after the last note had died away, it seemed as though the splendid discipline on which the Perfecto-Zizzbaum organization prided itself was to triumph. A few eyeballs rolled, and here and there you could hear the sharp intake of breath, but nobody moved. Then from without there came the sound of running footsteps, and the door burst open, revealing a haggard young assistant director with a blood-streaked face.

'Save yourselves!' he cried.

There was an uneasy stir.

'She's heading this way!'

Again that stir. Mr Schnellenhamer rapped the desk sharply.

'Gentlemen! Are you afraid of an unarmed woman?'

The assistant director coughed.

'Not unarmed exactly,' he corrected. 'She's got a sword.'

'A sword?'

'She borrowed it off one of the Roman soldiery in "Hail, Caesar". Seemed to want it for something. Well, good-bye, all,' said the assistant director.

Panic set in. The stampede was started by a young

Nodder, who, in fairness be it said, had got a hat-pin in the fleshy part of the leg that time when Miss Burwash was so worried over 'Hearts Aflame'. Reckless of all rules of precedence, he shot silently through the window. He was followed by the rest of those present, and in a few moments the room was empty save for Wilmot, brooding with folded arms; Mabel Potter, crouched on top of the filing cabinet; and Mr Schnellenhamer himself, who, too stout to negotiate the window, was crawling into a convenient cupboard and softly closing the door after him.

To the scene which had just concluded Wilmot Mulliner had paid but scant attention. His whole mind was occupied with the hunger which was gnawing his vitals and that strange loathing for the human species which had been so much with him of late. He continued to stand where he was, as if in some dark trance.

From this he was aroused by the tempestuous entry of a woman with make-up on her face and a Roman sword in her hand.

'Ah-h-h-h-h!' she cried.

Wilmot was not interested. Briefly raising his eyebrows and baring his lips in an animal snarl, he returned to his meditations.

Hortensia Burwash was not accustomed to a reception like this. For a moment she stood irresolute; then raising the sword, she brought it down with a powerful follow-through on a handsome ink-pot which had been presented to Mr Schnellenhamer by a few admirers and well-wishers on the occasion of the Perfecto-Zizzbaum's foundation.

'Ah-h-h-h-h!' she cried again.

Wilmot had had enough of this foolery. Like all the Mulliners, his attitude towards Woman had until recently been one of reverence and unfailing courtesy. But with four days' orange-juice under his belt, he was dashed if he was going to have females carrying on like this in his presence. A considerable quantity of the ink had got on his trousers, and he now faced Hortensia Burwash, pale with fury.

'What's the idea?' he demanded hotly. 'What's the matter with you? Stop it immediately, and give me that sword.'

The temperamental star emitted another 'Ah-h-h-h-h!', but it was but a half-hearted one. The old pep had gone. She allowed the weapon to be snatched from her grasp. Her eyes met Wilmot's. And suddenly, as she gazed into those steel-hard orbs, the fire faded out of her, leaving her a mere weak woman face to face with what appeared to be the authentic caveman. It seemed to her for an instant, as she looked at him, that she had caught a glimpse of something evil. It was as if this man who stood before her had been a Fiend about to Seize Hatchet and Slay Six.

As a matter of fact, Wilmot's demeanour was simply the normal one of a man who every morning for four days has taken an orange, divided it into two equal parts, squeezed on a squeezer, poured into a glass or cup, and drunk; who has sipped the juice of an orange in the midst of rollicking lunchers doing themselves well among the roasts and hashes; and who, on returning to his modest flat in the even-fall, has got to work with the old squeezer once more. But Hortensia Burwash, eyeing him, trembled. Her spirit was broken.

'Messing about with ink,' grumbled Wilmot, dabbing at his legs with blotting-paper. 'Silly horseplay, I call it.'

The star's lips quivered. She registered Distress.

'You needn't be so cross,' she whimpered.

'Cross!' thundered Wilmot. He pointed wrathfully at his lower limbs. 'The best ten-dollar trousers in Hollywood!'

'Well, I'm sorry.'

'You'd better be. What did you do it for?'

'I don't know. Everything sort of went black.'

'Like my trousers.'

'I'm sorry about your trousers.' She sniffed miserably. 'You wouldn't be so unkind if you knew what it was like.'

'What what was like?'

'This dieting. Fifteen days with nothing but orange-juice.'

The effect of these words on Wilmot Mulliner was stunning. His animosity left him in a flash. He started. The stony look in his eyes melted, and he gazed at her with a tender commiseration, mingled with remorse that he should have treated so harshly a sister in distress.

'You don't mean you're dieting?'

'Yes.'

Wilmot was deeply stirred. It was as if he had become once more the old, kindly, gentle Wilmot, beloved by all.

'You poor little thing! No wonder you rush about smashing ink-pots. Fifteen days of it! My gosh!'

'And I was upset, too, about the picture.'

'What picture?'

'My new picture. I don't like the story.'

'What a shame!'

'It isn't true to life.'

'How rotten! Tell me all about it. Come on, tell Wilmot.'

'Well, it's like this. I'm supposed to be starving in a garret, and they want me with the last remnant of my strength to write a letter to my husband, forgiving him and telling him I love him still. The idea is that I'm purified by hunger. And I say it's all wrong.'

'All wrong?' cried Wilmot. 'You're right, it's all wrong. I never heard anything so silly in my life. A starving woman's heart wouldn't soften. And, as for being purified by hunger, purified by hunger my hat! The only reason which would make a woman in that position take pen in hand and write to her husband would be if she could think of something nasty enough to say to make it worth while.'

'That's just how I feel.'

'As a matter of fact, nobody but a female goof would be thinking of husbands at all at a time like that. She would be thinking of roast pork ...'

'... and steaks ...'

'... and chops ...'

'... and chicken casserole ...'

'... and kidneys *sautés*.'

'... and mutton curry ...'

'... and doughnuts ...'

'... and layer-cake ...'

'... and peach pie, mince pie, apple pie, custard pie, and pie *à la mode*,' said Wilmot. 'Of everything, in a word, but the juice of an orange. Tell me, who was the half-wit who passed this story, so utterly alien to human psychology?'

'Mr Schnellenhamer. I was coming to see him about it.'

'I'll have a word of two with Mr Schnellenhamer. We'll soon have that story fixed. But what on earth do you want to diet for?'

'I don't want to. There's a weight clause in my contract. It says I mustn't weigh more than a hundred and eight pounds. Mr Schnellenhamer insisted on it.'

A grim look came into Wilmot's face.

'Schnellenhamer again, eh? This shall be attended to.'

He crossed to the cupboard and flung open the door. The magnate came out on all fours. Wilmot curtly directed him to the desk.

'Take paper and ink, Schnellenhamer, and write this lady out a new contract, with no weight clause.'

'But listen ...'

'Your sword, madam, I believe?' said Wilmot, extending the weapon.

'All right,' said Mr Schnellenhamer hastily. 'All right. All right.'

'And, while you're at it,' said Wilmot, 'I'll take one, too, restoring me to my former salary.'

'What was your former salary?' asked Hortensia Burwash.

'Fifteen hundred.'

'I'll double it. I've been looking for a business manager like you for years. I didn't think they made them nowadays. So firm. So decisive. So brave. So strong. You're the business manager of my dreams.'

Wilmot's gaze, straying about the room, was attracted by a movement on top of the filing cabinet. He looked up, and his eyes met those of Mabel Potter. They yearned worshippingly at him, and in them there was something which he had no difficulty in diagnosing as the love-light. He turned to Hortensia Burwash.

'By the way, my fiancée, Miss Potter.'

'How do you do?' said Hortensia Burwash.

'Pleased to meet you,' said Mabel.

'What did you get up there for?' asked Miss Burwash, puzzled.

'Oh, I thought I would,' said Mabel.

Wilmot, as became a man of affairs, was crisp and business-like.

'Miss Burwash wishes to make a contract with me to act as her manager,' he said. 'Take dictation, Miss Potter.'

'Yes, sir,' said Mabel.

At the desk, Mr Schnellenhamer had paused for a moment in his writing. He was trying to remember if the word he wanted was spelled 'clorse' or 'clorze'.

CHAPTER II

The Rise of Minna Nordstrom

THEY had been showing the latest Minna Nordstrom picture at the Bijou Dream in the High Street, and Miss Postlethwaite, our sensitive barmaid, who had attended the première, was still deeply affected. She snuffled audibly as she polished the glasses.

'It's really good, is it?' we asked, for in the bar-parlour of the Angler's Rest we lean heavily on Miss Postlethwaite's opinion where the silver screen is concerned. Her verdict can make or mar.

' 'Swonderful,' she assured us. 'It lays bare for all to view the soul of a woman who dared everything for love. A poignant and uplifting drama of life as it is lived to-day, purifying the emotions with pity and terror.'

A Rum and Milk said that if it was as good as all that he didn't know but what he might not risk ninepence on it. A Sherry and Bitters wondered what they paid a woman like Minna Nordstrom. A Port from the Wood, raising the conversation from the rather sordid plane to which it threatened to sink, speculated on how motion-picture stars became stars.

'What I mean,' said the Port from the Wood, 'does a studio deliberately set out to create a star? Or does it suddenly say to itself, "Hullo, here's a star. What ho!"?'

One of those cynical Dry Martinis who always know everything said that it was all a question of influence.

'If you looked into it, you would find this Nordstrom girl was married to one of the bosses.'

Mr Mulliner, who had been sipping his hot Scotch and lemon in a rather distrait way, glanced up.

'Did I hear you mention the name Minna Nordstrom?'

'We were arguing about how she became a star. I was saying that she must have had a pull of some kind.'

'In a sense,' said Mr Mulliner, 'you are right. She did have a pull. But it was one due solely to her own initiative and resource. I have relatives and connexions in Hollywood, as you know, and I learn much of the inner history of the studio world through these channels. I happen to know that Minna Nordstrom raised herself to her present eminence by sheer enterprise and determination. If Miss Postlethwaite will mix me another hot Scotch and lemon, this time stressing the Scotch a little more vigorously, I shall be delighted to tell you the whole story.'

When people talk with bated breath in Hollywood – and it is a place where there is always a certain amount of breath-bating going on – you will generally find (said Mr Mulliner) that the subject of their conversation is Jacob Z. Schnellenhamer, the popular president of the Perfecto-Zizzbaum Corporation. For few names are more widely revered there than that of this Napoleonic man.

Ask for an instance of his financial acumen, and his admirers will point to the great merger for which he was responsible – that merger by means of which he combined his own company, the Colossal-Exquisite, with those two other vast concerns, the Perfecto-Fishbein and the Zizzbaum-Celluloid. Demand proof of his artistic genius, his *flair* for recognizing talent in the raw, and it is given immediately. He was the man who discovered Minna Nordstrom.

To-day when interviewers bring up the name of the world-famous star in Mr Schnellenhamer's presence, he smiles quietly.

'I had long had my eye on the little lady,' he says, 'but for one reason and another I did not consider the time ripe for her *début*. Then I brought about what you are good enough to call the epoch-making merger, and I was enabled to take the decisive step. My colleagues questioned the wisdom of elevating a totally unknown girl to stardom, but I was firm. I saw that it was the only thing to be done.'

'You had vision?'

'I had vision.'

All that Mr Schnellenhamer had, however, on the evening when this story begins was a headache. As he returned from the day's work at the studio and sank wearily into an arm-chair in the sitting-room of his luxurious home in Beverly Hills, he was feeling that the life of the president of a motion-picture corporation was one that he would hesitate to force on any dog of which he was fond.

A morbid meditation, of course, but not wholly unjustified. The great drawback to being the man in control of a large studio is that everybody you meet starts acting at you. Hollywood is entirely populated by those who want to get into the pictures, and they naturally feel that the best way of accomplishing their object is to catch the boss's eye and do their stuff.

Since leaving home that morning Mr Schnellenhamer had been acted at practically incessantly. First, it was the studio watchman who, having opened the gate to admit his car, proceeded to play a little scene designed to show what he could do in a heavy role. Then came his secretary, two book agents, the waitress who brought him his lunch, a life insurance man, a representative of a film weekly, and a barber. And, on leaving at the end of the day, he got the watchman again, this time in whimsical comedy.

Little wonder, then, that by the time he reached home the magnate was conscious of a throbbing sensation about the temples and an urgent desire for a restorative.

As a preliminary to obtaining the latter, he rang the bell and Vera Prebble, his parlourmaid, entered. For a moment he was surprised not to see his butler. Then he recalled that he had dismissed him just after breakfast for reciting 'Gunga Din' in a meaning way while bringing the eggs and bacon.

'You rang, sir?'

'I want a drink.'

'Very good, sir.'

The girl withdrew, to return a few moments later with a decanter and siphon. The sight caused Mr Schnellenhamer's gloom to lighten a little. He was justly proud of his cellar, and he knew that the decanter contained liquid balm. In a sudden gush of tenderness he eyed its bearer appreciatively, thinking what a nice girl she looked.

Until now he had never studied Vera Prebble's appearance to any great extent or thought about her much in any way. When she had entered his employment a few days before, he had noticed, of course, that she had a sort of ethereal beauty; but then every girl you see in Hollywood has either ethereal beauty or roguish gaminerie or a dark, slumberous face that hints at hidden passion.

'Put it down there on the small table,' said Mr Schnellenhamer, passing his tongue over his lips.

The girl did so. Then, straightening herself, she suddenly threw her head back and clutched the sides of it in an ecstasy of hopeless anguish.

'Oh! Oh! Oh!' she cried.

'Eh?' said Mr Schnellenhamer.

'Ah! Ah! Ah!'

'I don't get you at all,' said Mr Schnellenhamer.

She gazed at him with wide, despairing eyes.

'If you knew how sick and tired I am of it all! Tired ... Tired ... Tired. The lights ... the glitter ... the gaiety ... It is so hollow, so fruitless. I want to get away from it all, ha-ha-ha-ha-ha!'

Mr Schnellenhamer retreated behind the Chesterfield. That laugh had had an unbalanced ring. He had not liked it. He was about to continue his backward progress in the direction of the door, when the girl, who had closed her eyes and was rocking to and fro as if suffering from some internal pain, became calmer.

'Just a little thing I knocked together with a view to showing myself in a dramatic role,' she said. 'Watch! I'm going to register.'

She smiled.

'Joy.'

She closed her mouth.

'Grief.'

She wiggled her ears.

'Horror.'

She raised her eyebrows.

'Hate.'

Then, taking a parcel from the tray:

'Here,' she said, 'if you would care to glance at them, are a few stills of myself. This shows my face in repose. I call it "Reverie". This is me in a bathing-suit ... riding ... walking ... happy among my books ... being kind to the dog. Here is one of which my friends have been good enough to speak in terms of praise – as Cleopatra, the warrior-queen of Egypt, at the Pasadena Gas-Fitters' Ball. It brings out what is generally considered my most effective feature – the nose, seen sideways.'

During the course of these remarks Mr Schnellenhamer had been standing breathing heavily. For a while the discovery that this parlourmaid, of whom he had just been thinking so benevolently, was simply another snake in the grass had rendered him incapable of speech. Now his aphasia left him.

'Get out!' he said.

'Pardon?' said the girl.

'Get out this minute. You're fired.'

There was a silence. Vera Prebble closed her mouth, wiggled her ears, and raised her eyebrows. It was plain that she was grieved, horror-stricken, and in the grip of a growing hate.

'What,' she demanded passionately at length, 'is the matter with all you movie magnates? Have you no hearts? Have you no compassion? No sympathy? No understanding? Do the ambitions of the struggling mean nothing to you?'

'No,' replied Mr Schnellenhamer in answer to all five questions.

Vera Prebble laughed bitterly.

'No is right!' she said. 'For months I besieged the doors of the casting directors. They refused to cast me. Then I thought that if I could find a way into your homes I might succeed where I had failed before. I secured the post of parlourmaid to Mr Fishbein of the Perfecto-Fishbein. Half-way through Rudyard Kipling's "Boots" he brutally bade me begone. I obtained a similar position with Mr Zizzbaum of the Zizzbaum-Celluloid. The opening lines of "The Wreck of the *Hesperus*" had hardly passed my lips when he was upstairs helping me pack my trunk. And now you crush my hopes. It is cruel ... cruel... Oh, ha-ha-ha-ha-ha!'

She rocked to and fro in an agony of grief. Then an idea seemed to strike her.

'I wonder if you would care to see me in light comedy? ... No? ... Oh, very well.'

With a quick droop of the eyelids and a twitch of the muscles of the cheeks she registered resignation.

'Just as you please,' she said. Then her nostrils quivered and she bared the left canine tooth to indicate Menace. 'But one last word. Wait!'

'How do you mean, wait?'

'Just wait. That's all.'

For an instant Mr Schnellenhamer was conscious of a twinge of uneasiness. Like all motion-picture magnates, he had about forty-seven guilty secrets, many of them recorded on paper. Was it possible that ...?

Then he breathed again. All his private documents were secure in a safe-deposit box. It was absurd to imagine that this girl could have anything on him.

Relieved, he lay down on the Chesterfield and gave himself up to day-dreams. And soon, as he remembered that that morning he had put through a deal which would enable him to trim the stuffing out of two hundred and seventy-three exhibitors, his lips curved in a contented smile and Vera Prebble was forgotten.

One of the advantages of life in Hollywood is that the Servant Problem is not a difficult one. Supply more than equals demand. Ten minutes after you have thrown a butler out of the back door his successor is bowling up in his sports-model car. And the same applies to parlourmaids. By the following afternoon all was well once more with the Schnellenhamer domestic machine. A new butler was cleaning the silver: a new parlourmaid was doing whatever parlourmaids do, which is very little. Peace reigned in the home.

But on the second evening, as Mr Schnellenhamer, the day's tasks over, entered his sitting-room with nothing in his mind but bright thoughts of dinner, he was met by what had all the appearance of a human whirlwind. This was Mrs Schnellenhamer. A graduate of the silent films, Mrs Schnellenhamer had been known in her day as the Queen of Stormy Emotion, and she occasionally saw to it that her husband was reminded of this.

'Now see what!' cried Mrs Schnellenhamer.

Mr Schnellenhamer was perturbed.

'Is something wrong?' he asked nervously.

'Why did you fire that girl, Vera Prebble?'

'She went ha-ha-ha-ha-ha at me.'

'Well, do you know what she has done? She has laid information with the police that we are harbouring alcoholic liquor on our premises, contrary to law, and this afternoon they came in a truck and took it all away.'

Mr Schnellenhamer reeled. The shock was severe. The good man loves his cellar.

'Not all?' he cried, almost pleadingly.

'All.'

'The Scotch?'

'Every bottle.'

'The gin?'

'Every drop.'

Mr Schnellenhamer supported himself against the Chesterfield.

'Not the champagne?' he whispered.

'Every case. And here we are, with a hundred and fifty people coming to-night, including the Duke.'

Her allusion was to the Duke of Wigan, who, as so many British dukes do, was at this time passing slowly through Hollywood.

'And you know how touchy dukes are,' proceeded Mrs Schnellenhamer. 'I'm told that the Lulubelle Mahaffys invited the Duke of Kircudbrightshire for the week-end last year, and after he had been there two months he suddenly left in a huff because there was no brown sherry.'

A motion-picture magnate has to be a quick thinker. Where a lesser man would have wasted time referring to the recent Miss Prebble as a serpent whom he had to all intents and purposes nurtured in his bosom, Mr Schnellenhamer directed the whole force of his great brain on the vital problem of how to undo the evil she had wrought.

'Listen,' he said. 'It's all right. I'll get the bootlegger on the phone, and he'll have us stocked up again in no time.'

But he had overlooked the something in the air of Hollywood which urges its every inhabitant irresistibly into the pictures. When he got his bootlegger's number, it was only to discover that that life-saving tradesman was away from home. They were shooting a scene in 'Sundered Hearts' on the Outstanding Screen-Favourites lot, and the bootlegger was hard at work there, playing the role of an Anglican bishop. His secretary said he could not be disturbed, as it got him all upset to be interrupted when he was working.

Mr Schnellenhamer tried another bootlegger, then another. They were out on location.

And it was just as he had begun to despair that he bethought him of his old friend, Isadore Fishbein; and into his darkness there shot a gleam of hope. By the greatest good fortune it so happened that he and the president of the Perfecto-Fishbein were at the moment on excellent terms, neither having slipped anything over on the other for several weeks. Mr Fishbein, moreover, possessed as well stocked a cellar as any man in California. It would be a simple matter to go round and borrow from him all he needed.

Patting Mrs Schnellenhamer's hand and telling her that there were still bluebirds singing in the sunshine he ran to his car and leaped into it.

The residence of Isadore Fishbein was only a few hundred yards away, and Mr Schnellenhamer was soon whizzing in through the door. He found his friend beating his head against the wall of the sitting-room and moaning to himself in a quiet undertone.

'Is something the matter?' he asked, surprised.

'There is,' said Mr Fishbein, selecting a fresh spot on the tapestried wall and starting to beat his head against that. 'The police came round this afternoon and took away everything I had.'

'Everything?'

'Well, not Mrs Fishbein,' said the other, with a touch of regret in his voice. 'She's up in the bedroom with eight cubes of ice on her forehead in a linen bag. But they took every drop of everything else. A serpent, that's what she is.'

'Mrs Fishbein?'

'Not Mrs Fishbein. That parlourmaid. That Vera Prebble. Just because I stopped her when she got to "boots, boots, boots, marching over Africa" she ups and informs the police on me. And Mrs Fishbein with a hundred-and-eighty people coming to-night, including the ex-King of Ruritania!'

And, crossing the room, the speaker began to bang his head against a statue of Genius Inspiring the Motion-Picture Industry.

A good man is always appalled when he is forced to contemplate the depths to which human nature can sink, and Mr Schnellenhamer's initial reaction on hearing of this fresh outrage on the part of his late parlourmaid was a sort of sick horror. Then the brain which had built up the Colossal-Exquisite began to work once more.

'Well, the only thing for us to do,' he said, 'is to go round to Ben Zizzbaum and borrow some of his stock. How do you stand with Ben?'

'I stand fine with Ben,' said Mr Fishbein, cheering up. 'I heard something about him last week which I'll bet he wouldn't care to have known.'

'Where does he live?'

'Camden Drive.'

'Then tally-ho!' said Mr Schnellenhamer, who had once produced a drama in eight reels of two strong men battling for a woman's love in the English hunting district.

They were soon at Mr Zizzbaum's address. Entering the sitting-room they were shocked to observe a form rolling in circles round the floor with its head between its hands. It was travelling quickly, but not so quickly that they were unable to recognize it as that of the chief executive of the Zizzbaum-Celluloid Corporation. Stopped as he was completing his eleventh lap and pressed for an explanation, Mr Zizzbaum revealed that a recent parlourmaid of his, Vera Prebble by name, piqued at having been dismissed for deliberate and calculated reciting of the works of Mrs Hemans, had informed the police of his stock of wines and spirits and that the latter had gone off with the whole collection not half an hour since.

'And don't speak so loud,' added the stricken man, 'or you'll wake Mrs Zizzbaum. She's in bed with ice on her head.'

'How many cubes?' asked Mr Fishbein.

'Six.'

'Mrs Fishbein needed eight,' said that lady's husband a little proudly.

The situation was one that might well have unmanned the stoutest motion-picture executive, and there were few motion-picture executives stouter than Jacob Schnellenhamer. But it was characteristic of this man that the tightest corner was always the one to bring out the full force of his intellect. He thought of Mrs Schnellenhamer waiting for him at home, and it was as if an electric shock of high voltage had passed through him.

'I've got it,' he said. 'We must go to Glutz of the Medulla-Oblongata. He's never been a real friend of mine, but if you loan him Stella Svelte and I loan him Orlando Byng and Fishbein loans him Oscar the Wonder-Poodle on his own terms, I think he'll consent to give us enough to see us through to-night. I'll get him on the phone.'

It was some moments before Mr Schnellenhamer returned from the telephone booth. When he did so, his associates were surprised to observe in his eyes a happy gleam.

'Boys,' he said, 'Glutz is away with his family over the week-end. The butler and the rest of the help are out joy-riding. There's only a parlourmaid in the house. I've been talking to her. So there won't be any need for us to give him those stars, after all. We'll just run across in the car with a few axes and help ourselves. It won't cost us above a hundred dollars to square this girl. She can tell him she was upstairs when the burglars broke in and didn't hear anything. And there we'll be, with all the stuff we need and not a cent to pay outside of overhead connected with maid.'

There was an awed silence.

'Mrs Fishbein will be pleased.'

'Mrs Zizzbeaum will be pleased.'

'And Mrs Schnellenhamer will be pleased,' said the leader of the expedition. 'Where do you keep your axes, Zizzbaum?'

'In the cellar.'

'Fetch 'em!' said Mr Schnellenhamer in the voice a Crusader might have used in giving the signal to start against the Paynim.

In the ornate residence of Sigismund Glutz, meanwhile, Vera Prebble, who had entered the service of the head of the Medulla-Oblongata that morning and was already under sentence of dismissal for having informed him with appropriate gestures that a bunch of the boys were whooping it up in the Malemute saloon, was engaged in writing on a sheet of paper a short list of names, one of which she proposed as a *nom de théâtre* as soon as her screen career should begin.

For this girl was essentially an optimist, and not even all the rebuffs which she had suffered had been sufficient to quench the fire of ambition in her.

Wiggling her tongue as she shaped the letters, she wrote:

> *Ursuline Delmaine*
> *Theodora Trix*
> *Uvula Gladwyn*

None of them seemed to her quite what she wanted. She pondered. Possibly something a little more foreign and exotic …

> *Greta Garbo*

No, that had been used. …

And then suddenly inspiration descended upon her and, trembling a little with emotion, she inscribed on the paper the one name that was absolutely and indubitably right.

> *Minna Nordstrom*

The more she looked at it, the better she liked it. And she was still regarding it proudly when there came the sound of a car stopping at the door, and a few moments later in walked Mr Schnellenhamer, Mr Zizzbaum, and Mr Fishbein. They all wore Homburg hats and carried axes.

Vera Prebble drew herself up.

'All goods must be delivered in the rear,' she had begun haughtily, when she recognized her former employers and paused, surprised.

The recognition was mutual. Mr Fishbein started. So did Mr Zizzbaum.

'Serpent!' said Mr Fishbein.

'Viper!' said Mr Zizzbaum.

Mr Schnellenhamer was more diplomatic. Though as deeply moved as his colleagues by the sight of this traitress, he realized that this was no time for invective.

'Well, well, well,' he said, with a geniality which he strove to render frank and winning, 'I never dreamed it was you on the phone, my dear. Well, this certainly makes everything nice and smooth – us all being, as you might say, old friends.'

'Friends?' retorted Vera Prebble. 'Let me tell you …'

'I know, I know. Quite, quite. But listen. I've got to have some liquor to-night …'

'What do you mean, *you* have?' said Mr Fishbein.

'It's all right, it's all right,' said Mr Schnellenhamer soothingly. 'I was coming to that. I wasn't forgetting you. We're all in this together. The good old spirit of co-operation. You see, my dear,' he went on, 'that little joke you played on us … oh, I'm not blaming you. Nobody laughed more heartily than myself …'

'Yes, they did,' said Mr Fishbein, alive now to the fact that this girl before him must be conciliated. 'I did.'

'So did I,' said Mr Zizzbaum.

'We all laughed very heartily,' said Mr Schnellenhamer. 'You should have heard us. A girl of spirit, we said to ourselves. Still, the little pleasantry has left us in something of a difficulty, and it will be worth a hundred dollars to you, my dear, to go upstairs and put cotton-wool in your ears while we get at Mr Glutz's cellar door with our axes.'

Vera Prebble raised her eyebrows.

'What do you want to break down the cellar door for? I know the combination of the lock.'

'You do?' said Mr Schnellenhamer joyfully.

'I withdraw that expression "Serpent",' said Mr Fishbein.

'When I used the term "Viper",' said Mr Zizzbaum, 'I was speaking thoughtlessly.'

'And I will tell it you,' said Vera Prebble, 'at a price.'

She drew back her head and extended an arm, twiddling the fingers at the end of it. She was plainly registering something, but they could not discern what it was.

'There is only one condition on which I will tell you the combination of Mr Glutz's cellar, and that is this. One of you has got to give me a starring contract for five years.'

The magnates started.

'Listen,' said Mr Zizzbaum, 'you don't want to star.'

'You wouldn't like it,' said Mr Fishbein.

'Of course you wouldn't,' said Mr Schnellenhamer. 'You would look silly, starring – an inexperienced girl like you. Now, if you had said a nice small part ...'

'Star.'

'Or featured ...'

'Star.'

The three men drew back a pace or two and put their heads together.

'She means it,' said Mr Fishbein.

'Her eyes,' said Mr Zizzbaum. 'Like stones.'

'A dozen times I could have dropped something heavy on that girl's head from an upper landing, and I didn't do it,' said Mr Schnellenhamer remorsefully.

Mr Fishbein threw up his hands.

'It's no use. I keep seeing that vision of Mrs Fishbein floating before me with eight cubes of ice on her head. I'm going to star this girl.'

'*You* are?' said Mr Zizzbaum, 'And get the stuff? And leave me to go home and tell Mrs Zizzbaum there won't be anything to drink at her party to-night for a hundred and eleven guests including the Vice-President of Switzerland? No, sir! *I* am going to star her.'

'I'll outbid you.'

'You won't outbid *me*. Not till they bring me word that Mrs Zizzbaum has lost the use of her vocal chords.'

'Listen,' said the other tensely. 'When it comes to using vocal chords, Mrs Fishbein begins where Mrs Zizzbaum leaves off.'

Mr Schnellenhamer, that cool head, saw the peril that loomed.

'Boys,' he said, 'if we once start bidding against one another, there'll be no limit. There's only one thing to be done. We must merge.'

His powerful personality carried the day. It was the President of the newly-formed Perfecto-Zizzbaum Corporation who a few moments later stepped forward and approached the girl.

'We agree.'

And, as he spoke, there came the sound of some heavy vehicle stopping in the road outside. Vera Prebble uttered a stricken exclamation.

'Well, of all the silly girls!' she cried distractedly. 'I've just remembered that an hour ago I telephoned the police, informing them of Mr Glutz's cellar. And here they are!'

Mr Fishbein uttered a cry, and began to look round for something to bang his head against. Mr Zizzbaum gave a short, sharp moan, and started to lower himself to the floor. But Mr Schnellenhamer was made of sterner stuff.

'Pull yourselves together, boys,' he begged them. 'Leave all this to me. Everything is going to be all right. Things have come to a pretty pass,' he said, with a dignity as impressive as it was simple, 'if a free-born American citizen cannot bribe the police of his native country.'

'True,' said Mr Fishbein, arresting his head when within an inch and a quarter of a handsome Oriental vase.

'True, true,' said Mr Zizzbaum, getting up and dusting his knees.

'Just let me handle the whole affair,' said Mr Schnellenhamer. 'Ah, boys!' he went on, genially.

Three policemen had entered the room – a sergeant, a patrolman, and another patrolman. Their faces wore a wooden, hard-boiled look.

'Mr Glutz?' said the sergeant.

'Mr Schnellenhamer,' corrected the great man. 'But Jacob to you, old friend.'

The sergeant seemed in no wise mollified by this amiability.

'Prebble, Vera?' he asked, addressing the girl.

'Nordstrom, Minna,' she replied.

'Got the name wrong, then. Anyway, it was you who phoned us that there was alcoholic liquor on the premises?'

Mr Schnellenhamer laughed amusedly.

'You mustn't believe everything that girl tells you, sergeant. She's a great kidder. Always was. If she said that, it was just one of her little jokes. I know Glutz. I know his views. And many is the time I have heard him say that the laws of his country are good enough for him and that he would scorn not to obey them. You will find nothing here, sergeant.'

'Well, we'll try,' said the other. 'Show us the way to the cellar,' he added, turning to Vera Prebble.

Mr Schnellenhamer smiled a winning smile.

'Now, listen,' he said. 'I've just remembered I'm wrong. Silly mistake to make, and I don't know how I made it. There *is* a certain amount of the stuff in the house, but I'm sure you dear chaps don't want to cause any unpleasantness. You're broad-minded. Listen. Your name's Murphy, isn't it?'

'Donahue.'

'I thought so. Well, you'll laugh at this. Only this morning I was saying to Mrs Schnellenhamer that I must really slip down to headquarters and give my old friend Donahue that ten dollars I owed him.'

'What ten dollars?'

'I didn't say ten. I said a hundred. One hundred dollars, Donny, old man, and I'm not saying there mightn't be a little over for these two gentlemen here. How about it?'

The sergeant drew himself up. There was no sign of softening in his glance.

'Jacob Schnellenhamer,' he said coldly, 'you can't square me. When I tried for a job at the Colossal-Exquisite last spring I was turned down on account, you said, I had no sex-appeal.'

The first patrolman, who had hitherto taken no part in the conversation, started.

'Is that so, Chief?'

'Yessir. No sex-appeal.'

'Well, can you tie that!' said the first patrolman. 'When I tried to crash the Colossal-Exquisite, they said my voice wasn't right.'

'Me,' said the second patrolman, eyeing Mr Schnellenhamer sourly, 'they had the nerve to beef at my left profile. Lookut, boys,' he said, turning, 'can you see anything wrong with that profile?'

His companions studied him closely. The sergeant raised a hand and peered between his fingers with his head tilted back and his eyes half closed.

'Not a thing,' he said.

'Why, Basil, it's a lovely profile,' said the first patrolman.

'Well, that's how it goes,' said the second patrolman moodily.

The sergeant had returned to his own grievance.

'No sex-appeal!' he said with a rasping laugh. 'And me that had specially taken sex-appeal in the College of Eastern Iowa course of Motion Picture Acting.'

'Who says my voice ain't right?' demanded the first patrolman. 'Listen. Mi-mi-mi-mi-mi.'

'Swell,' said the sergeant.

'Like a nightingale or something,' said the second patrolman.

The sergeant flexed his muscles.

'Ready, boys?'

'Kayo, Chief.'

'Wait!' cried Mr Schnellenhamer. 'Wait! Give me one more chance. I'm sure I can find parts for you all.'

The sergeant shook his head.

'No. It's too late. You've got us mad now. You don't appreciate the sensitiveness of the artist. Does he, boys?'

'You're darned right he doesn't,' said the first patrolman.

'I wouldn't work for the Colossal-Exquisite now,' said

the second patrolman with a petulant twitch of his shoulder, 'not if they wanted me to play Romeo opposite Jean Harlow.'

'Then let's go,' said the sergeant. 'Come along, lady, you show us where this cellar is.'

For some moments after the officers of the Law, preceded by Vera Prebble, had left, nothing was to be heard in the silent sitting-room but the rhythmic beating of Mr Fishbein's head against the wall and the rustling sound of Mr Zizzbaum rolling round the floor. Mr Schnellenhamer sat brooding with his chin in his hands, merely moving his legs slightly each time Mr Zizzbaum came round. The failure of his diplomatic efforts had stunned him.

A vision rose before his eyes of Mrs Schnellenhamer waiting in their sunlit patio for his return. As clearly as if he had been there now, he could see her swooning, slipping into the goldfish pond, and blowing bubbles with her head beneath the surface. And he was asking himself whether in such an event it would be better to raise her gently or just leave Nature to take its course. She would, he knew, be extremely full of that stormy emotion of which she had once been queen.

It was as he still debated this difficult point that a light step caught his ear. Vera Prebble was standing in the doorway.

'Mr Schnellenhamer.'

The magnate waved a weary hand.

'Leave me,' he said. 'I am thinking.'

'I thought you would like to know,' said Vera Prebble, 'that I've just locked those cops in the coal-cellar.'

As in the final reel of a super-super-film eyes brighten and faces light up at the entry of the United States Marines, so at these words did Mr Schnellenhamer, Mr Fishbein and Mr Zizzbaum perk up as if after a draught of some magic elixir.

'In the coal-cellar?' gasped Mr Schnellenhamer.

'In the coal-cellar.'

'Then if we work quick ...'

Vera Prebble coughed.

'One moment,' she said. 'Just one moment. Before you go, I have drawn up a little letter, covering our recent agreement. Perhaps you will all three just sign it.'

Mr Schnellenhamer clicked his tongue impatiently.

'No time for that now. Come to my office to-morrow. Where are you going?' he asked, as the girl started to withdraw.

'Just to the coal-cellar,' said Vera Prebble. 'I think those fellows may want to come out.'

Mr Schnellenhamer sighed. It had been worth trying, of course, but he had never really had much hope.

'Gimme,' he said resignedly.

The girl watched as the three men attached their signatures. She took the document and folded it carefully.

'Would any of you like to hear me recite "The Bells", by Edgar Allan Poe?' she asked.

'No!' said Mr Fishbein.

'No!' said Mr Zizzbaum.

'No!' said Mr Schnellenhamer. 'We have no desire to hear you recite "The Bells", Miss Prebble.'

The girl's eyes flashed haughtily.

'Miss Nordstrom,' she corrected. 'And just for that you'll get "The Charge of the Light Brigade", and like it.'

CHAPTER 12

The Castaways

MONDAY night in the bar-parlour of the Angler's Rest is usually Book Night. This is due to the fact that on Sunday afternoon it is the practice of Miss Postlethwaite, our literature-loving barmaid, to retire to her room with a box of caramels and a novel from the circulating library and, having removed her shoes, to lie down on the bed and indulge in what she calls a good old read. On the following evening she places the results of her researches before us and invites our judgement.

This week-end it was one of those Desert Island stories which had claimed her attention.

'It's where this ship is sailing the Pacific Ocean,' explained Miss Postlethwaite, 'and it strikes a reef and the only survivors are Cyril Trevelyan and Eunice Westleigh, and they float ashore on a plank to this uninhabited island. And gradually they find the solitude and what I might call the loneliness drawing them strangely together, and in Chapter Nineteen, which is as far as I've got, they've just fallen into each other's arms and all around was the murmur of the surf and the cry of wheeling sea-birds. And why I don't see how it's all going to come out,' said Miss Postlethwaite, 'is because they don't like each other really and, what's more, Eunice is engaged to be married to a prominent banker in New York and Cyril to the daughter of the Duke of Rotherhithe. Looks like a mix-up to me.'

A Sherry and Bitters shook his head.

'Far-fetched,' he said disapprovingly. 'Not the sort of thing that ever really happens.'

'On the contrary,' said Mr Mulliner. 'It is an almost exact parallel to the case of Genevieve Bootle and my brother Joseph's younger son, Bulstrode.'

'Were they cast ashore on a desert island?'

'Practically,' said Mr Mulliner. 'They were in Hollywood, writing dialogue for the talking pictures.'

Miss Postlethwaite, who prides herself on her encyclopaedic knowledge of English Literature, bent her shapely eyebrows.

'Bulstrode Mulliner? Genevieve Bootle?' she murmured. 'I never read anything by them. What did they write?'

'My nephew,' Mr Mulliner hastened to explain, 'was not an author. Nor was Miss Bootle. Very few of those employed in writing motion-picture dialogue are. The executives of the studios just haul in anyone they meet and make them sign contracts. Most of the mysterious disappearances you read about are due to this cause. Only the other day they found a plumber who had been missing for years. All the time he had been writing dialogue for the Mishkin Brothers. Once having reached Los Angeles, nobody is safe.'

'Rather like the old Press Gang,' said the Sherry and Bitters.

'Just like the old Press Gang,' said Mr Mulliner.

My nephew Bulstrode (said Mr Mulliner), as is the case with so many English younger sons, had left his native land to seek his fortune abroad, and at the time when this story begins was living in New York, where he had recently become betrothed to a charming girl of the name of Mabelle Ridgway.

Although naturally eager to get married, the young couple were prudent. They agreed that before taking so serious a step they ought to have a little capital put by. And, after talking it over, they decided that the best plan would be for Bulstrode to go to California and try to strike Oil.

So Bulstrode set out for Los Angeles, all eagerness and enthusiasm, and the first thing that happened to him was that somebody took his new hat, a parting gift from Mabelle, leaving in its place in the club car of the train a Fedora that was a size too small for him.

The train was running into the station when he discovered his loss, and he hurried out to scan his fellow-passengers, and presently there emerged a stout man with a face rather like that of a vulture which has been doing itself too well on the corpses. On this person's head was the missing hat.

And, just as Bulstrode was about to accost this stout man there came up a mob of camera-men, who photographed him in various attitudes, and before Bulstrode could get a word in he was bowling off in a canary-coloured automobile bearing on its door in crimson letters the legend 'Jacob Z. Schnellenhamer, President Perfecto-Zizzbaum Motion Picture Corp.'

All the Mulliners are men of spirit, and Bulstrode did not propose to have his hats sneaked even by the highest in the land, without lodging a protest. Next morning he called at the offices of the Perfecto-Zizzbaum, and after waiting four hours was admitted to the presence of Mr Schnellenhamer.

The motion-picture magnate took a quick look at Bulstrode and thrust a paper and a fountain pen towards him.

'Sign here,' he said.

A receipt for the hat, no doubt, thought Bulstrode. He scribbled his name at the bottom of the document, and Mr Schnellenhamer pressed the bell.

'Miss Stern,' he said, addressing his secretary, 'what vacant offices have we on the lot?'

'There is Room Forty in the Leper Colony.'

'I thought there was a song-writer there.'

'He passed away Tuesday.'

'Has the body been removed?'

'Yes, sir.'

'Then Mr Mulliner will occupy the room, starting from to-day. He has just signed a contract to write dialogue for us.'

Bulstrode would have spoken, but Mr Schnellenhamer silenced him with a gesture.

'Who are working on "Scented Sinners" now?' he asked.

The secretary consulted a list.

'Mr Doakes, Mr Noakes, Miss Faversham, Miss Wilson, Mr Fotheringay, Mr Mendelsohn, Mr Markey, Mrs Cooper, Mr Lennox and Mr Dabney.'

'That all?'

'There was a missionary who came in Thursday, wanting to convert the extra girls. He started a treatment, but he has escaped to Canada.'

'Tchah!' said Mr Schnellenhamer, annoyed. 'We must have more vigilance, more vigilance. Give Mr Mulliner a script of "Scented Sinners" before he goes.'

The secretary left the room. He turned to Bulstrode.

'Did you ever see "Scented Sinners"?'

Bulstrode said he had not.

'Powerful drama of life as it is lived by the jazz-crazed,

gin-crazed Younger Generation whose hollow laughter is but the mask for an aching heart,' said Mr Schnellenhamer. 'It ran for a week in New York and lost a hundred thousand dollars, so we bought it. It has the mucus of a good story. See what you can do with it.'

'But I don't want to write for the pictures,' said Bulstrode.

'You've got to write for the pictures,' said Mr Schnellenhamer. 'You've signed the contract.'

'I want my hat.'

'In the Perfecto-Zizzbaum Motion Picture Corporation,' said Mr Schnellenhamer coldly, 'our slogan is Co-operation, not Hats.'

The Leper Colony, to which Bulstrode had been assigned, proved to be a long, low building with small cells opening on a narrow corridor. It had been erected to take care of the overflow of the studio's writers, the majority of whom were located in what was known as the Ohio State Penitentiary. Bulstrode took possession of Room 40, and settled down to see what he could do with 'Scented Sinners'.

He was not unhappy. A good deal has been written about the hardships of life in motion-picture studios, but most of it, I am glad to say, is greatly exaggerated. The truth is that there is little or no actual ill-treatment of the writing staff, and the only thing that irked Bulstrode was the loneliness of the life.

Few who have not experienced it can realize the eerie solitude of a motion-picture studio. Human intercourse is virtually unknown. You are surrounded by writers, each in his or her little hutch, but if you attempt to establish communication with them you will find on every door a card with the words 'Working. Do not Disturb'. And if you push open one of these doors you are greeted by a snarl so animal, so menacing, that you retire hastily lest nameless violence befall.

The world seems very far away. Outside, the sun beats down on the concrete, and occasionally you will see a man in shirt sleeves driving a truck to a distant set, while ever and anon the stillness is broken by the shrill cry of some wheeling supervisor. But for the most part a forlorn silence prevails.

The conditions, in short, are almost precisely those of such a desert island as Miss Postlethwaite was describing to us just now.

In these circumstances the sudden arrival of a companion, especially a companion of the opposite sex, can scarcely fail to have its effect on a gregarious young man. Entering his office one morning and finding a girl in it, Bulstrode Mulliner experienced much the same emotions as did Robinson Crusoe on meeting Friday. It is not too much to say that he was electrified.

She was not a beautiful girl. Tall, freckled and slab-featured, she had a distinct look of a halibut. To Bulstrode, however, she seemed a vision.

'My name is Bootle,' she said. 'Genevieve Bootle.'

'Mine is Mulliner. Bulstrode Mulliner.'

'They told me to come here.'

'To see me about something?

'To work with you on a thing called "Scented Sinners". I've just signed a contract to write dialogue for the company.'

'Can you write dialogue?' asked Bulstrode. A foolish question, for, if she could, the Perfecto-Zizzbaum Corporation would scarcely have engaged her.

'No,' said the girl despondently. 'Except for letters to Ed., I've never written anything.'

'Ed.?'

'Mr Murgatroyd, my fiancé. He's a bootlegger in Chicago, and I came out here to try to work up his West Coast connexion. And I went to see Mr Schnellenhamer to ask if he would like a few cases of guaranteed pre-War Scotch, and I'd hardly begun to speak when he said "Sign here". So I signed, and now I find I can't leave till this "Scented Sinners" thing is finished.'

'I am in exactly the same position,' said Bulstrode. 'We must buckle to and make a quick job of it. You won't mind if I hold your hand from time to time? I fancy it will assist composition.'

'But what would Ed. say?'

'Ed. won't know.'

'No, there's that,' agreed the girl.

'And when I tell you that I myself am engaged to a lovely girl in New York,' Bulstrode pointed out, 'you will readily understand that what I am suggesting is merely a purely mechanical device for obtaining the best results on this script of ours.'

'Well, of course, if you put it like that …'

'I put it just like that,' said Bulstrode, taking her hand in his and patting it.

Against hand-holding as a means of stimulating the creative faculties of the brain there is, of course, nothing to be said. All collaborators do it. The trouble is that it is too often but a first step to other things. Gradually, little by little, as the long days wore on and propinquity and solitude began to exercise their spell, Bulstrode could not disguise it from himself that he was becoming oddly drawn to this girl, Bootle. If she and he had been fishing for turtles on the same mid-Pacific isle, they could not have been in closer communion, and presently the realization smote him like a blow that he loved her – and fervently, at that. For twopence, he told himself, had he not been a Mulliner and a gentleman, he could have crushed her in his arms and covered her face with burning kisses.

And, what was more, he could see by subtle signs that his love was returned. A quick glance from eyes that swiftly fell … the timid offer of a banana … a tremor in her voice as she asked if she might borrow his pencil-sharpener. … These were little things, but they spoke volumes. If Genevieve Bootle was not crazy about him, he would eat his hat – or, rather, Mr Schnellenhamer's hat.

He was appalled and horrified. All the Mulliners are the soul of honour, and as he thought of Mabelle Ridgway, waiting for him and trusting him in New York, Bulstrode burned with shame and remorse. In the hope of averting the catastrophe he plunged with a fresh fury of energy into the picturization of 'Scented Sinners'.

It was a fatal move. It simply meant that Genevieve Bootle had to work harder on the thing, too, and 'Scented Sinners' was not the sort of production on which a frail girl could concentrate in warm weather without something cracking. Came a day with the thermometer in the nineties when, as he turned to refer to a point in Mr Noakes's treatment, Bulstrode heard a sudden sharp snort at his side and, looking up, saw that Genevieve had begun to pace the room with feverish steps, her fingers entwined in her hair. And, as he stared at her in deep concern, she flung herself in a chair with a choking sob and buried her face in her hands.

And, seeing her weeping there, Bulstrode could restrain himself no longer. Something snapped in him. It was his collar-stud. His neck, normally a fifteen and an eighth, had suddenly swelled under the pressure of uncontrollable emotion into a large seventeen. For an instant he stood gurgling wordlessly like a bull-pup choking over a chicken-bone: then, darting forward, he clasped her in his arms and began to murmur all those words of love which until now he had kept pent up in his heart.

He spoke well and eloquently and at considerable length, but not at such length as he had planned. For at the end of perhaps two minutes and a quarter there rent the air in his immediate rear a sharp exclamation or cry: and, turning, he perceived in the doorway Mabelle Ridgway, his betrothed. With her was a dark young man with oiled hair and a saturnine expression, who looked like the sort of fellow the police are always spreading a drag-net for in connexion with the recent robbery of Schoenstein's Bon Ton Delicatessen Store in Eighth Avenue.

There was a pause. It is never easy to know just what to say on these occasions: and Bulstrode, besides being embarrassed, was completely bewildered. He had supposed Mabelle three thousand miles away.

'Oh – hullo!' he said, untwining himself from Genevieve Bootle.

The dark young man was reaching in his hip-pocket, but Mabelle stopped him with a gesture.

'I can manage, thank you, Mr Murgatroyd. There is no need for sawn-off shot-guns.'

The young man had produced his weapon and was looking at it wistfully.

'I think you're wrong, lady,' he demurred. 'Do you know who that is that this necker is necking?' he asked, pointing an accusing finger at Genevieve Bootle, who was cowering against the ink-pot. 'My girl. No less. In person. Not a picture.'

Mabelle gasped.

'You don't say so!'

'I do say so.'

'Well, it's a small world,' said Mabelle. 'Yes, sir, a small world, and you can't say it isn't. All the same, I think we had better not have any shooting. This is not Chicago. It might cause comment and remark.'

'Maybe you're right,' agreed Ed. Murgatroyd. He blew on his gun, polished it moodily with the sleeve of his coat, and restored it to his pocket. 'But I'll give her a piece of my mind,' he said, glowering at Genevieve, who had now retreated to the wall and was holding before her, as if in a piteous effort to shield herself from vengeance, an official communication from the Front Office notifying all writers that the expression 'Polack mug' must no longer be used in dialogue.

'And I will give Mr Mulliner a piece of *my* mind,' said Mabelle. 'You stay here and chat with Miss Bootle, while I interview the Great Lover in the passage.'

Out in the corridor Mabelle faced Bulstrode, tight-lipped. For a moment there was silence, broken only by the clicking of typewriters from the various hutches and the occasional despairing wail of a writer stuck for an adjective.

'Well, this is a surprise!' said Bulstrode, with a sickly smile. 'How on earth do you come to be here, darling?'

'Miss Ridgway to you!' retorted Mabelle with flashing eyes. 'I will tell you. I should have been in New York still if you had written, as you said you would. But all I've had since you left is one measly picture-postcard of the Grand Canyon.'

Bulstrode was stunned.

'You mean I've only written to you once?'

'Just once. And after waiting for three weeks, I decided to come here and see what was the matter. On the train I met Mr Murgatroyd. We got into conversation, and I learned that he was in the same position as myself. His fiancée had disappeared into the No Man's Land of Hollywood, and she hadn't written at all. It was his idea that we should draw the studios. In the past two days we have visited seven, and to-day, flushing the Perfecto-Zizzbaum, we saw you coming out of a building ...'

'The commissary. I had been having a small frosted malted milk. I felt sort of faint.'

'You will feel sort of fainter,' said Mabelle, her voice as frosted as any malted milk in California, 'by the time I've done with you. So this is the kind of man you are, Bulstrode Mulliner! A traitor and a libertine!'

From inside the office came the sound of a girl's hysterics, blending with the deeper note of an upbraiding bootlegger and the rhythmic tapping on the wall of Mr Dabney and Mr Mendelsohn, who were trying to concentrate on 'Scented Sinners'. A lifetime in Chicago had given Mr Murgatroyd the power of expressing his thoughts in terse, nervous English, and some of the words he was using, even when filtered through the door, were almost equivalent to pineapple bombs.

'A two-timing daddy and a trailing arbutus!' said Mabelle, piercing Bulstrode with her scornful eyes.

A messenger-boy came up with a communication from the Front Office notifying all writers that they must not smoke in the Exercise Yard. Bulstrode read it absently. The interruption had given him time to marshal his thoughts.

'You don't understand,' he said. 'You don't realize what it is like, being marooned in a motion-picture studio. What you have failed to appreciate is the awful yearning that comes over you for human society. There you sit for weeks and weeks, alone in the great silence, and then suddenly you find a girl in your office, washed up by the tide, and what happens? Instinctively you find yourself turning to her. As an individual, she may be distasteful to you, but she is – how shall I put it? – a symbol of the world without. I admit that I grabbed Miss Bootle. I own that I kissed her. But it meant nothing. It affected no vital issue. It was as if, locked in a dungeon cell, I had shown cordiality towards a pet mouse. You would not have censured me if you had come in and found me playing with a pet mouse. For all the kisses I showered on Miss Bootle, deep down in me I was true to you. It was simply that the awful loneliness ... the deadly propinquity ... Well, take the case,' said Bulstrode, 'of a couple on a raft in the Caribbean Sea ...'

The stoniness of Mabelle's face did not soften.

'Never mind the Caribbean Sea,' she interrupted. 'I have nothing to say about the Caribbean Sea except that I wish somebody would throw you into it with a good, heavy brick round your neck. This is the end, Bulstrode Mulliner. I have done with you. If we meet on the street, don't bother to raise your hat.'

'It is Mr Schnellenhamer's hat.'

'Well, don't bother to raise Mr Schnellenhamer's hat, because I shall ignore you. I shall cut you dead.' She looked past him at Ed. Murgatroyd, who was coming out of the office with a satisfied expression on his face. 'Finished, Mr Murgatroyd?'

'All washed up,' said the bootlegger. 'A nice clean job.'

'Then perhaps you will escort me out of this Abode of Love.'

'Oke, lady.'

Mabelle glanced down with cold disdain at Bulstrode, who was clutching her despairingly.

'There is something clinging to my skirt, Mr Murgatroyd,' she said. 'Might I trouble you to brush it off?'

A powerful hand fell on Bulstrode's shoulder. A powerful foot struck him on the trousers-seat. He flew through the open door of the office, tripping over Genevieve Bootle, who was now writhing on the floor.

Disentangling himself, he rose to his feet and dashed out. The corridor was empty. Mabelle Ridgway and Edward Murgatroyd had gone.

A good many of my relations, near and distant (proceeded Mr Mulliner after a thoughtful sip at his hot Scotch and lemon), have found themselves in unpleasant situations in their time, but none, I am inclined to think, in any situation quite so unpleasant as that in which my nephew Bulstrode now found himself. It was as if he had stepped suddenly into one of those psychological modern novels where the hero's soul gets all tied up in knots as early as page 21 and never straightens itself out again.

To lose the girl one worships is bad enough in itself. But when, in addition, a man has got entangled with another girl, for whom he feels simultaneously and in equal proportions an overwhelming passion and a dull dislike – and when in addition to that he is obliged to spend his days working on a story like 'Scented Sinners' – well, then he begins to realize how dark and sinister a thing this life of ours can be. Complex was the word that suggested itself to Bulstrode Mulliner.

He ached for Mabelle Ridgway. He also ached for Genevieve Bootle. And yet, even while he ached for Genevieve Bootle, some inner voice told him that if ever there was a pill it was she. Sometimes the urge to fold her in his arms and the urge to haul off and slap her over the nose with a piece of blotting-paper came so close together that it was a mere flick of the coin which prevailed.

And then one afternoon when he had popped into the commissary for a frosted malted milk he tripped over the feet of a girl who was sitting by herself in a dark corner.

'I beg your pardon,' he said courteously, for a Mulliner,

even when his soul is racked, never forgets his manners.

'Don't mention it, Bulstrode,' said the girl.

Bulstrode uttered a stunned cry.

'You!'

He stared at her, speechless. In his eyes there was nothing but amazement, but in those of Mabelle Ridgway there shone a soft and friendly light.

'How are you, Bulstrode?' she asked.

Bulstrode was still wrestling with his astonishment.

'But what are you doing here?' he cried.

'I am working on "Scented Sinners". Mr Murgatroyd and I are doing a treatment together. It is quite simple,' said Mabelle. 'That day when I left you we started to walk to the studio gate, and it so happened that, as we passed, Mr Schnellenhamer was looking out of his window. A few moments later his secretary came running out and said he wished to see us. We went to his office, where he gave us contracts to sign. I think he must have extraordinary personal magnetism,' said Mabelle pensively, 'for we both signed immediately, though nothing was further from our plans than to join the writing-staff of the Perfecto-Zizzbaum. I had intended to go back to New York, and Mr Murgatroyd was complaining that his bootlegging business must be going all to pieces without him. It seems to be one of those businesses that need the individual touch.' She paused. 'What do you think of Mr Murgatroyd, Bulstrode?'

'I dislike him intensely.'

'You wouldn't say he had a certain strange, weird fascination?'

'No.'

'Well, perhaps you're right,' said Mabelle dubiously. 'You were certainly right about it being lonely in this studio. I'm afraid I was a little cross, Bulstrode, when we last met. I understand now. You really don't think there is a curious, intangible glamour about Mr Murgatroyd?'

'I do not.'

'Well, you may be right, of course. Good-bye, Bulstrode, I must be going. I have already exceeded the seven and a quarter minutes which the Front Office allows female writers for the consumption of nut sundaes. If we do not meet again ...'

'But surely we're going to meet all the time?'

Mabelle shook her head.

'The Front Office has just sent out a communication to all writers, forbidding inmates of the Ohio State Penitentiary to associate with those in the Leper Colony. They think it unsettles them. So unless we run into one another in the commissary ... Well, good-bye, Bulstrode.'

She bit her lip in sudden pain, and was gone.

It was some ten days later that the encounter at which Mabelle had hinted took place. The heaviness of a storm-tossed soul had brought Bulstrode to the commissary for a frosted malted milk once more, and there, toying with – respectively – a Surprise Gloria Swanson and a Cheese Sandwich Maurice Chevalier, were Mabelle Ridgway and Ed. Murgatroyd. They were looking into each other's eyes with a silent passion in which, an observer would have noted, there was a distinct admixture of dislike and repulsion.

Mabelle glanced up as Bulstrode reached the table.

'Good afternoon,' she said with a welcoming smile. 'I think you know my fiancé, Mr Murgatroyd?'

Bulstrode reeled.

'Your what did you say?' he exclaimed.

'We're engaged,' said Mr Murgatroyd sombrely.

'Since this morning,' added Mabelle. 'It was at exactly six minutes past eleven that we found ourselves linked in a close embrace.'

Bulstrode endeavoured to conceal his despair.

'I hope you will be very happy,' he said.

'A swell chance!' rejoined Mr Murgatroyd. 'I'm not saying this beasel here doesn't exert a strange fascination over me, but I think it only fair to inform her here and now – before witnesses – that at the same time the mere sight of her makes me sick.'

'It is the same with me,' said Mabelle. 'When in Mr Murgatroyd's presence, I feel like some woman wailing for her demon lover, and all the while I am shuddering at that awful stuff he puts on his hair.'

'The best hair-oil in Chicago,' said Mr Murgatroyd, a little stiffly.

'It is as if I were under some terrible hypnotic influence which urged me against the promptings of my true self to love Mr Murgatroyd,' explained Mabelle.

'Make that double, sister,' said the bootlegger. 'It goes for me, too.'

'Precisely,' cried Bulstrode, 'how I feel towards my fiancée, Miss Bootle.'

'Are you engaged to that broad?' asked Mr Murgatroyd. 'I am.'

Ed. Murgatroyd paled and swallowed a mouthful of cheese sandwich. There was silence for a while.

'I see it all,' said Mabelle. 'We have fallen under the hideous spell of this place. It is as you said, Bulstrode, when you wanted me to take the case of a couple on a raft in the Caribbean Sea. There is a miasma in the atmosphere of the Perfecto-Zizzbaum lot which undoes all who come within its sphere of influence. And here I am, pledged to marry a gargoyle like Mr Murgatroyd.'

'And what about me?' demanded the bootlegger. 'Do you think I enjoy being teamed up with a wren that doesn't know the first principles of needling beer? A swell help-meet you're going to make for a man in my line of business!'

'And where do I get off?' cried Bulstrode passionately. 'My blood races at the sight of Genevieve Bootle, and yet all the while I know that she is one of Nature's prunes. The mere thought of marrying her appals me. Apart from the fact that I worship you, Mabelle, with every fibre of my being.'

'And I worship you, Bulstrode.'

'And I'm that way about Genevieve,' said Mr Murgatroyd.

There was another silence.

'There is only one way out of this dreadful situation,' said Mabelle. 'We must go to Mr Schnellenhamer and hand in our resignations. Once we are free from this noxious environment, everything will adjust itself nicely. Let us go and see him immediately.'

They did not see Mr Schnellenhamer immediately, for nobody ever did. But after a vigil of two hours in the reception-room, they were finally admitted to his presence, and they filed in and stated their case.

The effect on the President of the Perfecto-Zizzbaum Corporation of their request that they be allowed to resign was stupendous. If they had been Cossacks looking in at the office to start a pogrom, he could not have been more moved. His eyes bulged, and his nose drooped like the trunk of an elephant which has been refused a peanut.

'It can't be done,' he said curtly. He reached in the drawer of his desk, produced a handful of documents, and rapped them with an ominous decision. 'Here are the contracts, duly signed by you, in which you engage to remain in the employment of the Perfecto-Zizzbaum Corporation until the completion of the picture entitled "Scented Sinners". Did you take a look at Para. 6, where it gives the penalties for breach of same? No, don't read them,' he said, as Mabelle stretched out a hand. 'You wouldn't sleep nights. But you can take it from me they're some penalties. We've had this thing before of writers wanting to run out on us, so we took steps to protect ourselves.'

'Would we be taken for a ride?' asked Mr Murgatroyd uneasily.

Mr Schnellenhamer smiled quietly but did not reply. He replaced the contracts in the drawer, and his manner softened and became more appealing. This man knew well when to brandish the iron fist and when to display the velvet glove.

'And, anyway,' he said, speaking now in almost a fatherly manner, 'you wouldn't want to quit till the picture was finished. Of course, you wouldn't, not three nice, square-shooting folks like you. It wouldn't be right. It wouldn't be fair. It wouldn't be co-operation. You know what "Scented Sinners" means to this organization. It's the biggest proposition we have. Our whole programme is built around it. We are relying on it to be our big smash. It cost us a barrel of money to buy "Scented Sinners", and naturally we aim to get it back.'

He rose from his chair, and tears came into his eyes. It was as if he had been some emotional American football coach addressing a faint-hearted team.

'Stick to it!' he urged. 'Stick to it, folks! You can do it if you like. Get back in there and fight. Think of the boys in the Front Office rooting for you, depending on you. You wouldn't let them down? No, no, not you. You wouldn't let me down? Of course you wouldn't. Get back in the game, then, and win – win – win ... for dear old Perfecto-Zizzbaum and me.'

He flung himself into his chair, gazing at them with appealing eyes.

'May I read Para. 6?' asked Mr Murgatroyd after a pause.

'No, don't read Para. 6,' urged Mr Schnellenhamer. 'Far, far better not read Para. 6.'

Mabelle looked hopelessly at Bulstrode.

'Come,' she said. 'It is useless for us to remain here.'

They left the office with dragging steps. Mr Schnellenhamer, a grave expression on his face, pressed the bell for his secretary.

'I don't like the look of things, Miss Stern,' he said. 'There seems to be a spirit of unrest among the "Scented Sinners" gang. Three of them have just been in, wanting to quit. I shouldn't be surprised if rebellion isn't seething. Say, listen,' he asked keenly, 'nobody's been ill-treating them, have they?'

'Why, the idea, Mr Schnellenhamer!'

'I thought I heard screams coming from their building yesterday.'

'That was Mr Doakes. He was working on his treatment, and he had some kind of a fit. Frothed at the mouth and kept shouting, "No, no! It isn't possible!" If you ask me,' said Miss Stern, 'it's just the warm weather. We most generally always lose a few writers this time of year.'

Mr Schnellenhamer shook his head.

'This ain't the ordinary thing of authors going cuckoo. It's something deeper. It's the spirit of unrest, or rebellion seething, or something like that. What am I doing at five o'clock?'

'Conferencing with Mr Levitsky.'

'Cancel it. Send round notice to all writers on "Scented Sinners" to meet me on Stage Four. I'll give them a pep-talk.'

At a few minutes before five, accordingly, there debouched from the Leper Colony and from the Ohio State Penitentiary a motley collection of writers. There were young writers, old writers, middle-aged writers; writers with matted beards at which they plucked nervously, writers with horn-rimmed spectacles who muttered to themselves, writers with eyes that stared blankly or blinked in the unaccustomed light. On all of them "Scented Sinners" had set its unmistakable seal. They shuffled listlessly along till they came to Stage Four, where they seated themselves on wooden benches, waiting for Mr Schnellenhamer to arrive.

Bulstrode had found a place next to Mabelle Ridgway. The girl's face was drawn and despondent.

'Edward is breaking in a new quart of hair-oil for the wedding,' she said, after a moment of silence.

Bulstrode shivered.

'Genevieve,' he replied, 'has bought one of those combination eyebrow-tweezers and egg-scramblers. The advertisement said that no bride should be without them.'

Mabelle drew her breath in sharply.

'Can nothing be done?' asked Bulstrode.

'Nothing,' said Mabelle dully. 'We cannot leave till "Scented Sinners" is finished, and it never will be finished —never . . . never . . . never.' Her spiritual face was contorted for a moment. 'I hear there are writers who have been working on it for years and years. That grey-bearded gentleman over there, who is sticking straws in his hair,' she said, pointing. 'That is Mr Markey. He has the office next to ours, and comes in occasionally to complain that there are spiders crawling up his wall. He has been doing treatments of "Scented Sinners" since he was a young man.'

In the tense instant during which they stared at each other with mournful, hopeless eyes, Mr Schnellenhamer bustled in and mounted the platform. He surveyed the gathering authoritatively: then, clearing his throat, began to speak.

He spoke of Service and Ideals, of Co-operation and the Spirit That Wins to Success. He had just begun to touch on the glories of the Southern Californian climate when the scent of a powerful cigar floated over the meeting, and a voice spoke.

'Hey!'

All eyes were turned in the intruder's direction. It was Mr Isadore Levitsky, the chief business operative, who stood there, he with whom Mr Schnellenhamer had had an appointment to conference.

'What all this?' demanded Mr Levitsky. 'You had a date with me in my office.'

Mr Schnellenhamer hurried down from the platform and drew Mr Levitsky aside.

'I'm sorry, I.G.,' he said. 'I had to break our date. There's all this spirit of unrest broke out among the "Scented Sinners" gang, and I thought I'd better talk to them. You remember that time five years ago when we had to call out the State Militia.'

Mr Levitsky looked puzzled.

'The what gang?'

'The writers who are doing treatments on "Scented Sinners". You know "Scented Sinners" that we bought.'

'But we didn't,' said Mr Levitsky.

'We didn't?' said Mr Schnellenhamer, surprised.

'Certainly we didn't. Don't you remember the Medulla-Oblongata-Glutz people outbid us?'

Mr Schnellenhamer stood for a moment, musing.

'That's right, too,' he said at length. 'They did, didn't they?'

'Certainly they did.'

'Then the story doesn't belong to us at all?'

'Certainly it doesn't. M-O-G has owned it for the last eleven years.'

Mr Schnellenhamer smote his forehead.

'Of course! It all comes back to me now. I had quite forgotten.'

He mounted the platform once more.

'Ladies and gentlemen,' he said, 'all work on "Scented Sinners" will cease immediately. The studio has discovered that it doesn't own it.'

It was a merry gathering that took place in the commissary of the Perfecto-Zizzbeaum Studio some half-hour later. Genevieve Bootle had broken her engagement to Bulstrode and was sitting with her hand linked in that of Ed. Murgatroyd. Mabelle Ridgway had broken her engagement to Ed. Murgatroyd and was stroking Bulstrode's arm. It would have been hard to find four happier people, unless you had stepped outside and searched among the horde of emancipated writers who were dancing the Carmagnole so blithely around the shoe-shining stand.

'And what are you two good folks going to do now?' asked Ed. Murgatroyd, surveying Bulstrode and Mabelle with kindly eyes. 'Have you made any plans?'

'I came out here to strike Oil,' said Bulstrode. 'I'll do it now.'

He raised a cheery hand and brought it down with an affectionate smack on the bootlegger's gleaming head.

'Ha, ha!' chuckled Bulstrode.

'Ha, ha!' roared Mr Murgatroyd.

'Ha, ha!' tittered Mabelle and Genevieve.

A perfect camaraderie prevailed among these four young people, delightful to see.

'No, but seriously,' said Mr Murgatroyd, wiping the

tears from his eyes, 'are you fixed all right? Have you got enough dough to get married on?'

Mabelle looked at Bulstrode. Bulstrode looked at Mabelle. For the first time, a shadow seemed to fall over their happiness.

'We haven't,' Bulstrode was forced to admit.

Ed. Murgatroyd slapped him on the shoulder.

'Then come and join my little outfit,' he said heartily. 'I've always room for a personal friend. Besides, we're muscling into the North Side beer industry next month, and I shall need willing helpers.'

Bulstrode clasped his hand, deeply moved.

'Ed.,' he exclaimed, 'I call that square of you. I'll buy a machine-gun to-morrow.'

With his other hand he sought Mabelle's hand and pressed it. Outside, the laughter of the mob had turned to wild cheering. A bonfire had been started, and Mr Doakes, Mr Noakes, Miss Faversham, Miss Wilson, Mr Fotheringay, Mr Mendelsohn, Mr Markey and the others were feeding it with their scripts of 'Scented Sinners'.

In the Front Office, Mr Schnellenhamer and Mr Levitsky, suspending their seven hundred and forty-first conference for an instant, listened to the tumult.

'Makes you feel like Lincoln, doesn't it?' said Mr Levitsky.

'Ah!' said Mr Schnellenhamer.

They smiled indulgently. They were kindly men at heart, and they liked the girls and boys to be happy.

P. G. Wodehouse in Penguins

The writer who has been called (by Sean O'Casey) 'English literature's performing flea' and who was already selling stories and lyrics in the first decade of the century, is still performing magnificently in his eighties.

The immortal series featuring Bertie Wooster and his man, Jeeves, received a new lease of life when 'The World of Wooster' appeared on television. Now, with a new television series, in which Ralph Richardson stars, the reading public is likely to be cadging invitations to Blandings Castle in the hope of meeting Clarence, ninth Earl of Emsworth, and his weighty pig.

They can be met in the following Penguins:

Blandings Castle

Full Moon

Galahad at Blandings

Heavy Weather

Leave it to Psmith

Lord Emsworth and Others

Pigs Have Wings

Service with a Smile

Summer Lightning

Uncle Fred in the Springtime

In all over twenty books by P. G. Wodehouse are available in Penguins.

Not for sale in the U.S.A.